Castles
in the
Sand

For: Ron

a Many thanks for

your input & encouragement ...

Best Wishes Always,

Castles
in the
Sand

A novel by
Annie Daylon

McRAC Books
British Columbia • Canada

Published by McRAC Books, British Columbia, Canada.

This book is a work of fiction. All names, characters, places, organizations, and events portrayed in this book are either products of the authors imagination, or are used fictitiously. Any resemblance to actual events or persons, living or dead, is entirely coincidental.

ISBN-13: 978-0-9866980-1-9
ISBN-10: 0-9866980-1-6

McRAC Books Trade Paperback Edition.
First Printing, March 2013.
Printed in the United States of America.

Cover photo of English Bay, Vancouver copyright © Eva Kondzialkiewicz.

For David
(always)

"Safe upon the solid rock the ugly houses stand:
Come and see my shining palace built upon the sand!"
~Edna St. Vincent Millay

ACKNOWLEDGMENTS

The seed for *Castles in the Sand* was a short story, one based on a twenty-four hour contest prompt from Ontario's Wynterblue Publishing. I am grateful to all who hold such contests; they provide writers with opportunities to hone their craft. A special nod of thanks to Maggie Kirton and the staff at Wynterblue.

Draft one of *Castles in the Sand* emerged during National Novel Writing Month, an annual November event in which thousands of writers participate. Thanks to the folks at NaNoWriMo for providing this worldwide pen-to-paper community.

The voice for *Castles in the Sand* materialized during an online course titled *Voice and Viewpoint*. Thank you Gloria Kempton for your excellent instruction. Thank you also to instructors—Rachelle Gardner, Chuck Sambuchino, Sara Megibow, Jane Friedman and James Scott Bell—for their webinars which covered everything from structure to synopsis to query. Thank you also to authors/coaches Terri Valentine and Richard Krawiec for support, encouragement, and suggestions during content editing.

Castles in the Sand won the mainstream genre of the 2012 Houston Writers Guild Novel Contest. Thank you to Roger Paulding and the staff of the Houston Writers Guild for providing this opportunity.

Thank you to early readers, Ron Kandle and Lillian Day, and to the Chilliwack Writers' Group for their support while this novel was in its infancy.

A special thank you to author/editor/designer Michael Hiebert for content and copy editing and for cover design. It was a pleasure to work with someone of such caliber; he is a rare combination of meticulous detail, phenomenal talent, and generous spirit.

1

ON THE VERGE

January, 2010

I have to stay on the verge of sleep. Just on the verge. Can't let my body slip over the threshold. Too damn scary.

My long-held conviction—that the homeless are a stationary lot, staking out territory on a corner, steadfast until some third party herds them along—is gone. Vanquished my first night on the street when fear goaded me into motion. Since then, I meander at night, all night, seeking the security of daybreak.

This night, however, is different. Hungover and exhausted, I am motionless, lying on the sidewalk, my very marrow impregnated with cold despite the heating vent beside me. On the verge of sleep. Trying to convince myself that the concrete is a pillow-top mattress, that Sarah is sleeping next to me, and that our Bobby is down the hall, dreaming of Dory and Nemo . . .

"Hey, you! What do you think you're doing?"

My body jumps and my eyes pop open. Some guy in a puffy, white jacket hovers over me. A marshmallow. A goddam talking marshmallow. My heart pounds. *The watch. Do I still have it?* I grab for my wrist. Yes. Still there. Relief gushes, and I yank at my sleeve until the watch is hidden. *It's safe, my gift from Sarah, safe.* My heart rate slows, but not much; the marshmallow lingers.

I squint to shield my eyes from the streetlight. "I'm trying to sleep. What does it look like I'm doing?"

"Not here, bud. There are shelters, you know."

Great. Another Good Samaritan determined to clean up Vancouver streets. Damn city's going all out to prevent Olympic tourists from tripping over the homeless. I glare at this latest do-gooder and stifle a comeback. Then I drop my gaze to the pigeons strutting the sidewalk. Huh. The little bastards have red feet. Never noticed that before. The way they dart around, seems they'd get crushed by all these people. Yep. The beautiful people are here, scurrying to the office or the Skytrain, or the bus stop. I take a deep breath so I can suck in the Starbucks. Love the smell of Starbucks. The beautiful people all carry Starbucks.

Wind rushes my face as a city bus passes. The bus engine grumbles, preparing to halt at the next stop. *Whooossssssh.* Air brakes.

Damn. The city is awake.

Won't be long before the bolts on the door of the shoe boutique behind me twist open. Three bolts. Every morning. Like clockwork. *Click. Click. Click.* Pretty soon, the whole fleet of designer shops flanking Robson Street will reel in the first cash of the day.

Might as well move. No point in arguing with the marshmallow. Sighing, I scramble to my feet and linger over the heating vent, *my* heating vent that was hard to find, harder to claim.

"Way to go, bud," says Marshmallow Man. "Do you need any help?"

I ignore him. Help, my ass. *Saw the way you looked at me,* bud, *with the corner of your mouth pulled up in contempt. Screw you.* I choke back the urge to spit at him. My mouth is so dry I probably couldn't form a spit wad anyway. I deliberately stick my butt in the direction of his face as I bend over to gather my stuff.

I heft my backpack over my shoulder, turn toward Stanley Park, walk about a block, and then do an about-face. The park washrooms are at least twenty-five minutes away and I need one *now.* I pick up my pace.

Marshmallow Man is still talking at me as I hurry past. Idiot. I push up my tattered sleeve and glance at my watch. Seven-thirty. It's a dangerous time for alleys but my bladder won't wait.

At the next corner, I veer around a bakery and go toward the green Dumpster at the back. I hide behind it, take a leak, and let out a long sigh. Relief doesn't last; as soon as that need is met, before I can zip my jeans, my stomach growls. Time to hunt.

The smell of fresh-baked bread wafts up my nose. My mouth waters. Bakeries throw out stuff. Day-old stuff. Easy pickings. I dislodge my backpack and conceal it in the bushes nearby. Then I scramble up the side of the Dumpster, jump in, and fumble through paper and plastic. At the sound of voices, men's voices, I freeze. *Am I safe here?* The hair on my neck stands up. I slowly lower myself to my haunches and hold my breath. The voices get louder.

"My ex-wife's new boyfriend damn near got himself killed last night."

"How the fuck did that happen? "

"People on bicycles gotta look out for big, red pickup trucks. Hard to see people on bicycles."

"Yeah, right. Especially in that big, red pickup you drive." His laughter rumbles through me like vibrations from a passing freight train. My heart speeds up.

"Shut up, you damn fool. I was with *you* last night, remember?"

"Oh yeah, what was it we were doing?"

A rat scuttles past me and I jump back, splaying my body against the side of the Dumpster. Oh, God. I squeeze my eyes shut and freeze in place, wedged to the wall like a magnet to steel.

"What the hell . . . ? Did you hear that?"

"I don't hear nothing. Jesus, you're jumpier than a . . . "

"Ssssh! Just listen, will ya?"

My heart thunders in my ears and sweat pours off my brow. My lungs are about to explode. Don't breathe. Don't dare breathe.

"Hmmph. Nothing. Probably just a rat. Let's get the hell outta here."

Footsteps pound, thump, then fade. Certain they are gone, I gulp in air. Then I inch forward and peer out. No one in sight. Relieved, I wrap my fingers around the edge of the Dumpster and flip myself over the side with athletic skill bred from chronic fear. I land with knees bent, head down. When I unfold my body, a Goliath fist slams toward me. The stench of stale nicotine hits first. Then bones crunch and pain shoots through my face. Blood spurts into my mouth. I lurch back, bang into the Dumpster, spew teeth, and collapse to the ground.

My body grunts in response to the thumping kicks that land on my torso. Gruff fingers poke and prod, searching. A triumphant "aha!" tells me they have discovered my watch. *Sorry, Sarah.* There is no physical pain now, only crushing sadness. Strange. They pick me up, swing me, and toss me. I am a rag doll, flying. I land with a thud, back in the garbage. Rats scurry over me and up the wall of the Dumpster. Laughter rumbles. Feet hammer. Then . . . stillness.

I want to open my eyes. Can't. Can't move. Know where I am, know what's around me, but can't move. My body is a shell, useless as a flashlight with the batteries ripped out. Maybe this is the end. And maybe I don't give a damn. Bobby. Bobby's castle. What did I do with Bobby's castle?

I must have blacked out completely because the next thing I know I'm on some kind of gurney. Men in uniform are leaning over me. Jesus! Cops. I thrash about like a freshly-landed sockeye. Muscular arms, a whole octopus of them, pin me down.

"Relax, bud," says a voice.

I turn my head. Marshmallow Man. Only this time he's red and white. There's blood on his puffy jacket. Must be my blood. The son of a bitch pulled me out of the Dumpster. I go limp now, allowing the uniforms to stick me and wrap me and wheel me to an ambulance. For some reason, Marshmallow Man stays at my side.

A memory flashes. Bobby's castle. "Backpack," I utter.

Marshmallow Man leans in. "What's that, bud?"

"Backpack. In bushes by Dumpster."

"Oh, yeah, right. I remember your backpack. Listen, the ambulance is going to take you to St. Paul's. I'll look for the backpack and then I'll find you, okay?"

Trust you? Why should I trust you, bud? I struggle to get up but the octopus arms are having none of that.

"Let him get the backpack," says one of the uniforms. "He'll take it to the hospital."

Huh. Guess this guy knows Marshmallow Man. Relieved, I nod. The uniforms lift me and load me onto the ambulance. Safe now—no thugs, no rats, no stench of rotting garbage. The last thing I notice is a nametag sewed onto a uniform bent over me. I focus on it and allow myself to float away . . .

2

ANGEL TATTOO

I jump from sleep, sweating, heart racing. Light glares overhead. Used to that. Always sleep under streetlights. Always wake up cold and stiff, *rigor-mortis* stiff. No comfort on sidewalks. But I'm warm now. Molded to a cloud. I inhale and my nose twitches. Antiseptic. Memory is triggered and my heart rate slows.

"Mister? Are you awake? Mister?" A female voice.

I turn my head and scrutinize her with my one good eye. Middle-aged nurse. Dark hair, streaked with grey. Tattoo on neck. An angel tattoo. Huh. Appropriate.

"What is your name, Mister? Can you tell me your name?" She straps a blood pressure cuff on me and stares long and hard at my arm. Looking for track marks, no doubt. She can look all she wants. None there. "Can you tell me your name, Mister?"

Fat chance. Did I say that out loud? Guess not. She's still staring at me.

"Vladimir," I mutter. I knew a Vladimir once. Liked the man. Liked the name. Means "renowned prince," he told me. I used to be a prince.

"Vladimir, huh?" She raises an eyebrow. "Any possibility you have a last name?"

Rhetorical question. We both know it.

She sighs. "Okay, Vladimir-with-no-last-name, the doctor will be in to see you shortly. You can rest for a while." She touches my hand and I recoil. "It's okay; you're safe here." She reaches for my hand again.

This time I don't pull back. Instead, I look into her eyes. I see compassion there, not pity. Probably no difference to most people. Would have been none to me a few months back before I started living out of garbage cans. But now? Now I think compassion gives hope. And now, as I stare at the nurse with the angel tattoo, I'm sucking in hope like a black hole sucks up light. I want to smile at her. I try, but the pain hits and I remember why I'm here. She withdraws her hand and I am lost, disoriented, like I was cut off in mid-sentence during a phone call. Hope oozes away. Blackness returns and settles in.

"I have to go now. You just rest." She turns and walks away.

Rest. My eyelids droop. One of them anyway. The other is swollen shut. My brain is still. Sounds travel to my ears, hospital sounds. The thud of rubber soles on linoleum, the clatter of trays being loaded onto a cart, the white noise of simultaneous conversations, a moan of pain, a jolt of laughter. Everything feels safe, comfortable. Like listening to a movie soundtrack. Nothing really affects me. It's not like the street where whispers and footsteps can make adrenaline gush. I want to float here for a while, but something niggles at me. What am I trying to remember?

"Hey, bud, I'm back."

That's it. Bobby's castle. My good eye snaps open. My backpack is there, in the hands of Marshmallow Man. I grab it, unzip the side pocket, and shove my hand in.

"Ouch!" I pull back. I try again with my left hand, the one without the IV needle attached to it. I grope. There it is. With the small, plastic castle safely clutched in my fingers, I fall back against the pillow. A deep breath. Feels good. I take another, deeper. Pain slices my ribcage.

"Is that all you wanted, bud? I could have gotten that out for you. They tell me your name is Vladimir? Is that right?"

Annoying little shit. "Get lost. I'm done with you."

"Sorry, bud, I'm not done with you."

Damn. Guess this time I did say the words out loud. The problem with living inside my head is that I'm not sure what leaks out and what doesn't.

"What the hell do you want, *bud*?" I demand.

"The name's Steve. And you're my project."

"Nobody's project. Go away."

"No can do."

"Why the hell not?"

"Need your help."

"Don't need yours."

"You did today."

Couldn't argue that one. "Thanks. Now, get lost."

"Sure." He turns away.

I sigh with relief. But the son of a bitch pulls up a chair and parks his butt in it.

"What the . . . ?"

"Now," says Steve as he pulls a small notebook from his back pocket, "let's talk." He clicks his pen. "Vladimir, huh? How did you come up with that one?"

I open my mouth to lay into him but he grins and I am disarmed. Is there something familiar in his smile? Maybe, maybe not. Maybe I'm just lonely, starved for company, like a prison inmate surfacing from solitary. Maybe I don't want him to walk away like the nurse did. Whatever. I decide to shut up and listen.

"Okay, so, as I was telling you, my name is Steve. Steve Jameson. I'm a grad student, doing research on the homeless for my thesis. Been interviewing people, but can't get the info I want. Seems that street people tell me everything about sex and drug and alcohol habits and nothing about family. Interesting. Why is that, Vladimir?"

Maybe because it's none of your damn business. I shrug. "Don't do drugs." I look straight at him.

The damn fool's eyes light up. He doesn't know I am toying with him.

"Can we skip the alcohol and sex and go right to the family?"

I turn away and an audible sigh escapes Steve's lips.

"Darn," he mutters.

A squeak of rubber sole on linoleum marks the entrance of the doctor. Chair legs scrape the floor as Steve rises and moves both chair and self out of the way.

" Vladimir," reads the doctor from the chart she has pulled from the tray table. "Can you sit up at all?"

I struggle into a seated position. It hurts like hell, but I don't show it.

She pushes a button to raise the head of the bed. I am grateful, but don't show that either. Then she touches my face; I flinch.

"You will need a few stitches above that eye," she announces. "I guess you don't want to tell me what happened."

I look at her. There's no compassion in that face. Silence is golden.

"Fine then. We'll just get those stitches in, and send you to Imaging for a CT scan and an X-ray of your ribs. You'll probably be on your way in a few hours."

I cover my face with my free arm. "On your way." Small statement. Great disappointment. It reminds me of Bobby. Five-year-old Bobby with his little face scrunched up, ready to cry. The time I took him to visit a school friend of his. I got the dates mixed up, and his friend wasn't home. A minor screw-up on my part . . . Lord knows I made far greater mistakes where my family was concerned. But this tiny error stabs me. "This is what disappointment feels like, son," I had told him. I would have given anything, *anything,* to take away Bobby's pain, to feel it for him. Well, I'm feeling it now . . . I'm just like Bobby. A disappointed five-year-old. I don't want to be "on my way." I want to stay here on the soft, clean bed with the bright light overhead.

The doctor lowers my arm and, at warp speed, sews me up. Her shoes whine their way out of the room. The nurse with the angel tattoo reappears.

"Vladimir," she says, her soft, comforting voice sliding around me, like she's wrapping me in a down-filled quilt, "do you know about the homeless shelters? There's one not too far from here. I think you should go there."

I say nothing.

"For the night, at least," she adds, anxiety creeping into her voice. "I know someone over there, and I can phone ahead for you. It is just a few blocks away. What do you think?"

Again, nothing.

"Please, Vladimir." Her voice is a whispered prayer now. Makes me wonder who the other Vladimir is, the one I remind her of.

"I'll take him there." Steve pops into view like a movie star doing a cameo. *Damn it all! Where's the white cowboy hat, Steve?*

"That okay with you, Vladimir?" asks the nurse.

I shrug. Somehow, that is enough for her.

"Well, that's settled then." All business now, she helps me into a wheelchair, tucks a blanket on my lap, and we head off to Imaging.

"I'll be waiting," calls Steve.

Don't doubt that for a second, bud.

The wheelchair creaks and rolls, creaks and rolls. To the elevator. *Ping!* The doors slide open and we glide on. The nurse presses the button for the second floor and then stands behind me, leaning on the wheelchair.

I expect conversation—okay, I expect a monologue from my angel companion—maybe some probing. But, no. There is only silence, simple and peaceful, a calming shroud, jostled a bit by the *whir* of the elevator. A short *whir* for a short ride. *Ping!* Damn. Too short.

The doors open and a wall of stifling heat wallops me. We push into it, becoming one with it as we navigate the wide, polished hallway. The angel nurse parks my chair outside a swinging door, locks my wheels and orders me to wait. She disappears then, and I linger, as ordered, and sleep, as needed.

My body jerks when someone unlocks my wheels. A different nurse, male and burly, mutters a hello as he reverses my chair, lines it up with the swinging door and thrusts it through, into the X-ray room.

The whole X-ray/CT scan thing takes a while. Okay with me. The longer the better. At least a couple of hours before the angel nurse comes to claim me. She wheels me back to the ER, removes my IV, and is about to help me up when the PA system barks an order. The only word I make out is "Stat!". Then the nurse is gone. *Pouf!* So much for angels.

I manage to get myself from the wheel chair onto the bed, unassisted. When I realize I'm actually *looking* for Steve, I laugh. Tried to get rid of him and now I'm sorry he's gone. Whatever. I know I'm leaving too, so I pull my shirt from the blue plastic bag on the bed.

"There you are. How are you doing, bud? Want me to help you with that?" Steve barrels in, grabs my shirt, and holds it while I put my arm through the sleeve. Then he does up my buttons.

Jesus! What am I . . . two?

"Where's the nurse? She didn't help you? Well, at least, you got the IV out of your hand. Bet that feels better, doesn't it?"

Maybe I should tell him that if he wants to interview people, he should wait for them to answer his freaking questions. Screw it. Let him figure it out for himself.

"There you go, all done." Steve stands back and surveys the job he did. "Now, do we have to wait for results of X-rays or are we free to go?"

The nurse scurries into the room. "Well, all done. You're free to go."

What was she doing? Standing outside waiting for her cue?

"You will be sore for a while," she says. "Just take care. Steve here is going to take you to the shelter for tonight. Right, Steve? You can't stay there during the day, but you probably know about the library. You can go there in the morning. The library has a nice indoor foyer; it's safe there and you can rest." She insists that I sit in the wheelchair, passes me my backpack, and keeps talking to Steve as she walks us to the exit. Once there, she helps me up and turns around. "Good luck," she says to me. "Thank you," to Steve.

We amble away, Steve and me. He is constantly checking to see if I am there, if I am okay, if I *am* . . . period. Part of me likes being on an invisible leash. Part of me craves being on my own. Since every step causes me to cringe in pain, the leash wins. For now.

I know it's not far to the shelter. Steve mutters something about not having his car. About streets closed preparing for Olympics anyway. About how it's better to use the bus. Or the Skytrain. Yada. Yada. Yada.

Shut up, Steve. Don't care.

It's almost dusk now, and I wonder where the day went. How much time had I spent sleeping, waiting, in the Dumpster, in the hospital? We stop and start, Steve hovering like a nervous new mother. Like Sarah with Bobby. I hold tighter to my backpack and smile on my good side. Steve thinks I'm smiling at him.

"There. That's more like it. You're looking better already. Here, let's sit at the bus stop for a minute or two, just to be sure you're okay."

I oblige. We both sit there, staring at the passersby. Here, at the bus stop, with Steve by my side, I'm a regular person. Almost. Feels good until a homeless man passes, pushing a bulging shopping buggy. My stomach lurches. I used to feel sorry for people like that. Jesus! Who the hell am I kidding? Sorry, my ass. Contempt is more like it. Shiftless vagrants. A blight on the postcard beauty of Vancouver. Scraggly hair, dirty clothes, yellow teeth.

"Hummph!" I hold back a laugh. Stick my tongue into the empty space in the side of my mouth where two teeth used to be. Maybe yellow teeth are better than no teeth. Still, I don't want a shopping cart. There's no hope left when you have a shopping cart. No hope. I don't belong with the shopping cart crowd. "Let's. Get. Out. Of. Here." My body trembles as I spit the words.

Steve rockets to his feet, helps me to mine, and we continue on our way. "After I get you settled in," he says, "I'll go away. But I promise I'll come back in the morning as soon as they open and I'll take you wherever you want. The library works for me if it works for you. We can talk . . . "

I stop dead. "What do you want from me?"

Steve is still walking. Words still pouring out of him. " . . . because I don't have classes tomorrow, and I can help . . . " Yada. Yada. Yada. He's waving his hands around like he's conducting a goddam symphony. He halts abruptly, swings around, and marches back to me.

"What do you want from me?" I demand again.

He is standing about a foot away, looking up at me. I notice how small he is. The man can't be more than a hundred thirty pounds soaking wet. Mid-twenties, I'm guessing.

He runs a hand through his blond brush cut and lets out a sigh. "I want to help. Like I told you, I have to interview . . . "

"Why me?"

"Don't know." He shrugs his shoulders and shivers.

For the first time, I notice he is not wearing his puffy jacket. A warm January, yeah, but he must be bloody freezing.

"Maybe you just looked like you needed someone," he says, folding his arms.

I narrow my one good eye. Something familiar about that face staring into mine, about the way those arms are crossed. I don't know what. The only thing I do know is that Marshmallow Man is a liar.

3

SAFETY IN NUMBERS

I am curled up on a cot in the homeless shelter. Not like the hospital. No rest and relaxation here. I've been in a shelter before. No such thing as safety in a shelter where a hundred or so men are locked up together without walls. Folding cots lined up tight, claustrophobic tight. I figure prison would be safer; at least there, the addicts and the crazies have their own cells. Here, they can show up at your bedside any second. I clutch my grey wool blanket and jump at every sound.

Eventually, fatigue overrides fear and I doze off. In and out of sleep. Waiting for daylight. Intending to be out first thing. All the while, I'm trying to figure out the Steve guy. Tomorrow, I have to go to the library because there's really nowhere else for me. I can't avoid Steve if I go to the library. Yeah. He's gonna find me. Guess I'll just string him along until I'm healthy enough to be on my own.

When morning comes, I pick up my belongings and, head low, shuffle with the crowd toward the exit. My need to get out of here escalates with every step. I'm halfway there—to the door, to open air, to freedom—when I hear it: rumbling, freight-train laughter. Jesus! I freeze. My heart trips, pounds, races. My body starts shaking. Maybe I imagined the sound, I tell myself. But then I hear it again. Muffled. Coming from outside. Definitely him. One of the thugs who attacked me.

The departing horde prods and pushes me, but I resist, sidle out of it, plop onto a chair, and hug my backpack. Safe. No one can see this chair from the door. I can't leave, not now. Got to hang around until the place is empty. Until the thug is sure everyone's gone. Can't risk him seeing me. Oh, God! Maybe they're both here. Outside, trolling for victims. I don't know their faces but they know mine. Maybe they came to finish me off.

I unzip the backpack, pull out the plastic castle, and hold it in my palm, gripping it so hard that my hand hurts. Someday, I want to return this castle to Bobby. Someday, I want to see my son. I don't want to die at the hands of two thugs.

Suddenly, my perspective on the Steve thing changes. I hope the hell he shows up. *Hurry up, Steve. Safety in numbers. Hurry up.* My right knee is bouncing like a jackhammer. I inhale, hold my breath. *Don't throw up. Just don't throw up.* I squeeze my good eye shut. Someone approaches, stops in front of me, just stands there. I open my eye. White sneakers. Blue jeans with a crease—razor-sharp. I slowly raise my head until I see a blond brush cut. I exhale in a whoosh. There is a God.

"Sorry, I'm late, bud. Missed the bus. Ready to go?"

I look around. Most people are gone. I nod and stand. Keeping my head low, I walk fast, very fast. To the door. Through the door. Onto the sidewalk.

Laughter rumbles. "Well, well, well! Will ya look at that?"

"I'll be damned." The second voice.

Christ! They're both here. I pick up my pace and look over my shoulder repeatedly, like an experienced beat cop on the downtown east side. Terrified, I try to run. My chest burns and my head pounds. Damn near pass out. Have to settle for walking. Speed walking.

"Hey! Wait for me. What's the rush?" Steve catches up with me. One last shoulder check shows me that the thugs have turned back. I slow down.

"Who set a fire under you? You sure heal quick, bud."

I grunt. *Fear trumps pain,* bud. The fear dissipates now and relief surges through me. I let out a sigh. Safe. For the moment. Don't know about tonight or tomorrow. But I'm here now: safe and alive and, damn it all, I want to stay that way.

"As I was saying, you sure heal fast."

Jesus. He's still talking.

"Want to get some breakfast before the library, bud? I could go for a cup of coffee. Maybe a muffin. What about you?"

I stop and look at Steve. Don't trust him, but so what? Don't trust anybody. Need to stay alive. Need to get healthy. Need to get to Bobby. Marshmallow Man is looking pretty good right now.

"Suppose you're one of them Starbucks people, are you?" I ask.

"Prefer Tim Hortons, actually. McDonald's even."

"Egg McMuffin sounds good."

"Great idea. Library doesn't open 'til ten."

We go to the McDonald's that's not too far from where we first met and sit by a window. I look out at my heating vent across the street. Not mine anymore. A human form lies there, under a blue sleeping bag. Maybe I can reclaim the spot tonight.

Steve passes me an Egg McMuffin. My stomach growls. Despite the pain in my jaw and the absence of teeth, I manage to chomp down on it, inhale it.

Steve is about to take a first bite of his Egg McMuffin when he notices that mine is gone already. He returns his to its container and slides the whole thing across the table.

"All yours, bud."

"Stop that."

"Stop what?"

"Calling me 'bud.' "

"Why does that bother you?"

"Derogatory."

" 'Derogatory?' " His eyes widen. "Guess I *am* being derogatory."

"Duh."

"Sorry, bu . . . , oops, I mean, Vladimir. If that's your real name."

Sharp one, Steve. I polish off the last of the food and sip my coffee. "Vladimir will do."

"Okay, Vladimir. Wanna tell me how you ended up here?" He has his notebook out again.

"We just walked here from the shelter."

"Humor intact." Steve is actually writing this down. "You know what I mean."

"Why should I tell you anything?"

"*Because* . . . right now, you need me. *Because* if you wanted to die you would have walked toward those guys who started to follow you rather than waiting for me to help you. And you were waiting for me, weren't you?"

My good eye flashes. I say nothing.

"Figured as much. I study people, you know. Want me to report those thugs?"

I shake my head. "No."

"Why the heck not?"

I sniff. "If you mean 'hell,' just say it."

"Why the hell not?"

Steve's a quick study. "Can't ID 'em. Didn't see 'em." Now I'm a poet. Sarah would be proud.

"Then what made you so scared?"

"Didn't see 'em. Heard 'em. I remember their voices, their laughter. It was them."

"Oh, I see." For some reason, relief flickers across Steve's face. "So, you sure you don't want me to report them?"

I shrug. "Need more coffee."

"Okay. I get it. No cops." He twirls his pen. "So then . . . back to my question. How did you end up here?"

"Coffee?" I hold up my empty mug.

"Yeah. Yeah. Suppose you want another Egg Mc Muffin, too?" Steve drops his pen, plants both hands on the table, pushes off. He's standing over me now. "Good Lord, you do, don't you? Well, I'll get you one, but I got to warn you, that stuff will harden your arteries." He pauses then and laughs out loud. "Guess that was a ridiculous statement."

I'm smiling, inside and out. Steve walks to the counter and returns a few minutes later with coffee and two more Egg McMuffins. He sits.

"I guess it all goes back to the funeral," I say. Steve's posture morphs from relaxed to rigid. He reclaims his pen.

"What funeral, Vladimir?"

"Did I say that out loud?"

"You know darn well you did. What funeral?"

"Well, once upon a time . . ."

Steve's sigh is loud, rushed, like a kettle reaching its boiling point. "Yeah, yeah. And they all lived happily ever after . . . " He shakes his head and clicks his pen, repeatedly. "Can we get some semblance of reality here?"

I say nothing.

"Well?"

Still nothing.

Steve rises. "If you need more food, I'll get it for you. Other than that, I guess there's no point in my staying, is there?" He turns toward the door.

My heart races and my head reels. I clutch my gut. I can't be sick, here, at McDonald's, for Christ's sake. I open my mouth and words spew like projectile vomit. "The name's Justin." Jesus! Am I desperate or what?!

Steve does an about-face and reclaims his seat. "That's more like it. Justin, huh?"

"Yeah." I gulp. "Justin. And the funeral . . . "

"What funeral?"

"It was twenty years ago."

Steve opens his mouth and then closes it again. He takes a deep breath, holds it, and waits.

"Twenty years ago," I say again, more to myself than to Steve. Has it really been that long?

Steve exhales, long and slow. "How old were you, Justin?" he asks, almost in a whisper.

"Eighteen."

"You want to tell me whose funeral we're talking about?"

4

FAMILY OUTING

August, 1990

I gobble my lunch and leap from the kitchen table. "Gotta go pack!"

"Can't it wait, dear?" Mom has that soulful look in her eyes again.

I hesitate.

"Let him go, Jen." Dad waves his hand, a light gesture of dismissal. "He's excited about university. Let him pack."

Mom swallows and blinks. She takes a deep breath and exhales in an inaudible sigh. She nods.

I grin, give her a quick hug, and vault toward the stairs. I'm halfway up when I hear Dad's voice, a usually-steady baritone, jump to a trembling tenor. "Nametags?" he says.

I stop dead and tilt an ear toward the kitchen.

"Jennifer Wentworth," he continues, "did you just say that you sewed *nametags* into Justin's underwear?"

I cringe, grab the stair rail, and fold my body over it. *Please say you didn't do that, Mom.*

"Of course, I did, Jason," says my mother. "How on earth is he going to keep track of his stuff in that residence?"

I roll my eyes and race to my room. I keep the door open so I can hear the rest of my parents' conversation. *God knows what else Mom did.*

"He's eighteen years old, for Pete's sake, woman—in a few days he will be a university freshman. He's not going to a kids' summer camp." Bet any money that Dad is shaking his head now. "You sure do pamper that son of yours."

"Me pamper him? Who got him the sports car for his sixteenth birthday, Jason? What about that sundial *you* constructed for his homework when he was in the sixth grade? He still has that thing, you know."

Note to self: get sundial out of waste basket.

"And while we're at it, who bought him the top-of-the-line computer?" Mom continued. "The video games? All I did was to put tags in his underwear."

"Oh, is that all? I seem to remember him getting lots of As at school for those speeches *you* wrote for Toastmasters!" Dad laughs, loud. Just throws his laughter across the room, like a baseball heading for home plate. Mom catches it, echoes it.

"Okay, so we both spoil him. But he is our only child, Jason. S-o-n and s-u-n."

"Yeah, yeah. Son and sun. I get it. You don't have to spell it out for me, Jen. You do say that *all* the time, you know."

"I know. I'm going to miss him." Mom sobs a little.

Instinct kicks in and I spring for the door, determined to make her smile. But, before I even get out of my room, reality pierces and I freeze in position like a miler waiting for a starting gun. Huh. What's the point? I can't fix this. Mom, *and* Dad . . . my world, yes, but, in a few days, I'm leaving. A sense of loss washes over me and I scan my room, trying to find . . . what? Don't know. Still the urge to rush to them pulses through me. Maybe I'm not ready to let go, to grow up. I have always depended on my parents. I'm sure they'll be there for me, even after I leave, but . . .

"I'm going to miss him, too," Dad says, "but we'll be fine, Jen. *He'll* be fine."

It's my turn to sigh now. Resigned, I close my bedroom door.

I grope through suitcases and extract underwear. Sure enough, there it is—JUSTIN WENTWORTH—plastered on every pair. *Damn it all, Mom.* I find my nail clippers and grapple with the threads.

"Justin?" My father's voice.

Racing to the waste basket, I yank out the sundial and put it on my desk. Then I go back to the underwear mission.

"In my room, Dad. Come on up."

Seconds later, Dad pushes open the door. "Son, your mother and I . . . " He stops suddenly. "Well, it's a good thing I came up instead of your mom. Break her heart to see this."

"Can you believe it? She must have used Crazy Glue along with the thread. I'd be a laughingstock . . . ." I swerve to look at him. "You won't tell her, will you?" I hold my breath.

"Hell, no! Gotta pick your battles in life, Son. No need to walk into that one."

I exhale. "Thanks, Dad." Good. Now I wouldn't have to go through the whole *I'm sorry, Mom* routine. Done that many times. Too many times. I never really felt sorry. Never wanted to hurt her either. Just hated the drama.

My father waves his hand in the air. "No worries, mate," he says. Dad thinks he is Crocodile Dundee. "Anyway, I came up to tell you that your mother and I are going out to a movie this evening. You can come if you want."

I shake my head. "Don't think so. Only a few days left at home and lots to do. Packing and all. What are you going to see? *Crocodile Dundee II* still playing?"

"Doesn't matter. Your mother's turn to pick, God help me."

I grin. "Try *A Fish Called Wanda*. You both might like that."

"That the one with John Cleese?"

"Yup. And Jamie Lee Curtis."

Dad nods. "Not a bad idea. Maybe I'll bring that up. Well done, Son." He slaps me on the back. "We'll be off in about a half hour. Come on down if you change your mind." He turns to leave. "By the way, I really don't mind if you throw out the sundial. It has served its purpose, don't you think?"

I smile and nod. "No fooling you, is there?"

"Saw it in the waste basket earlier today." There's that baseball laugh again. "See you later."

He heads downstairs and I go about my business. Removing tags, keeping this, tossing that. Outside, rain is pelting down, drumming the rooftop, reminding me of camping days: Mom, Dad, and me—in the Airstream. Seems it rained only at night on those trips. I remember being lulled to sleep, many times, by the rhythm of rain on the roof. In the mornings, the sun would appear and Dad and I would get the fishing rods ready while Mom made breakfast. Huh. I can almost smell the bacon . . .

"Son?" Dad calls from the foot of the stairs. "We're off to the movie. Sure you don't want to come?"

I open my mouth, intending to say I'd rather stay, but only a sigh comes out. In a few days, I'm leaving home. In a few days. Not now. I seize a jacket from the mountain of clothes on my bed. "Be right there!"

I charge through the door and barrel down the stairs, two steps at a time. At the bottom, I grab the cap of the newel post; it comes off in my hand. I stumble, almost falling into the arms of my father before I manage to right myself.

"Guess you never did get around to fixing that one, Dad!"

"Tomorrow, son. I'll do it first thing tomorrow." He grins at me.

Returning his smile, I nod and replace the cap. I dash to the front door and yank it open. A blast of wind and rain whacks me in the face. "Whoa! Are you two sure you want to go to the movies this evening?"

"It'll be fine, son. No worries," says Dad.

"It'll be nice to have a family outing. Maybe our last for a while." Mom's eyes are tear-filled . . . again.

I feel my heart sink a little and I turn from her. "University is only thirty miles away . . ."

Dad intervenes, clapping me on the shoulder. "Women. Go figure." He rolls his eyes at me as he guides us through the door. We race to the car; I hold the passenger door for Mom and then jump into the back seat.

"Seat belts," says Mom. "Precious cargo."

Huh. She's been saying that forever. "Precious cargo." I'm not a kid anymore, but her voice and her words still warm me. I smile to myself, glad that I'm going with them. She's right: could be the last family outing for a while.

After the movie, we emerge, laughing, into darkness. The rain has stopped. Not a breath of wind. The streets are slick with water which slithers into streams and gurgles into drains. I inhale; the air smells fresh. A clean slate.

"Hey, the weather's really turned around. How about we grab some Chinese food before we head home?" Dad's holding his car keys, waiting for a reply.

"Sounds good to me," I say.

Mom nods and Dad pockets his keys. We cross the street to Nanking Gardens where we decide to dine in. Nothing unusual about the fare: pineapple chicken, beef and broccoli, chicken fried rice. Completes the family outing. Mom is all smiles when we leave.

We climb aboard the car.

The next thing I know, it's raining again. Just a little, but I'm drenched to the skin. And I'm standing at the side of the road, talking to a police officer. "No, I don't know why we didn't fasten our seat belts, Dad and me," I'm saying. "Mom did. I'm sure Mom did. She always does. She always reminds us . . ."

"I'm sorry, son," says the officer.

I don't want to turn toward the car, but I do. Mom is still in it, latched into her seat. Is that a tree branch impaling her chest? Why don't I feel anything? I look at the driver's seat. It is empty. "Where's Dad?" I ask no one in particular.

"I'm sorry, son," the officer says again.

I slowly rotate my head until I am looking into the officer's face.

"I guess you and your father were thrown clear," he continues. "Your father didn't make it, son."

This is a dream, that's what it is, a dream. *Wake up, damn it. Wake up.* I shake my head, but I don't wake up. I'm trapped here. "It was a family outing," I say. My voice sounds like it's coming from another planet. "I'm leaving for university in a few days. Just a family outing."

5

FINAL GOODBYES

August, 1990

I have no clue how to behave here. I stand where they tell me to, on a beige carpet in a big room that feels like a church. My throat is tight. I loosen my tie but it doesn't help. Everyone stares at me like I am a slide under a microscope in Mr. Smith's eighth grade biology class. I wonder if that frog felt any pain the day I slit him open. I shudder and shake my head. My eyes dart around the room.

Folding chairs. Lots of them. On every side. No, just three sides. People sit, stand, squirm. The chairs squeak. Loud. Or maybe it is just the room is so quiet that every sound jumps at me. Whatever. Squeaks and whispers, that's all I hear until Mom's friend, Nancy, walks in and starts howling like a freaking banshee. I pull up one corner of my mouth in contempt. I want to turn away, but I don't. That would mean looking at the fourth wall. Can't do that. If I do, I might start believing all this stuff. Nothing feels real yet and I'm okay with that.

Someone puts a coffee and a sandwich in my hands. In the viewing room? I frown. It doesn't seem right to eat here. But that Jim Thompson is eating, damn him, the fat pig.

"Total ignoramus," Mom used to say. "Whatever you do in this world, Justin, don't be like him."

Okay, Mom. I don't eat or drink.

Mr. Cormier from next door approaches me. "*Je suis désolé,* Justin," he says. "I am so sorry for your loss." He nods slightly and keeps his hands folded in front of him.

"Thank you, *monsieur.*"

Mr. Cormier moves slowly away and I watch him. He knows how to act. A good man, Mr. Cormier. Dad always said so.

Someone else comes near, the man who runs the place. The funeral director. He touches my arm and looks up at me. "It's time, Justin." He removes the coffee and sandwich from my hands and passes them off to a woman who whisks them away. "Do you wish to say your final goodbyes before we close the caskets?"

I don't move until Debra slips her arm through mine. *Thank God.* Debra is here. She has always been here, ever since seventh grade. Friend and girlfriend. I can rely on Debra. I turn toward her and our eyes collide. Hers are dilated, eerie, like a troll doll. A shiver snakes its way down my spine. I gulp and nod, thankful that I am not alone.

My neck hurts. I raise my free hand to rub the ache away and I catch a whiff of Old Spice. Dad's Old Spice. It lingers on the sleeve of my suit which is not my suit, but Dad's suit. *Dad loves this suit.* Out of the corner of my eye, I notice a piece of lint on the sleeve of this, Dad's dark blue suit. *Mom uses sticky rollers to remove lint.*

"It's time," repeats the man.

As I turn toward the matching caskets, reality knifes my gut: Dad *loved* this suit; Mom *used* sticky rollers. *There. I corrected my verb tense. Wouldn't my English teacher be proud?* I quiver. Must be something wrong with me. Verb tense? Where the hell did that come from? Maybe I am just losing it.

The funeral director begins ushering people out of the room. I remember Mr. Cormier's movements. A good man, Mr. Cormier. Squeezing Debra's arm to my side, determined never to let her go, I fold my hands in front of me, lower my head and walk slowly toward the coffins to . . . what was it the man said? Oh yes, " . . . say my final goodbyes."

6

A SPARE ROOM

January, 2010

I keep my head low, focused on the sidewalk. I'm counting lines, avoiding cracks as Steve and I walk along. At our destination—the library—he opens the door and holds it for me. I saunter toward a bench; he follows. We sit and I look directly at him.

Steve's face is glowing like he won the freaking lottery or something. Huh. Don't get that. Whatever. Don't care. My stomach is full for the first time in weeks. I need a meal ticket and I need safety. No way I'm going to a shelter tonight. Maybe not for many nights. Too scary in the shelter. Should I risk the street? Maybe there's another option. Maybe I should keep Steve talking, interested. Maybe he has a spare room. Maybe he'll let me use his spare room.

"Where do you live?" I ask.

"Doesn't matter. What happened after your parents' funeral?"

You want answers, you give answers, bud. In protest, I swerve away from him and stare at the armrest on the bench: wrought iron, lacquered, black. Strange design: a complete circle, big enough to stick my head through. Maybe even my whole torso. Okay, maybe not *my* whole torso, but certainly Sarah's. I touch the armrest and flinch from the chill.

"Okay, okay," says Steve. "I live on Nicola, a few blocks from English Bay."

I grin, just a little. English Bay. Huh. I know that area. Sold a few condos there. Marshmallow Man has money. *Tell me more,* bud. I erase my smile as I turn toward him and wait. No rush. Nowhere to go.

"It's a two bedroom condo."

"Got a roommate?"

"No. I live alone." *Tap, tap, tap* goes his pen as he flicks it against his notebook.

I have pushed enough for now. Gotta give him something. "Went to university."

"UBC?"

"No. Not here. New Brunswick. Mount Allison."

"New Brunswick? That's a long way away. Why there? You from there?"

I nod.

"Your parents, too? They die there?"

Another nod.

"So, you going to tell me what this Mount Allison place was like?"

Not now, Steve. Even though I am already there. In autumn. Seeing the trees. Meeting Sarah. Want to be alone now. "I'm tired. Need to rest." I start to spread out on the bench. Steve moves to accommodate me. I forget he is even there.

"Okay," he sighs.

7

SARAH

October, 1991

Cold air blasts me when I try to exit Hart Hall. "Damn!" I shut the door, drop my books on the radiator and zip up my jacket. Shoving my books under my arm, I yank at the door again, dart through, and jam my hands into my pockets. Once outside, I shrug. Not so cold. Kinda like going swimming. Better just to plunge in and keep moving.

What the hell was that professor talking about this morning? And where the hell was my brain when I signed up for Early English Lit? Geoffrey Chaucer, for Christ's sake. I shake my head. Too late to transfer. Guess I'll just continue pretending like I'm getting everything that's going on—just watch everybody and smile my way through. Always been good at that. I yawn. Coffee. I need coffee.

Out of the corner of my eye, I notice red, yellow, and brown dripping all over the place. Really like it—trees and autumn and all. And Mount Allison campus. It's peaceful here, like in the park back home. From small town to small university. Good choice, especially after Mom and Dad died. I shudder and throw my eyes out of focus, making the colors of the leaves blur together. Instantly think of that impressionist guy—Monet or was it *Manet*? Whatever. Anyway, I remember that watercolor I saw in Fine Arts 101 last year and I smirk. At least I learned something in that course. Skipped so many classes I damn near failed it. The wind blasts again, snaking under my jacket, biting my skin, forcing me to walk faster. Okay, so it *is* cold. Damn near freezing. Coffee.

There's a pile of leaves near the bottom of the steps to the Student Center. A quick glance around proves that the area is clear of groundskeepers, so I give the leaves a kick. They fly into the air and rain down on someone going by.

I cringe. "Jesus! I'm *so* sorry!"

A grey-haired man—a professor maybe—brushes leaves from the shoulders of his camel overcoat and then stares at me, his face vacillating between accusation and dismissal.

"I really didn't see you there." My heart speeds up. "Are you okay . . . sir?" I lean forward, waiting for his reply.

He shrugs and smiles. "No harm done, young man." As he goes on his way, I let out a relieved sigh.

Got to pay more attention, Wentworth. I barrel up the steps to the Student Center. I can smell the coffee now. Love that smell. I inhale deeper, head into the cafeteria and approach the service counter. As usual, Sally is there.

"Mornin', Justin," she says. "Managed to get out of bed in time for class this morning, did ya?" She grins and a series of vertical lines pop out on her face. They intersect the horizontal lines that time has already put there, and the result is a crosshatch pattern.

Tic-tac-toe. I really want to say that but don't dare. "You don't miss a thing, do you, Sally?"

Sally chuckles and tucks a strand of grey hair underneath her hairnet. "See all, know all—that's me. The usual?"

"Absolutely."

"Well, have a seat and I'll give a shout when it's ready."

"Thanks." I go to my regular spot next to the counter, put my books on the table, remove my jacket, toss it on a chair, and sit. I like sitting here, alone. Don't understand why some people hate eating or going to movies by themselves. I don't get that at all.

I glance at my watch. Lots of time before my next class. I reach for my binder and flip to the notes from English Lit. The door wheezes open, prompting me to look up. A young, very young, blonde girl comes in. I raise one eyebrow and then chastise myself for feeling even a twinge of interest. She can't be more than thirteen. A girl from town, maybe. High school kid. What is she doing on campus? She heads toward the far end of the room.

"Order's ready," calls Sally. I turn, pull a five dollar bill from the pocket of my jeans and go to the counter.

"Thanks, Sally. Keep the change."

Sally rings in the sale and pockets the change. "Thank you, Justin." She beams.

With a plate of cinnamon toast in one hand and coffee in the other, I go back to my table. As I sit, I hear Sally chatting with another waitress.

"Lovely young fellow, isn't he, Mary? So polite."

My lips curve into a wide grin. Time to eavesdrop.

"You know he lost his parents, don't you?" Sally continues.

Ouch. The grin disappears and I gulp. Maybe I should move to another table.

"Yeah. I heard. Such a shame. But you'd never know he's been through a thing like that. Every time I see him, he has a smile on his face."

I squirm, grab my jacket, and slide to the edge of my chair. *Hold on a sec, Wentworth. They'll shut up soon enough.* I wait.

"Yep. Charm the socks off Satan, that one. Life just doesn't seem fair, does it? Well, anyway, his folks must have left him with a bundle: he always gives me a tip. Can you imagine?"

"That's so nice of him, Sally. Most of the kids are broke. Them that have a few bucks don't even say thank you, never mind leave a tip." She giggles. "Here's an idea: maybe I should serve him tomorrow!"

Sally laughs outright. "Sure. In the meantime, how about serving the one at the counter?"

Footsteps scurry. Conversation's over.

Relieved, I drop my jacket and slide back in my seat. I nod, pleased that they like me, that I made them laugh. But still, don't think I'll be eavesdropping again anytime soon. I turn and scan the room. Don't see the blonde anywhere, so I figure she left. I shrug. Too young anyway.

I wrap both hands around my coffee cup until I feel its warmth in my fingers. Scan some notes as I sip my coffee. Then I reach for a triangle of cinnamon toast, shake a dusting of sugar from it, and take a bite. When I look up again, the young, very young, blonde is standing in front of me. With her is

Nathan—a short guy with big eyes and a nervous laugh—who lives on my floor in Truman House.

"Hey, Justin. This here's Sarah. She's in my Psych class." Nathan deposits his books on the table. "Coffee, Sarah?" he asks as he heads to the counter.

"Sure. Black, please." With a wave of her hand, Sarah flicks back her long hair. She smiles at me and her eyes flash deep blue. Sapphire blue.

"Have a seat, Sarah." I notice her chipped front tooth. "How was Psych class?"

"Not bad, I guess. Elective. Have to take it. English Lit is my major. I'm a sophomore." The plastic chair across from me scrapes the floor as Sarah pulls it out. She plops into it. "What about you?"

"European History. Soph."

"Cool. You planning to teach?"

"Haven't really given it much thought. How about you?"

"Teaching?" She scrunches up her nose. Damn cute. "Maybe. But I think that what I really want is to work in a library. I love books . . . could spend hours in the Bell Library just staring at the stacks. Reading is the best. Yeah, you read a good book and you've got a friend for life." She clamps her lips together and nods as if she has just figured that out.

I open my mouth to speak but she is still talking.

"Right now, I'm happy just being a sophomore. Yeah, being a sophomore is pretty good. Now, last year . . . " she points a nail-bitten finger in my direction . . . "that was a completely different matter. Frosh week—the whole initiation thing—scared me half to death." She plunks her elbows on the table, rests her head in her hands, and locks her eyes with mine.

I sit still and hold my breath, certain that she is about to reveal some deep, dark secret.

"Decided to hide out for the second half of it." Her voice is whispered, as soft as brushed velvet. Makes my skin shiver. A good feeling.

"I figured some annoying sophomore would come and drag me out of the dorm and paint my face green or something," she says. A grin creeps across her lips and sparks of silver dance in her eyes. Without warning, she leans back, throws her hands up and then claps them together.

I drop my toast.

"Turns out it didn't matter; no one even noticed I was missing," she says airily.

I laugh and the sound bounces across the table. She echoes my laughter, just like Mom did with Dad. My eyes widen and I inhale sharply. We stare, wordless.

White noise—shuffling feet, chattering voices, clattering cutlery—closes around us like rushing water. I can't move. Don't want to. Want to sit here forever, eyes riveted to hers . . . .

Sarah takes a deep breath, extracts her gaze from mine, and drops her eyes to the table.

Disappointed, I release a long, silent sigh.

"Anyway," she says, "I couldn't believe my luck. And now that I'm a soph, I'm hiding out again . . . having nothing to do with all that hazing stuff. Hard enough for the frosh around here." Abruptly, she jumps up. "Now, where's my coffee? That cinnamon toast looks good! Got to get me some of that!" She heads to the counter.

I stare after her. Then I grab my binder and drop it on my lap to cover up my boner. Huh. A few words from a perky, chipped-tooth blonde, and I'm ready for action. I continue to watch her. Pretty skinny, I decide. Can't be more than a hundred ten pounds. Short. Cute. And definitely looks younger than her age. And those eyes. So blue. So perfect. And that laugh . . . the way it echoed mine. What I would give . . . *Jesus, Wentworth. What are you thinking? Debra would have a fit.*

That did it. Didn't need the binder anymore so I put it back on the table. Debra. I am involved with Debra. Not too serious except for the fact that we are engaged to be engaged . . . whatever that means. How the hell did that happen?

By the time Nathan and Sarah return with their coffee and cinnamon toast, I have dismissed my interest in Sarah. I keep my focus on Nathan, talk to Nathan, don't glance into Sarah's eyes again. I'm sure I'll meet many cute blondes, many cute, blue-eyed blondes, but I have Debra. Debra knew Mom and Dad; she remembers Mom and Dad. She is all I have left. The closest thing to a relative. My palms are sweating now and my heart is hammering. I don't want surprises. No uninvited blondes walking through the door. No distractions. Straight path. Being with Debra is good. Familiar.

Nathan is blabbing away, making no sense. Time to leave. "Darn." I look at my watch and shrug into my jacket. "Got to get to class. See you later." I lump my books together, grab my cup and plate and stumble away. The back of my neck hurts like hell. I drop my dirty dishes into one of the bins near the exit, reach up and rub my neck. Doesn't help. Damn it all. As I head through the door, I think of Sarah's sparkling eyes. I smile and the ache disappears.

8

STEVE'S PLACE

January, 2010

Guess I dozed off here. I'm pretty tired and my body seems sorer than it did earlier. Not surprising. The library benches are like the ones in the park: curved slats, fine for sitting but not for lying down. I grab the wrought iron armrest, pull myself up, and look all around. A long yawn escapes me.

What now? Daylight's fading. Steve's not here, but I don't panic. He'll show up. Guaranteed. Still have to get him to invite me to his place. I sit on my hands, rock, wait. Maybe I should go to the washroom. No. Don't want to miss Steve. People are scurrying—ants—all around me. No Steve. *Where the hell are you, Steve? Where the hell are you?*

"Here I am." Steve is in front of me.

I exhale. I try to look indifferent, all the while wondering if I was thinking out loud again. If I was, he knows I'm desperate. Maybe he knows that anyway.

"You were asleep so I took off for a while," says Steve. "Things to do, you know. Wanna talk some more?"

I shake my head. "Washroom."

"Sure. I'll walk with you, and I'll watch your backpack if you want." He holds up a plastic bag. "Brought you some shaving stuff, some soap, a toothbrush."

"Thanks. Don't think I could brush my teeth just yet." I pull up my lip and display the gap where my teeth used to be.

"Darn! That must hurt."

"If you mean 'damn' then say it."

"Damn! That must hurt."

Now we have a running joke, Steve and me. In my other life, I would have liked him. But now, I just need him. "Give me the toothbrush anyway. In a couple of days, I'll use it. Need a new one."

"What about the soap? A shave?"

"I'll take the soap. No need to shave. The beard keeps me warm."

"Yeah, about that . . . you don't have to live on the street."

"Yeah, yeah. Shelters, I know."

"No, not shelters, Vladimir, Justin, whatever. Not shelters. My place."

I look at the floor. This is too good. I wonder what his angle is. "What do you mean . . . your place?"

"Not permanent, you know. Just long enough for you to heal a bit. For me to get my research. I give you shelter. You give me info. It's not charity. It's a barter system. What do you think?"

My heart is doing calisthenics. I nod like a bobble head on the dashboard of a car. I pick up my backpack, jump to my feet, and head toward the exit.

"Hey! I thought you wanted to go to the washroom."

I'm already at the door. This time my bladder can wait.

"Hey!" Steve calls again.

I stop when I realize that I don't know exactly where I'm going. I turn and wait for my meal ticket. We exit, walk a block, and board the number five bus that is just sitting there like it knew we were coming. Steve pays. I follow him down the aisle and sit beside him. A short ride. Off the bus at Denman and Davie. A short wait. Onto another bus. We exit near Nicola, walk a couple of blocks downhill and enter an apartment building.

Steve's condo is a corner unit on the second floor. The living room looks familiar. Maybe I sold a condo here. Or maybe it's just the red and green, plaid couch. Have I seen that couch before? Steve leads me down the hall, past the den, to my room, my very own room with a double bed.

I am excited until I go to the window and peer into the alley below. A city alley with a green Dumpster, the sight of which makes my stomach churn. So close. So damn close. Only a wall separates me from my reality. I take a few deep breaths. At least, there *is* a wall. And, for now, that is enough. I am safe. I turn toward the bed and walk to it like I am entering heaven. Nirvana. I sit on the edge, slowly, tentatively, half-afraid it will dissolve beneath me. It gives a little, but remains. Encouraged, I lie down and close my eyes. Then I am gone. Asleep. Blackness. Then dreams.

9

AND, AND, AND . . .

May, 1992

What's the matter with you lately?" Debra snatches the remote from my hand and slides to the other side of the red and green plaid couch. With a defiant sweep, she switches off the TV.

"Hey! Give that back!" I jump up. We scramble. She tosses. The remote thuds into a nearby armchair. I eye it, ready to pounce.

"Don't even think about it!"

I groan and plop next to her on the couch

"Good . . . you can watch hockey any old time. Now . . . tell me what's wrong."

"Nothing's wrong, Deb. Nothing. Tough shift at work, that's all."

"Work, my ass. You haven't said two words in the past hour. What's going on?"

I turn and look into her eyes, shiny, black eyes that are wide and questioning, just like they were at the funeral when she clung to my elbow. Damn.

Deb has always been there, ever since seventh grade. My parents loved her like a daughter. I swallow. Do I want to lose her? Who will help me remember my family? *And why can't I get Sarah out of my head?*

"Deb, we're in your parents' home." I put an arm around her. "I don't think it's appropriate . . ."

She sloughs off my arm, shoots up from the couch, and stands, glaring, fists on hips. "Okay then, so when is it appropriate, Justin?" She throws her arms out to the side. "Not *he*-ere."

God, the girl is dramatic. Have to give her that.

"Not when we're at that godforsaken Y you're living in." She is pacing the floor now. I move my head from side-to-side, watching.

"Not when you're tired. Not in the park, not at McDonald's, not at the Mall . . . when, Justin? When?" She stops and turns toward me. "Tell me that!"

I shrug. The hockey game is in the third period. Tie game, too. I glance at the TV. *Huge* mistake.

"Forget the game, Justin!" She waggles a finger in my face. "You have to set a time!"

I snap. "Set a time . . . and a date—right?"

She jumps back like I've slapped her.

My gaze plummets to the carpet. Well, I screwed up there. Definitely. Couldn't stall anymore after that one. Time to rock and roll. I lean forward, grab her hand, and hold it tight. "Sit down, Deb."

"Hmmph!"

"Please." I tug repeatedly . . . and gently. I do *not* want to do this, to hurt her. But I can't pretend anymore. Not fair. Not right. So I smile and tug, tug and smile.

Bit by bit—head, shoulders, torso, legs—she wilts.

Damn. She knows what's coming.

When her body plops like a rag doll beside me, I take a deep breath. Then another. "You know I just turned twenty, Deb."

"So did I, and, quite frankly, I expected a ring for my birthday." Her lower lip quivers.

Oh God, the tears are coming. I squirm, release her hand and angle my body to face the door. "I'm not ready for marriage."

"What? But, but, but . . . you said we'd get married when you sold your parents' home. You got money. Tons of money!"

Damn! When she gets on about something, her voice whines like wind through storm-whipped trees.

"We can afford a ring," she continues, "and, and a wedding . . . and, and a house . . . and a car, and . . . "

My eyes widen. An EXIT sign flashes in my head. On, off, on, off. "A ring *and* a house *and* a car *and, and, and* . . . " She wants stuff, lots of it. *And* I've always given her stuff. Maybe *all* she wants is stuff. The way out—the easy way out—is through the stuff. I pivot toward her.

"I'm broke, Deb."

She hiccups back a sob and gapes at me. Jaw down to her chest. "What do you mean—broke? The house? The garage sale? The cars? You can't be broke!" Sniffing, she wipes her eyes on her sleeve. "Your parents gave you presents, all the time! Expensive stuff. They even gave *me* stuff." She shakes her head. "Uh-uh! I'm not buying this 'broke' business!"

My gaze returns to the door. "I *am* broke. My parents were in debt."

"Look at me, Justin."

Oh God, what now? I don't move.

She reaches over, cups my face with her hands and rotates my head toward her. "Huh!" She drops her arms. "You're lying," she whispers. "You get a streak in your eyes when you lie, you know. I just *can't* believe you'd try to lie to *me!*"

I keep my voice even; can manage that easily because I'm *not* lying . . . not about the debt anyway. "No lies, Deb. Maybe it seems that way because I can hardly believe it myself. But Mr. Cormier—Dad's executor, Dad's friend—he handled all the lawyer stuff for me and explained it all to me. My parents overspent. Simple as that. They lived beyond their means . . . Mr. Cormier said so. Why do you think I'm working at a bakery for the summer?"

She stares into my eyes again, making my heart race like it did before every final exam I ever wrote. I clench my jaw and harden my gaze.

"Mr. Cormier. Hmmm. Of course, I remember him," she says slowly. Her head tilts to the side and tiny lines crease her brow. "Your neighbor, right? The one whose wife was really ill?"

I nod, relieved that, for a few seconds, I am free of scrutiny.

"He told you about the debt? And you believe him?" She shakes her head and puts one hand out, palm facing me. "Wait. Don't answer that. Your parents were good people and I'm sure they chose an honest man. What matters here is that you have a job, a decent job." Her eyes go back to probing mine.

I squirm.

"And, and . . . you came back for me, didn't you?" she asks, wide-eyed.

"Of course I did; you're my bond to my family, Deb." Seems like the right thing to say, but the EXIT sign begins to strobe again. Damn. What now? I plunge. "Maybe, after I finish university and make some money, maybe we'll get married someday, but . . . " Damn! Another screw up! What if she goes for the "married someday" bit? Chained. I'll be chained. Forever.

"Oh, I see." Debra shrugs and looks away. "So you really are broke?"

Now my jaw was on the couch. Who the hell is this girl? "All this time, this was about money?"

Her head snaps back toward me. "Jesus, Justin! I don't give a damn about the money. I'm not that kind of girl, and you know it. I just wanted to see how far you'd go . . . " Her voice drops to a whisper. "You've met someone, haven't you?"

I open my mouth to deny, but nothing comes out. Oh, shit. This is not the way I want things to go. What can I say to her? *Deb, you're a wonderful person . . . but you're not Sarah.* Yeah, right.

After a few excruciatingly silent seconds, Debra looks down and tugs at the bottom of her cashmere sweater. "Darn! Is that mascara on my sleeve? Gotta change." She straightens, rises, and marches to the door. Once there, she pauses and peers over her shoulder.

The look she shoots me is as pointed as an icicle. Hits right between my eyes. Major brain freeze.

"You know the way out." Debra tosses her head, sending her pony tail into a whipping frenzy, and stomps away.

As I stumble to the door, I wonder if I should go back. Talk to her. At the door, I hesitate. The doorknob is cold to the touch. I recoil, but grab it again and twist. The door opens. One foot lands on the stoop. Then the other. The door creaks shut behind me. My lips curl upward and I propel myself down the steps, jumping from the second last step and landing on the sidewalk, feet together, firmly planted. My smile widens. I turn and break into a canter. I'm running free, nothing but the warm wind of spring on my face and whispers of Sarah on my mind.

10

BARRY GIBB

January, 2010

Who's Sarah?"

"Huh?" I jump. We're in Steve's kitchen. I'm minding my own business. Sitting at the table. Enjoying the smell of bacon that Steve is frying.

"Who's Sarah?"

I scan my brain. Had I left anything with that name on it in my backpack? Uh uh. Only had one thing—the watch with the engraving—and that was gone. I stare at my naked wrist and remember huge hands groping and clawing. I shudder as I turn toward Steve.

"Who told you about Sarah?"

"You did."

"Not a chance." Did I? Maybe. Not sure.

"Okay. Technically, you did. Actually, I overheard you. You were dreaming, maybe. Said the name a lot. I think you were even singing it at one point."

"Oh." Okay, *that* I can buy. I remember dreams. Movie-style dreams. Everything shows up. Vivid color. "I dream a lot. It helps me to stay connected or something. Easy to lose touch in the streets."

"That makes sense. Who's Sarah?"

"When's breakfast?"

Steve laughs. "Okay, I'll leave it for now. Maybe later?" He puts a plate of bacon and eggs in front of me. "Here." He plunks another plate on the table. "Have some toast, too."

"Twist my arm." I grab a slice of toast and lay on a thick coat of butter and strawberry jam. "If it's Smucker's, it has to be good." My knife stops in midair and a sob escapes me. Bobby floats in front of my face. "*If it's Smucker's, it has to be good, Daddy.*" My knife clatters to the table.

"Justin! What the heck is the matter? Justin!" Steve grabs my arm. I slap his hand away, shake my head, and retrieve my knife.

"Nothing. Nothing's wrong. Everything's fine." I chomp down on the toast, but I taste nothing. Not a damn thing. My whole body quivers. Need a drink. Need a drink. I scan the open-concept condo, looking for a liquor cabinet. Maybe over there, in the hutch beside the framed picture that is supposed to be Jesus Christ. Looks like one of the Bee Gees. Huh. Interesting. I look back at Steve.

He's still gawking at me. Speechless, for a change.

"Don't you have to go to work or take a class or something?" *That's a hint, bud.*

"Jeepers! Forgot. I have an appointment with a prof this morning. Are you sure you're okay? Should I just leave you here on your own?"

"*Jeepers!* I think I can handle it." Now get the hell out so I can find something to numb this pain. Wait. Did I say that last part out loud? Guess not. He's leaving. Trusting sort, isn't he? Wonder if the place has security cameras. I actually look around to check.

My eyes fall back on the Barry Gibb picture. That explains it. Marshmallow Man's a born-again. He trusts me. Didn't people learn anything from that Elizabeth Smart story? Go figure. I move to the hutch, open the doors, and rifle through all contents. No booze. Of course not. Born-again. Maybe I'll have more luck finding money. Where would he keep money? His bedroom? The den?

The den's closer, so that's my next stop.

First thing I see is the ficus tree. Instantly, a vision of Sarah pierces my mind and heart. *Can't give it a massive haircut, Justin, just a few leaves at a time,* she's saying as she preens and prunes her ficus. Damn, she loved that thing.

I shake off the memory before it can own me and turn toward Steve's solid oak computer desk. No, not desk, *armoire*, for Christ's sake, with its doors swung as wide as a whore's legs. I rummage through shelves and niches. No money. Damn. The four-drawer file cabinet—also oak, also open—is equally barren.

Anything else in this room? Nope, nothing but that pathetic-looking tree. The memory emerges again. *Sarah. Sarah. Sarah.* Sarah and her shears, trimming branches. Sarah and me, repotting the ficus. This time, I let mind dwell on the past, and sadness floods my eyes. I rein in tears as I stare at Steve's ficus which, unlike me, openly weeps, shedding leaves onto the carpet. Sighing, I turn and walk away.

I go back to my quest. Kitchen's next, then the bedroom.

In the kitchen, I rip drawers open and slam them shut. As I am heading out of the room, intent on searching Steve's bedroom, I go by the fridge and notice money waving from behind a magnet. Two twenties. Damn. Has this been here the whole time? There is a note attached:

> *This is for you. Take what you need.*
> *Extra key on table by door. Have a good one. S.*

"Thanks, Steve." I take the money and leave. I know I need a shower but I need this more.

It's a short walk uphill to Davie Street, to the nearest liquor store. Huh. Short walk, my ass. My body is a wreck. Hurts like hell. The walk won't feel short to me but it doesn't matter. I need a drink. Need trumps pain.

Walk. Walk. Walk. As fast as I can. I end up clutching my ribs for the last block to ward off the pain that stabs me with every intake of breath. Need a drink.

Finally, I arrive; I push through the door and pace the aisles, looking for the cheapest bottle. I spot one, pick it up, and cradle it. Calmness descends now because I know that pain is temporary. I take a deep breath and head to the checkout, keeping my head low as I pass over my money.

The cashier gives me my booze in a brown paper bag. I grab it and charge for the exit. Am almost there, home free, when a voice behind me yells, "*Monsieur!*"

I turn.

"Sorry, *Monsieur*." The cashier rushes to me and passes me some change. "I forgot to give you back the money."

My head jerks like he's dealt me an upper cut. I stare at the money in my hand, mutter my thanks and exit, stumbling over my own feet. Damn it all. Stone-cold sober and I still can't walk straight.

I stagger along, hugging my bottle, wracking my brain. *What the hell is going on here? What the hell? What the hell? What the . . .* Halfway to the bus stop, the "*what the hell*" mantra fades and another materializes: "*Monsieur . . . give you back the money. Monsieur . . . give you back the money. Monsier . . . give you back the money.*" I'm almost at the bus stop when my bewilderment crumbles, bringing me to an abrupt halt in the middle of the sidewalk. *Mr. Cormier.* Goddamn it. *Mr. Cormier said those very words.*

I thought I'd buried the memory of my last visit with my parents' executor. Why is it coming up now? The French accent? The money reference? And why would it damn near knock me off my feet? Clueless, I throw my free hand in the air. I lurch forward, arrive at the bus stop, and plop down on the bench.

I shake my head and, without removing the brown-paper-bag disguise, I unscrew the cap on the booze. One thing for sure: memories are cropping up since I met Marshmallow Man. Makes sense, I guess. Sold my life story for food and a roof, didn't I? Yep. Sure did. But does that mean I have to exhume every relic? Steve's not here now, is he? He's not asking about Cormier. I raise the bottle. Take a couple of swigs. The alcohol coats my throat, warms my chest, and numbs my pain. But it does nothing to still the memory which races round and round and round in my head.

11

BE MASTER, NOT SLAVE

September, 1992

It's the very last day of summer vacation. My bus leaves for Mount Allison University in a few hours. My Junior year already. Huh. Where has the time gone?

I needed to come here today, to Douglas Avenue. I steered clear of this place all summer; I figured I couldn't live here anymore, so why bother? Still, the urge to see it's been haunting me, day and night, night and day, so here I am. Perched on the sidewalk, gawking like a fool.

The house has new windows, and it's been painted, grey. It used to be white, used to be mine. My eyes are stinging.

I swallow a lump in my throat. Gotta get away from here before I'm sucked into a chasm. I pivot.

Out of the corner of my eye, I spot Mr. Cormier, my former neighbor, standing on his porch, leaning on his cane. An unexpected warmth surges through me and I raise my arm in a wave. But he doesn't notice.

"Mr. Cormier!" I yell.

He veers toward me, almost losing his balance in the process. "*Mon Dieu!* Justin?"

"Yeah!" Smiling, I race to his steps and bound up. "Sorry if I startled you. It's really good to see you. *Comment ca va?*"

"*Bien, merci.* I am fine," Mr. Cormier says in a trembling voice. He shifts his cane to his left side, and extends his right hand. His eyes meet mine and then plummet to the doorstep. Puzzled, I look down at the doormat. *Bienvenue,* it says. Huh. I don't feel welcome.

Regardless, I reach out and grasp his hand firmly, like my dad taught me. He flinches. I slacken my grip. Damn. I know I surprised him, but he's shaking like a scared puppy, and sweat is sluicing off his forehead. Is he going to pass out or something? "Are you okay, Mr. Cormier?"

He releases my hand and steps back. Panting, he fumbles to locate the pocket of his red, flannel shirt. His quivering fingers excavate a tissue, and he mops his brow.

My heart thumps against my ribcage. Should I rush into the house, find a phone?

Suddenly, he re-pockets the crumpled tissue and speaks again, this time in a voice that is as smooth as a glass lake. "*Moi, ca va bien.*" He straightens his stance. His body is still.

"Are you sure? I can call someone . . . "

"*Non!*" He sucks in a deep breath. He waves a hand, dismissing my concern. "*Bien.* I'm fine," he says as he exhales. Abruptly, he tilts his head to one side and glances toward my old house. "It is the memories that bring you back, *oui?*"

Sidetracked, disarmed, I nod. Tears flood my eyes and heat rushes my face. I blink, turn my head, and gulp. Damn it all. A man of twenty can't cry.

"Such a sad thing. *Difficile, non?*"

I nod again.

"*Oui, oui. Très difficile.* I can see that." We linger, silent.

On the street behind me a car zooms by, horn blaring. Mr. Cormier jumps into action like a cartoon character, vehemently shaking a fist in the direction of the vehicle. "What are they thinking, these young drivers? *Stupide!*"

"Yeah, I guess so," I mutter, not caring at all, just grateful for the distraction.

Mr. Cormier turns back to me and heaves a lengthy sigh. "Two years already." He shakes his head. "You come into my house, Justin. We will have the coffee and we will talk. *D'accord?*"

The impulse to flee resurfaces, but my feet are heavy, like blocks of concrete. "I don't know."

"Ah, *oui, je comprends, je comprends.* Then I will talk and you will be the ears, eh? *Viens* . . . the coffee is made already." Mr. Cormier puts a hand on the small of my back and steers me inside.

I reach for the screen door; it creaks open and clatters shut behind us. We walk through the cramped foyer to the kitchen, which is smaller than I remember. Still yellow though. Faded now.

"*Assieds,* Justin, *assieds.*"

The chair grumbles as I drag it from under the table. I plop down and lean back.

Mr. Cormier picks up the coffee pot and fills two mugs. He sets the mugs on the table, one at a time, and works his way into a chair across from me. "I am sorry," he says.

I look at him, puzzled. "Sorry? *Pourquoi*, Mr. Cormier? Why are you sorry?"

"*Tu aimes ta maison.*" He rests his cane against the table, and puts his hands out, palms up. "I try to be good neighbor, to help, to take care of the *maison* for you while you go to the *université.*" He points a finger at me. "You are young man. You should not be worrying about guarding house to honor parents." Using both hands, he clasps and hoists his mug. "*Non*, that's not the proper thing at all."

"You have nothing to apologize for, Mr. Cormier." I cross my arms and sit still, eyeballing the blue *fleur-de-lis* on my mug.

Mr. Cormier extends one hand and pats my arm. "You are good to say this, young man. But I feel not so good. First, you lose your *famille* . . . and then your home." He withdraws his hand.

I look up. Raw pain glimmers in those eyes of his. I tilt my head. It's been two years . . . why such fresh hurt? Why such concern for me? I don't know what to say, so I say nothing.

"A man needs home and family," he says. "It is hard to lose everything, all at once." He slumps in his chair, as if suddenly tired. "Your father, he depend on me. I try to help, but the thieves, you know, they rob your house. I deal with it, with *les gendarmes* and all seems well. But the thieves, they come back. It is too much for me." He holds both hands out, palms up. "I am not so young like I used to be when you ran up and down Douglas Avenue, Justin. My *famille* . . . gone, too." He points to a photograph attached to the fridge. "You see? My daughter, she marry and move away long ago. She has her own *famille* now." He looks back at me, eyelids drooping.

I gaze at the picture: woman, man and little boy. "Sorry, Mr. Cormier. I don't remember your daughter; she was a lot older than me. Is that your grandson?"

He nods and his eyes light up.

"*Quel âge?*"

"Ah . . . *Il a sept ans*, seven . . . already." He raises his mug and takes a sip. The gleam in his eyes slips away as suddenly as it appeared; a vacant stare slides in. "The time, she flies," he says and plops his mug down. Coffee sloshes; it trickles down the side of the mug, creating an inkblot puddle.

I extract a blue, paper napkin from the diner-style holder on the table. I slide the napkin across to him.

He ignores it. "I am alone, too," he whispers.

I lean closer.

"*Ma femme*, she was so sick when you leave here two years ago; like your parents, she is gone now." He pauses and makes the sign of the cross. "I know of loss, Justin. No, I am not so young anymore."

I scrutinize his face. Many lines. Close to seventy now, I figure. That's not so old, is it? But he's always limped. His family is gone. Those things—illness and loss—are hard. That I know about. Especially the loss part. I was gutted when my parents . . . A dagger of pain pierces my chest. I grip the edge of the table with both hands and force myself to breathe slowly. I squeeze my eyes shut; unwanted images—darkness, rain, blood—claw at the outskirts of my mind. *Go away. Go away. Go away.* I push, push, push them back until they are obscured, buried, where they belong. The pain dissipates. I sigh with relief and open my eyes.

Mr. Cormier, face drained of color, shakes his head. His hand trembles as he reaches for the blue napkin and drops it onto the coffee spill. We both glance down, watching as liquid bleeds into paper, saturating it.

In synchronized motion, we raise our heads. Our eyes meet but he turns away.

I frown. Okay, so what now? Maybe I should shut up, get the hell out before entombed memories escape again and take another stab at me. Maybe I should man up and offer reassurance to him: he is *not* responsible for the loss of my parents' house. As I grapple with indecision, a whispered memory slides past my ear. "A good man, Mr. Cormier." Dad's voice. I shiver. Dad always said that. *Okay, Dad, okay. I get it. I'll give it a shot.*

I take a deep breath and charge from my mute state like a sprinter from a starting block, racing, racing, racing to get the words out as fast as I can. "Mr. Cormier you have nothing to apologize for I had to sell my parents' home you know that it had nothing to do with thieves I had no choice my parents were in so much debt how could I possibly earn enough to pay those bills . . . ?" Out of breath, I stop, suck in air and whoosh it out.

A shadow flickers across his face.

Huh. I squint, like I'm trying to read the fine print on a medicine bottle. Am I just a blithering idiot here? What's the point of all this? Say something, Mr. Cormier, damn it. Anything . . .

The telephone rings, slashing the silence. He ignores it. I glance toward the phone on the counter behind him. Still he ignores the phone. I lean forward, about to move toward it. He puts a hand up, palm toward me. I wait. When the last ring fades, he says, "I wish . . . "

"Yes?"

"I wish I could give you back the money." He places a hand over his mouth and looks away.

"Give back the money? What are you talking about? Why should you be concerned about giving back money?"

His shoulders rise and fall, a deliberate shrug. He offers no explanation.

I revert to letting words tumble. "Look, Mr. Cormier, I appreciate every-thing you did for me. I couldn't be here to, as you say, *guard* the house. It was hard for me to sell my home but, under the circumstances, the house was a burden. If it wasn't for you, I wouldn't even have known how bad things were." I grab my coffee mug and grip the damn thing so hard that my fingers blanch. "Not you or anybody else could get money for me. Sometimes I find it hard to believe that my parents were reckless with money but . . . they overspent. I had to sell the house." I put the coffee mug down and whip my arms wide. "What else could I do? The accident alone was hard enough . . . but the debt? I *had* to pay the debt. Two mortgages, three car loans, eight credit cards . . . all maxed. Bank accounts dry as a desert." My gut is churning.

"Hmmm." Mr. Cormier finally turns his head in my direction and lowers his hand. He nods. "*Je comprends.*" He bites his lower lip.

"Exactly what do you understand?"

"Hmmm," he repeats. He inhales sharply and opens his mouth.

Here it comes, whatever the hell it is. I freeze.

But he merely shakes his head, snaps his jaws shut, and shifts in his chair.

"What were you going to say?"

He shrugs. "*Je comprends . . . tout.* Everything: loss, debt, anger." He leans so close that his breath is one with mine. "You are like your parents, Justin, always the giving and the spending." He pulls back, just a little. "Maybe you can be more careful with the money than they were, eh?"

What the hell? I open my mouth to protest, but no words form.

"Your parents, they spend too much, they give away too much," he continues. "Then they leave." He puts his hand over his heart. "You have the sadness, but the anger, too, *non?*"

I clench my jaw and swallow the lump in my throat.

"Loss. It is *difficile, non?* A tough time for you, *oui?* You know, your parents did not plan to leave. They did not plan debt for you. They love you. They want everything for you. They think that they would be here for a long time. But life? No guarantees. You love someone and you plan for long life together. But life steals your plans. Accidents. Sickness. You try everything to keep your plans, but life is cruel." He lowers his eyes. "Life is cruel," he repeats, in a murmur and I sense that somehow he is no longer talking to me, or about me.

"Mr. Cormier," I begin . . .

Suddenly, his head snaps up. "I am old man, Justin, but you? You are young. *You* have lots of time to make the money; *you* can earn the money." His volume increases and his voice quivers like that of an excited kid on Christmas. "You do not need for parents to leave you money. You can make the money . . . *oui?*" He claps his hands together. "Ah, *oui, c'est ca!*" He stares at me, eyes shining.

I raise my eyebrows. "Why are you so concerned about this?"

Immediately his eyes darken and he looks away again. His index and middle finger begin a slow drum roll on the table. Faster and faster they tap, louder and louder, and then, abruptly, stop. He pulls his hand from the table and crosses his arms.

Silence falls between us like a stage curtain. I tug at the neck of my T-shirt.

Eventually, he turns to face me. His eyes are fixed, decisive. "Maybe parents should teach children about the money," he says in a low-pitched monotone. "Maybe you will have more anger because parents spoil you." He raises his right arm and stabs a finger in my direction. "They give too many toys, they make things easy, and then . . . " he shrugs and crosses his arms again . . . "they leave."

My face burns and my right knee bounces. Hmmmph! Maybe I am angry with my parents, but that's my business. *Fuck you, Mr. Cormier!* I clench my jaw. *Got to get the hell out of here before I explode.*

"Thanks for the coffee," I blurt. "Got to go. Don't bother to see me out." I plant my hands on the table and push myself into a standing position.

Mr. Cormier grabs my arm. He doesn't let go so I concede, bending until we are eye to eye. Regret floods his face; his whole body is shaking. "Be careful with the money, Justin. You are young man; you can get by in the world. But save the money. You never know when you will need . . . Be master, not slave, to the money." His eyes flash, sending a tremor through me.

My gaze expands, then tapers to a glare. "You have no right . . . "

"You are young man," he says again, tightening his grip on my arm. "You can earn whatever you need. I cannot give the money back. You must learn to be master, not slave . . . "

I shake off his hand, swerve, and stomp to the door. "*Au revoir,*" I call over my shoulder as I exit the house.

Mr. Cormier mutters something else but I choose not to hear. I storm down the front steps wishing I had gone with my first instinct and stayed away. *Give the money back, give the money back . . . what the hell? Maybe Debra was right in questioning my trust for him.* I shake my head, dismissing the thought. Dad trusted him . . . "*a good man, Mr. Cormier.*" When I get to the sidewalk, I glance back at his house and see something I did not notice before: a small sign on the lawn. FOR SALE BY OWNER. Huh. Guess he's losing his home, too. Whatever . . . I'm out of here. I pick up my pace.

I head for the bus station, retrieve my belongings from a locker and prepare to board the bus to Mount Allison. Not coming back here. Never coming back. Had enough. I'm going to the only home I know now. Mount Allison. Back to school. And, hopefully, to Sarah.

12

DON'T NEED AA

January, 2010

So, who's Sarah?"

I'm splayed out across the red and green couch, barely awake. "Huh?"

"I see you found the money." Steve waves an empty bottle in my face. "Wanna go to Alcoholics Anonymous? I'm sure I can find a meeting someplace."

"Huh! Don't need AA."

"Okay. Maybe later." Steve thuds his way to the kitchen. The clinking of glass tells me that he has deposited my empty into his blue recycle bin. My foggy brain makes connections: deposit, recycle, income. Later, I'll relieve Marshmallow Man of his bottles and cans.

"You've been talking in your sleep again." Steve is still in the kitchen and his voice is loud. Not helping my head any. When he returns, he plunks down in the armchair beside the couch. "Who's Sarah?"

"Need sleep." *Shut the hell up, Steve.*

"The deal was that you get a place to stay. And I get your story. Remember? Now, I figure this Sarah person must be important because you talk to her—and about her—in your sleep. So, who's Sarah?"

Damn. I sit up, stretch a bit. "This could take a while."

"It's only one o'clock. We have lots of time."

"Lunch?"

"Stalling?"

"Starving."

Steve eyes me suspiciously. "Okay, sandwiches first, then Sarah. Deal?"

"Relentless son of a bitch, aren't you?

"Yes."

"What happens if I don't talk?"

"Someone else can haul you out of a Dumpster tonight."

"Jesus Christ!"

"My Lord and Savior."

"Figured as much. Saw the Barry Gibb picture." I point to the wall.

Steve's eyes widen. He smiles. Capped teeth. White as Chiclets. He throws back his head and laughs loud. "Good one. Actually, the picture is from my mother. She figures I'll make it to church more often if Jesus is staring at me." He laughs again and shakes his head. "Barry Gibb. Perfect. Does look like him, I'll give you that." He jumps up and heads to the kitchen. "I'll get the sandwiches. Peanut butter and jelly do for you?"

I flinch. Don't want to see the Smucker's jar again. "Got any bananas?"

"Yep. Peanut butter and banana coming up. Be right back."

Good. Now I have a few minutes to figure out a way to change the subject. But there are no minutes. Steve returns with the bread, the peanut butter, the bananas, plates, knives—everything on a tray. I guess this is self-serve. Damn.

"You go ahead. Start making your sandwich. And start talking. Who's Sarah?" He pulls out his notebook.

I reach for the bread. "Met Sarah my sophomore year at Mount Allison."

"Did you date her? Sleep with her? Marry her? What?"

"All of the above."

"Keep talking."

"Met her my sophomore year."

"You said that already. Did you date her right away?"

"No. I was seeing someone else."

"Okay, okay, so after you broke up with Debra, then what?"

My hangover vanishes. Alert now, I snap my head toward Steve and look him straight in the eye. "How did you know about Debra?"

Steve's eyes flash. "You told me about her . . . the funeral story, remember?" he says, dropping his notebook. "Give me that." He takes the slice of bread from my hand and begins slathering peanut butter onto it.

Told him about her? Did I? Possible, I guess. Yeah, I told him about the funeral. Debra was there. She was always there then. Always. Yeah. I guess I told him. "Let's see. After *Debra* . . . " I continue to watch Steve, to gauge his reaction when I say Debra's name for the second time, but he has moved on. "Oh, yeah. In the fall—junior year, I guess—I went back to Mount Allison and asked Sarah out."

"Went well?"

"Yeah."

"Am I going to have to drag every word out of you?"

"Maybe I'm the strong, silent type."

"Strong, my foot. Silent? Definitely. Better start talking. Temperature's dropping. It might even snow. A person could freeze his butt off on the streets tonight."

How much does he know about Debra? I lean back and take a bite of my sandwich. Good peanut butter. Unprocessed. "100% Natural." Says so on the jar. Steve likes the real stuff. I look around. It's comfortable here. Safe, too. I might as well talk, let the words Steve wants to hear leak out of my head. They're swirling around in there all the time anyway. I'm stuck in the past. My past. In a time warp. With Steve, without Steve . . . what the hell's the difference? Can't go forward. Might as well go back. I made the decision already anyway. Back at the shelter when those two thugs showed up, I chose Steve. I chose this. Me and Steve. Steve and me. There's no other way, really. Only thugs and Dumpsters and filth and cold.

I close my eyes and drift back to Mount Allison. To Sarah. It feels good, living it again.

13

SMALL. NAIL-BITTEN. PERFECT.

September, 1992

I'm thrilled to get out of Moncton. There's nothing there for me anymore: parents, home, Debra—all gone now. Yeah . . . I'm glad to get back to Mount Allison. This is where I belong.

I'm on campus early because I'm a member of the CP—campus police. I do the job for money mostly, but am proud to wear that yellow leather jacket, too. Everybody notices us, knows who we are. Makes it easy to get attention.

There's not much in the way of crime here. Sometimes all we do is show freshmen or visitors around, but I like that, too. Maybe for a purely selfish reason: focusing on other people helps me to keep dark memories where they belong . . . buried.

My plan is to settle in and look up Sarah. Learning her full name—Sarah Marie Greene—is easy enough; I just thumb through the yearbook until I locate her class picture. As soon as the student rosters are posted, I'll uncover which residence she's in. There's no hurry; the bulk of the student population is not due to arrive for a few days.

But Sarah Marie Greene shows up early.

I'm sitting in the foyer of Harper House women's residence, just shooting the breeze with the guys and in she walks. I damn near fall off my chair.

Instantly, I tighten my biceps. Maybe I should take off my jacket? Show off a bit? Huh. It suddenly occurs to me that all the freaking bench presses I did this summer were in preparation for this moment, for meeting Sarah.

"Sarah! Hi! What are you doing back so early?" There! That sounds pretty casual. My palms are sweaty and my heart is thumping. I notice something different about her. The hair is the same, long, straight, maybe blonder? No, that's not it.

She grins.

Ah. The tooth. No longer chipped. Cuter now than ever.

"Justin! Good to see you." Sarah does a hop-skip toward me and plops into a chair. "I'm a volunteer for the Junior Class Welcoming Committee. Have to be here early to plan events but, apparently, the rooms in my wing aren't ready yet . . . I can't get in. What about you?"

"Campus police." I throw my arms to the side to show off my jacket. Okay, so I flex a bit, too. "We *have* to be here early." Don't know to say next, but I open my mouth anyway and the words just tumble out. "You can stay in my room if you want." Damn it all . . . am I an idiot or what?

Sarah jumps up and narrows her eyes. "I don't think that will be necessary." The frost in her voice makes me shiver. She crosses her arms. "I only have to wait a couple of hours, you know. The custodian here is great; he let me put my suitcases into my closet already. I have to get going. Good-bye." She spins around, marches to the double-door exit, thrusts one door open, and walks out.

I just sit there, stunned.

"I guess she told you," jokes my CP partner.

My face burns. "Guess so." Hold on a minute! Is that it? I waited all summer and that's it? No way. I shoot out of my chair and charge for the door.

"You're a glutton for punishment, Wentworth," my partner calls.

As I exit, I turn, grin, and salute.

Once outside, I spin around, spot Sarah, and start to run. "Sarah! Wait up!" She doesn't turn, so I continue to run until I catch up with her. I put a hand on her shoulder.

She shakes it off, swings around, and glares at me.

I recoil. "Sarah, I'm sorry. I didn't mean anything by that comment back there. I was only trying to help. Sometimes my tongue moves faster than my brain."

Sarah remains stationary for a few seconds and then tilts her head to one side. She bites her lower lip.

Indecision? Maybe there's hope for me after all.

"You want to go to a movie tonight?" As soon as those words escape me, I cast my eyes skyward and throw my hands in the air. "Damn, now the evidence is there for sure. I *am* a complete idiot." Convinced that that was the end of everything, I start to turn. But, out of the corner of my eye, I see her mouth curve upward. I pause.

Sarah giggles and flicks back her hair. Then she stares straight at me, dead serious. "I thought you had a girlfriend or were engaged or something."

I open my mouth and close it again. Don't want to blurt out too much, too soon. I've done enough of that in the last few minutes. I figure if I keep it short, I'll be okay. "Not anymore," I say, slowly. "That ended this summer."

"Oh, I'm sorry to hear that."

Did her eyes just light up?

She presses her lips together. "Hmmmmmm. Well, I guess if that's the case, we could go to a movie. What's playing?"

How the heck would I know? I hadn't thought that far ahead. But why would I? I didn't even know she was here. "Well, to be perfectly honest, I don't have a clue but it won't be too hard to find out; there's only the Vogue theater and it only has one screen." My throat feels dry. "I really don't care what the movie is, Sarah," I squeak out. I inhale and clear my throat. "The truth is that I have wanted to ask you out for a while. I haven't even given any thought to what we should do. I opened my mouth and 'movie' was the first thing that came out of it."

"The first thing?"

I roll my eyes. "Okay, not the first thing. The first sensible thing, maybe."

"*Maybe?*"

Okay, definitely then." I smile. "*I* really don't care what the movie is . . . do you have any ideas?"

"Hmmm. I've been waiting to see *A League of Their Own*. It came out this summer. Do you think it could be playing at the Vogue?"

"Maybe." Total chick flick. But it would be worth it to spend time with Sarah. "I'll check the times and call you. What's your number?"

Sarah pauses, stares, and then breaks eye contact for a few seconds. When she looks back, she smiles. "You know what? I don't care about the movie either. Why don't we go for a walk on campus? The leaves are turning; it's really pretty." Quickly she adds, "Or we can just hang out at the Student Center and chat if you want."

I'm grinning like a kid on a carousel now. "I like autumn, too, Sarah."

"A walk it is then."

"What time should I pick you up?"

"I think you already have." She laughs and begins to walk away. I stand still.

Sarah turns. "Are you coming or what?" The twinkle has returned to her eyes. I fall into step beside her.

"Darn!" I come to an abrupt halt.

"What is it now?" says Sarah.

"Have to run back, get one of the other guys to work my shift. Will you wait?"

Sarah raises her eyebrows.

"Just two minutes," I plead.

"I'm counting," says Sarah, looking at her watch and tapping her foot.

Two minutes takes a lifetime. But then I'm back, walking with Sarah. Life's looking up. Tricky at first, though. I don't know what to say. It seems she doesn't either. Small talk, I tell myself. Small talk is safe: weather, summer, school. When we run out of that, I turn to campus details: colors of leaves, red brick of Centennial Hall, and ivy-covered trellises on the walls.

"It may seem silly but I always feel like someone is comforting me when I walk by Centennial Hall," says Sarah.

"No, it's not silly at all. That feeling is exactly what made me choose this place. Somehow I knew I would need to be in a place that made me feel comfortable. I visited here before my parents died." Jesus! Why did I say that? Too soon for that!

Sarah freezes. "Your parents? When? How?"

I open my mouth to answer. My throat tightens. No words come out. Oh, God. My heart is racing. How am I going to handle this? I don't want to face that morbid curiosity again. So sick of people gawking at me like I'm some kind of freak. Maybe I should mutter an excuse and leave, just get my sorry butt back to my room and stay there. Permanently. I turn toward her.

Her eyes, wide and shining, latch onto mine. Instantly, my brain ceases its rambling and my heart slows its pace. For the first time, I want to talk about everything. I actually *want* to talk.

"My parents died in a car accident two years ago," I begin, "just before I started my first year here. It was the hardest thing I ever . . . "

My voice cracks like it did when I was a teenager. I gulp and open my mouth to try again. Nothing comes out.

Sarah grabs my hand and pulls me through the door of the Bell Library, up the stairs, past the book stacks, and into a private study room.

Each study room has a window that looks out into the center of circular-shaped building. People looking out, people looking in. She maneuvers me into a chair, my back to the window, and sits opposite. Then she reaches into the pocket of her jacket, pulls out a wad of folded tissues, and places them on the table. For some reason, that simple gesture amuses me. I have no intention of crying.

"Now, tell me," she commands.

After a deep breath, I obey.

"My parents wanted to go out to the movies one evening. It was just before my freshman year at Mount A. and I wanted to stay home to pack." Instantly, I am transported back . . . to my room, to the patter of the rain, to the memories of camping in the *Air Stream.* Even to the nametags. I smirk. "I was actually removing nametags from my underwear."

Sarah raises her eyebrows.

I wave my hand in dismissal. "Never mind. It was a *mom* thing."

Sarah smiles, nods, and waits, eyes glistening.

I blink and stare at the table. "Anyway, I decided to go with my parents. A movie. Then a Chinese restaurant. A family outing."

A memory flashes: me, standing on the roadside, dripping, talking to a cop. A shudder rips through my body. I fold my arms and huddle inside my yellow CP jacket. "I don't remember anything about the accident, but, apparently, the roads were slick from the rain. Dad missed a sharp turn. Don't know how because he had driven it a million times." I shrug. "We wound up in a ditch. Dad and I were thrown clear. My mom . . . " I shake my head to get rid of the image of my mother impaled in the passenger seat. "My mom died instantly, and my dad . . . " Another image sparks—my father's face, not the stubbly, grinning face I knew intimately, but a bloated and bruised replica. *Enough.* I shake my head, unfold my arms and begin drumming my fingers on the table. No more of that. No need to talk about the counseling either. The Elizabeth-Kubler-Ross-stages-of-grief stuff. Been through them all. Truth was, I had bounced erratically from one stage to another. Repeatedly.

Sarah is facing me, giving me her full attention. I don't know when she took my hand; just know that she is holding it.

"I think you're amazing," she whispers.

I widen my eyes.

"Despite all that pain, you're moving on with your life." She sweeps her left hand through the air. "You made it here, to university. You are studying. Working on a future rather than dwelling on your loss. You are a remarkable guy."

"Oh. I don't know if that's true. I'm just trying to do what my parents wanted for me. Didn't know what else to do." I should shut up at this point, but I just keep talking. "Trying to behave the right way. Don't know if . . . "

Sarah squeezes my hand. "Ssh. No explanations necessary here." She locks her eyes on mine. "I'm so sorry for your loss, Justin."

A knife of pain shoots through my throat: sudden, sharp, then gone. My eyes flood with tears. I grab at the tissues. I drop my head to the table and offer no resistance to the sobs that erupt from my body.

"I know now why I am drawn to you," murmurs Sarah, as she runs her hand through my hair. "You are like the autumn, all the color and all the sadness, too."

We sit like that for a while. I don't know how long. When I raise my head, she is still looking at me. For now, I am calm. For now, I am free. Sarah came and pain left. I drop my eyes to her hand and stare at her fingers. Small. Nail-bitten. Perfect.

14

BETRAYAL

January, 2010

So when did you and Sarah get married?"

"Huh?"

"You and Sarah . . . wedding? When?"

"Oh, junior year. End of junior year. At Mount Allison Chapel."

"So that would be the spring of 1994—right?" Steve is making copious notes. "In New Brunswick." He looks up. "Were you drinking then?"

"Not really. Wine or beer once in a while. Booze came later . . . in Vancouver."

"Yeah, so how on earth did you end up in Vancouver, anyway? Sarah from here?"

I shake my head. "She was born and raised in a town called Ajax, in Ontario. And we ended up here the same way every Canadian from east of the Rockies does. Visited. Liked all the green. Wanted to escape winter."

Steve grins. "Makes sense. Did the same thing myself."

"Oh. And where are you from, Steve?"

"East of the Rockies." Steve closes his notebook. "Let's take a breather. Want to go to the Old Spaghetti Factory in Gastown? It's not that far away. We can walk if you're up for it; if not, we can take the bus."

I point at the peanut butter jar. "Just ate, didn't we? No way I'm going to Gastown today. I'm injured, remember?" Huh. *East of the Rockies.* Why is Steve being vague? Don't know, but a CAUTION sign flashes inside me. What's that about? I'm off the street. Safe here, isn't it? I catch myself looking over my shoulder. Stupid. Nothing there but the wall. Maybe I just don't trust anyone. Don't? Or *can't?* Whatever.

" 'East of the Rockies' covers a lot of ground, Steve. Where, exactly, are you from?" *Are you trying to hide something,* bud?

"I'm from Ontario. Toronto, to be exact." He suddenly reopens his notebook. "Come to think of it, if Sarah's from Ontario, why didn't she just go to the University of Toronto?"

I shrug. "She visited Mount Allison on an exchange program. Liked it. Wanted to get away from home."

Steve looks at me quizzically.

"Okay. Okay. Her father took off . . . she was twelve, maybe thirteen . . . not sure. He was there one minute, gone the next. Sarah was devastated. Marian—her mother—got married again to a man named Thomas Harrington. Sarah tolerated him, until she found out that her mother had been dating him for years. Said she couldn't look at Marian after that without picturing a red *A* plastered across her chest."

"Huh?"

I sniff. "Yeah, that was my reaction, too, until Sarah explained. Hester Prynne? *The Scarlet Letter?* Sarah was an English Lit major."

Steve nods. "So Sarah felt betrayed. Did she ever go back?"

I shake my head. "Not after we met. Before that? To Ontario, yes. Home, no. She stayed with friends in Ottawa, and worked at a bookshop during summer vacations. We invited Marian to our wedding. She showed up. No Thomas though. Marian and Sarah barely spoke to each other. Sarah said it would be a frosty day in hell before she would cross the threshold of her mother's house again."

"And where is Sarah now?"

I busy myself studying the peanut butter jar.

"Okay, then. Would I be right in assuming that hell has frozen over?" He pauses.

Got nothing to say here, bud.

"Guess we're done with that for now. How about this . . . why did you and Sarah get married?"

"Forever." The word just pops out. Huh.

"You want to explain that one?"

"Want to? The question is . . . can I?" *Forever.* The word pings at my brain. I squint, concentrating hard like I'm trying to remember a locker combination I haven't used in eons. Seconds pass. Nothing. I slump into the chair. "No, don't think I can explain . . . never really thought about . . . " Without warning, my slouched spine jolts into an upright position. I nod and smile as, one by one, the tumblers click into place.

04/07

Monday appt 11:8 am - Pain seems to carry self-pity. I learns a sense of
limitations (physical). And to get is current anguish outside
of self. Music, poetry, friends, pursuits, all I've heard because I'm incapacitated weeks

* Overnight pain level #7. Bruised, stressed muscles the 2 the 3/14
... sterility ... reason on nonsense - maybe!
... life ... rhythm - Knuckovers to accept = placebo not placebo. =
If self face seems to be growing more receptive - works to accept - It =
that a good description of face in pain)   I liked the place
to the mirror up to last two years. Managing my own pain
will help to get that I've learned face work back. Patience is the
lesson to learn. Acceptance is another one

15

FOREVER

December, 1993

The snow crunches underfoot as I make my way across campus to Palmer Hall. I squint at the glare of the sun and shiver at the bite of the wind. Despite nature's attempt to push me along, I pause at the bottom of the footpath that leads to Sarah's residence. I look up.

Palmer Hall—semicircular, Gothic-Tudor, sandstone—is *the* senior building on campus now and is rife with the proverbial shipwreck of old age. I've heard rumors that it's just about dead in the water; maybe it is . . . but it won't be replaced during Sarah's time at Mount Allison. Thank goodness. Sarah loves this place. Puts it right up there with Shakespeare and Mozart. Should last forever, she says.

Thoughts of Sarah do for me what components of winter cannot: urge me onward. I sprint to the entry, stamping snow off my boots as I yank the door open. I scale the stairs to the fourth floor, dash down the hallway, and, at Sarah's room, come to a halt. The door is ajar. I push it. It recedes and there she is, my Sarah, clad in cut-off jeans and a tank top, leaning against the window, prying at its stubborn latch. My eyes pop and my lips part, but I don't speak. Instead, I scrutinize her every curve. I shrug off temptation and replace it with concern. "Sarah! What are you doing? It's freezing out there."

She spins toward me. "But not in here! Just look at that thermometer . . . 45 degrees. That's Celsius! Help me get this window open."

I kick off my boots, step inside and oblige, prodding at the window until it gives. I turn to her. "Can't you just turn the heat down? Or call the janitor?"

"The thermostat is useless, nothing but wall decor. And the janitor can't do anything with these old pipes." She picks up a book and slaps the radiator. As if in self-defense, the radiator responds with a repetitive clang.

Sarah tosses the book onto her desk and throws her hands in the air. "Hear that? How would you like to live with that racket, night and day?"

I smile. We're in familiar territory now, Sarah and me. There's no need for me to worry about her blustering; like the recalcitrant radiator, she is just overheated. And I get a kick out of watching her fume. *Better hide that smile, Wentworth.* I put my hand over my mouth . . . not fast enough, though.

"I saw that! Easy for you to grin . . . you weren't the one trying to use a hair dryer this morning. Apparently, residents are not supposed to . . . "—here she pauses to make quotation marks in the air— " ' . . . synchronize the usage of small appliances.' " She plants her hands on her hips. "Janet and I blew a fuse . . . literally! My hair's still wet, for heaven's sake." To make a point she tosses her head.

I squint as tiny droplets of water spray my face.

"And yes," she continues, "*before* you ask, the janitor replaced the fuse . . . about ten minutes ago."

I wipe my face with my sleeve and wave a hand in dismissal. "Yeah. Yeah. Yeah. You could have moved to Harper Hall this year . . . no such problems there."

"Smartass!" She plops into her chair and props her feet up on her desk. With a kick, she sends her flip-flops soaring, one at a time. One of them flies past my ear.

"Hey! Watch it!"

She grins. "Oops! Sorry."

"Like hell you are."

"Well, maybe I'm not." She stretches her arms high and then stifles a yawn. "No harm, no foul. Take off your coat and stay a while."

"Gladly. Damn, it is hot in here." I toss my jacket onto her bed and plop down beside it. My elbow slams down on a paperback. "Ouch." I pull it out— *Pride and Prejudice.* "What is it with you and classic novels anyway?"

She tilts her head. "That's easy. Great literature lasts. That one was published in 1813. I like things that have staying power."

I flip through the pages. "Think I'd like this?"

"No reference to the Toronto Maple Leafs there, Justin," she says with a smirk.

I lob the book at her.

She catches it. "Thanks. I have to write a report on it." She opens it to the front page and immediately lets out a tortured sigh.

Baffled, I blink. "Disillusioned? So soon? You just picked up the book."

She bites her lower lip, and a shadow crosses her face.

Uh oh. My desire to tease morphs into a need to soothe. "Just tell me," I say, serious now. "What's bothering you?" I lean forward and push stray tendrils of damp hair from her face.

Her hand closes over mine, stays there for a few seconds; she squeezes my fingers and then releases them. She sighs again. "I've read this book before, Justin, and it is great. It's just that the opening gets to me, every time. Listen to this . . . " She sits upright and, in exaggerated tones, reads, "It is a truth universally acknowledged that a single man in possession of a good fortune must be in want of a wife." She tilts her head and peers at me, eyebrows raised.

"So? Didn't people marry for money and status back then? Why does that upset you?"

"Huh." She flicks her hair back. "It's not the *then*; it's the *now*."

Grinning, I shove my hand into my jeans pocket and pull out the lining. "Well, *now* I just happen to be broke, but I'll rob a Brinks truck for you, if that's what you want."

She rolls her eyes and manages a weak smile. "Thanks . . . I'm no gold digger; but my mother . . . that's a different story."

I scratch my head. "I'm drawing a blank here. I thought your family was *not* well off."

"And you thought right. We were practically Dickensian. My dad did not have a great work ethic. Bugged the heck out of my mother. That's why she set her sights on the moneyed and powerful Thomas." She waves the novel in the air. " 'Single man . . . good fortune . . . in want of a wife.' "

"She actually said that about him?"

"Didn't have to. I watched her . . . spending money, maxing out credit cards, always wanting more, regardless of how much we had."

Her words slash at old wounds and I sit, frozen, feeling blood drain from my face.

Sarah's intake of breath is instantaneous, sharp. She extends a hand, caresses my thigh. "How thoughtless of me! Your parents . . . I'm so sorry, Justin."

"It's . . . " I clear my throat and start again. "It's okay." I pat her hand. "Yeah, my parents overspent, but I don't think they meant to leave me in debt. They didn't plan well . . . wanted to give me everything. Is that so wrong?"

"No, of course not." She leans back in her chair. "But it's just all *stuff*, you know?"

"But you're still angry with your mother about buying all the *stuff*?"

Her eyes flash with indignation. "Aren't you angry with your parents?"

I shrug off the question. No way I'm going there. I redirect. "You think your dad left because your mom spent too much money?"

Sarah sniffs and drops the book. "Money, shmoney. He left because she was having an affair with Thomas." Pain flickers in her eyes and she lowers them. "It's just that when he left, he left both of us." Inhaling deeply, she puts her hand up, palm facing me. "Enough of that." She grabs a letter from the top of her desk. "At least my mother is happy now . . . if this letter is any indication. She has a *new* Persian rug, *new* central vacuum, *new* custom Mercedes, *new* gold membership in an exclusive country club . . . all the *stuff* she ever wanted." She tears the letter into tiny pieces and tosses it into the waste basket under her desk. " Hmmmph! Damned if I'll ever go back there."

I stare at her as she resorts to her telltale habit: nail-biting. I reach out, pull her hand from her mouth, her body from the chair. Without resistance, she follows my lead and plops onto the bed beside me. I hug her close and, feeling the tautness in her body, run my fingers up and down her arm.

Relaxation gradually overtakes her; she sinks into me and sighs, extending her feet out in front of her. The small tattoo on her instep comes into view. I smile. Huh. The tattoo. The key to Sarah. I sigh, knowing, understanding that what she needs is permanence. Can I give her that? I think so, because that's what I need, too. I whisper to her, "Tell me about the tattoo."

She examines the indelible marks and smiles. "You've heard that story many times."

"Tell me again."

She tilts her head and looks up at me. "Really?" She claps her hands together, jumps off the bed, and retrieves a photo album from the bookshelf above her desk. Her body is trembling with excitement as she thumbs through it. "Here it is." She sits cross-legged on the bed and holds the open photo album so we both can see.

"This is Rocky. A Pomeranian cross. Rescued from a shelter. I was only six when we got him." She looks at me again, her blue eyes blurring with tears.

I massage her shoulders and plant a kiss on the top of her head.

She drags her hand across her eyes. "Sorry. Can't look at these pictures without getting emotional. He died just before I left home."

"I know."

"Yeah. He always followed me around like an apostle and, when he wanted my attention, he planted his front paws on my left foot. Wouldn't budge until I acknowledged him." She runs her hand over the page. "When he got sick, I bought an ink pad and made an imprint of those paws. I wanted to keep him with me . . . forever. So I went to a tattoo parlor. Am glad I did." She dropped her feet over the side of the bed and stared down at the tattoo. "Forever," she whispered. "When I make a commitment, it's for keeps, Justin."

My cue. I reach for my jacket and extract a small, black-velvet box from an inside pocket. I hold it in front of her face and stare into her eyes, now wide with surprise. "I was going to keep this until Christmas, but now seems right." I open the box. "I don't have a lot to offer you yet . . . "

She shakes her head. "Doesn't matter. I'd live in a garage to be with you. Forever."

I pull her closer. "Forever sounds good to me, Sarah."

16

WALKING, TALKING

January, 2010

I stare at a blurred spot on the carpet.

Steve is quiet for a minute. Then, in a low voice, he says, "Forever, huh?"

"Can you believe she was only six when she got the dog? A rescuer at six. Of course, her parents had something to do with it, but she chose that dog." I drag my arm across my face. "Damn it all, she rescued me, too."

Steve gets up from the armchair, walks toward me, and puts a hand on my shoulder. "Sorry, Justin."

I shake his hand off. "You're sorry? I'm the one who screwed it all up."

Steve lets out a long sigh. He steps back. "Everybody screws up, bud." He paces back and forth in front of me.

I watch him out of the corner of my eye; I know he's searching for words, wanting to offer something . . . advice, maybe.

He comes to a standstill and faces me. "Look . . . are you sure you don't want to go to the Old Spaghetti Factory or something?"

Huh. I'll be damned. Steve doesn't know what to say. I never thought that would happen.

"I know you're injured, but we can take our time," he continues. "Walk or take the bus. Up to you. If you don't want to go, that's okay. I can just organize some notes."

Walk. Bus. Bus. Walk. *Who cares?* I'm still thinking about Sarah's tattoo, her forever tattoo. *I screwed up. All my fault.* Damn. Damn. Damn. My nostrils flare and my heart races. I raise my head and glare at Steve. Words erupt. "Leave me alone, *bud*," I yell in a voice so loud it scares even me.

Steve's face is ashen. He steps back, hands up, palms facing me. After a few frozen seconds, he emits a sigh, long and low, like a slow tire puncture. He then shakes his head, turns, and walks away.

Instant remorse slides through me. Damn. Didn't mean to shout. I'm mad at myself, not him. "Sorry," I mutter, just loud enough for him to hear.

"No problem." He waves a hand as he saunters down the hall.

"I'm just sick of everything: talking, walking, taking the bus," I call out. Huh. Come to think of it, why is it always the bus? Where the hell is his car? Why doesn't the moneyed Marshmallow Man have a car?

I stare at his back. "Steve?"

He spins. "Yeah?"

"How come you don't have a car?"

"Where did you get that idea?" Steve pulls a key with a BMW tag from his pocket, waves it at me, and then retraces his steps. He angles off toward the door and hangs the key on a hook.

"We're always taking the bus."

Nodding, Steve moves closer and stands beside the couch. "Oh yeah. That. Tons of traffic because of Olympics. Street closures all over the place." He raises his shoulders, holds them, drops them. An explicit shrug. "Nowhere to park."

"Guess that makes sense."

"Yep. It does." Steve grins like he's anxious to please. He starts walking backwards, toward the den. "We can take the car if you want, bud. Especially if you're not well."

"It doesn't matter."

"Fine." Steve turns. "You have a nap or something. Sleep the whole day away if you want. We'll go to Gastown tomorrow. Bus, car, whatever you prefer."

He slides into the den and I slide into sleep.

17

DEAD CENTER

June, 1994

Sarah and I are in Vancouver's oldest neighborhood, Gastown, on the south shore of the Burrard Inlet, not far from the cruise ship terminal. The tang of sea salt infiltrates the air and makes my nose twitch. I'm staring at the statue of Gassy Jack Deighton—seaman, boat captain, and barkeep—who set up the first saloon here in 1867. Where the whiskey flowed, the people followed: Vancouver was born. I glance at my brochure and spot a passage about the transition of Gastown from shipping port to industrial center. I begin to read aloud, very loud, so that Sarah can hear over the flurry of chatter from a horde of elementary school children who are swarming Gassy Jack's statue like a colony of ants.

"Read it again, Mister! She's not listening!" yells one little boy whose teacher instantly shushes him and ushers him away. At his prompt, I blink and look at Sarah who is rotating slowly, eyes as wide as a kid at Christmas. I smile and follow her sight line, taking in row upon row of Victorian buildings that now form a backdrop for contemporary urban lifestyle.

"It's a collision of yesterday and today." Sarah claps her hands together to illustrate her point. When the nearby steam clock spits, hisses, and whistles, she freezes in position and emits a tiny squeal. "Quarter to twelve . . . oh, let's go!" She points to the clock which is just a couple of blocks away. "I want to be there right at noon so we can hear the Westminster Chimes." She darts off, threading her way through the crowd. I shove my brochure into one pocket, pull my camera from another, and trail her.

Once there, I raise the camera. "Okay, but you have to pose for me while we're here. Stand in front of the clock."

Sarah obliges. "Just like a model on *The Price is Right*!" She waves her hands in front of the clock. Passersby pause to watch.

"Would you like me to take a picture of both of you?" asks one short, rotund lady who's cuddling a very young puppy.

"Oh, a puppy . . . can I hold it while you take our picture?" The lady smiles and hands Sarah the puppy.

"A retriever, right? What's his name?" Sarah hugs the dog.

"*Her* name is Lady," says the woman. "My granddaughter just saw *Lady and the Tramp* and she insisted I call her Lady. And yes, it's a golden retriever. The movie Lady is a cocker spaniel, but my granddaughter didn't seem to care. Was more concerned with the fact that I wasn't feeding the dog spaghetti. Now, show me how to work this camera."

Once she's taken the picture, the stranger reclaims her dog.

"Bye, Lady," waves Sarah. "I think we should get a dog . . . someday. I loved my little Pom, Rocky, but I could love a big dog, too. . . . just like that one."

"Maybe, someday. Right now, I am more interested in the spaghetti idea. There's an Old Spaghetti Factory down the block. Wanna go?"

Sarah opens her mouth to reply. The steam clock interrupts, pumping out the Westminster Chimes. We stand there until the last echoes fade and then she latches onto my arm. "Spaghetti sounds good. Lead on."

We stroll along the cobbled sidewalk to the green door of the Old Spaghetti Factory. We step inside. The host scurries to greet us; he seats us in the railway car that sits in the heart of the restaurant. The waiter appears with the menu but I wave it away. "Spaghetti and meatballs for both," I tell him and then glance at Sarah. "Tomato sauce for you?"

She nods.

"Tomato sauce for both, please."

"Certainly," says the waiter. "Do you want salads with that?"

In synchronized motion, we shake our heads.

"But I'll have a glass of red wine, please . . . the house wine will do," says Sarah.

The waiter gives Sarah a puzzled look and then writes down the order.

"Just a Diet Coke for me, please," I say.

"Excuse me, sir," the waiter clears his throat. "Are you her legal guardian? If you are, you must know that I can't serve wine to a minor."

Sarah's face splits into a wide grin. "But I'm twenty-three years old."

I try to hide my smirk as I scrutinize my wife who, with hair in pigtails and face devoid of make-up, looks like she just stepped off a high school campus. Sarah gropes through her purse, searching for ID. By the time she presents proof of age, her face is red; the waiter's face is redder. I clamp my lips together to keep from laughing out loud.

The waiter skitters off and Sarah finds her indignation. "I don't look that young! Minor indeed!"

I take her hand . "Ah, but you do look that young. In fact, the very first time I saw you, I wondered what a kid like you was doing on a university campus. Instantly felt like some kind of pervert!"

"But that was years ago. I'm an old, married woman now."

"Married, yes. Old, definitely not. And you can stop pretending to be up-set." I shake my head slowly. "Not falling for it. If anybody should be upset it's me: people are always accusing me of robbing the cradle. Wait till we actually are older. Wonder what they'll say about a stunning young woman being with an old geezer?"

"Now it's you who is fishing for compliments, Justin Wentworth. And I'm happy to oblige . . . "

The waiter, a different waiter, deposits beverages and bread on our table. Sourdough bread, a small loaf with a serrated knife standing upright like Excalibur, in the center.

"Thank you," says Sarah. He dashes off, wordless; she extracts the knife and begins sawing slices. "Guess the other waiter is hiding out in the kitchen."

"Can't say that I blame him." My mouth waters as the aroma of fresh bread wafts toward me. I reach for the container of butter. "Now, let's get back to me. You were saying . . . "

"Oh, yes. You." She passes me two pieces of bread." You are not now, or never will be, an old geezer. You are a very handsome man, Justin. Five-foot-eleven is just the right height. Dark, wavy hair never hurt anybody. And you have those brown, puppy-dog eyes that reach the soul."

I wince. Jesus. Puppy-dog eyes. Mom used to say that to Dad. In fact, that's one of the last things she said . . . at the restaurant, the Chinese restaurant, the night they . . . the floor beneath me is quicksand now, sucking me down, down, into the past. *Shake it off, Wentworth.* I clutch my knife and focus on slathering whipped butter onto bread.

Sarah leans across the table and touches my arm. "Justin? Is something wrong?"

I relinquish the knife, grateful to take her hand instead. I grip like a vise. My breath is coming in quick gasps so I slam my eyes shut, deepen my air intake and breathe out slowly, repeating the procedure until the floor thickens, then solidifies. When I open my eyes, I see that Sarah's face is pale with concern. Without saying a word, I let go of her hand, pat it, and resume buttering bread.

Sarah rubs her fingers and then stretches them. She sighs, leans back, and runs her thumb and forefinger up and down the stem of her wine glass. She takes a sip. "Those eyes of yours betray you, Justin. Doubt. Fear. I don't really know what it is. At this point, I am not sure you do, either. Maybe someday, when you figure it all out, you'll share it with me. That's up to you. Just know that I am here if you need me."

I nod and turn away. I stare at the exterior window. I know it is sunny outside, but the stained-glass window is blue, dark blue, and has specks of clear glass in it. Looks like a windshield on a rainy night. My body squirms.

"Well, never mind that," says Sarah. She glances toward the entrance to our railway-car dining room and sits up eagerly. "Here comes the spaghetti." Her voice drops to a whisper. "Another new waiter. What the heck did we do to the last one?" She grins.

I stare at my Diet Coke as the waiter plops down the plates. We refuse the offer of grated parmesan, but before he leaves, I order a glass of wine.

Sarah reaches across, places her hand over mine. "Justin . . . "

I pull away and force a weak smile. "Spaghetti smells good. A toast to my beautiful, young—very young—wife." We clink glasses.

Sarah focuses on her spaghetti, begins twirling long strands onto a spoon.

My appetite has gone. With my fork, I poke at the meat balls, making the little bastards *do-si-do* around my plate. When the waiter brings my wine, I gulp it. The warmth trickles down my throat, soothing me. I sigh. Suddenly hungry, I impale a meatball and wolf it down. Then I slide back into being here, enjoying my time with Sarah.

A short time later, as we are leaving the restaurant, I spot a sheet of newspaper, carried along by the wind. For a few seconds, it soars. Then it hits a lamppost and drops to the sidewalk where it is trampled by passersby. A young man in a puffy jacket picks up the paper and scrunches it into a ball. He tosses. The crumpled sphere arcs through the air and falls, dead center, into a nearby garbage can.

18

STEVE'S VOICE

January, 2010

I'm flying through the air, arms and legs flailing. *Thump!* What the hell . . . ? The stench of rotting garbage assaults my nostrils. Jesus! I'm back in the Dumpster. Back in the goddamn Dumpster.

I command my body to move but it doesn't respond. But wait—this is a dream, isn't it? Yeah, a dream. Relief surges through me. A dream. That means I can wake up at any time. So . . . why don't I? Something is keeping me here. Something, but what? Something I need? Something I need to know? Irritation niggles, claws, rips at my brain. What? What? What?

Suddenly, laughter rumbles and my focus shifts. Time to listen. Just listen. I hear voices, two voices. I know those voices. The thugs who beat me and tossed me. Wait a minute. There are three voices now. Who's the third? The one saying, "Thanks, guys. Where is he? In the Dumpster? You got to be kidding me! You were only supposed to scare him, not kill him!"

I jump up, wide awake. *Steve's voice.* That was Steve's voice. Jesus Christ! That was Steve's voice. I'm shaking now, *grand mal* tremors and my whole body is raining sweat. I wrap my arms around my torso and rock back and forth, back and forth. I have to remember that dream. Have to remember every second of it before the whole thing disappears into my subconscious.

I struggle to remember, but struggling doesn't work. So I sit still, release the effort and wait. The fuzzy images begin to focus and I wait some more, aiming for high definition. *Click.* I've got it. As easy as pushing a button on the TV remote.

I plow through the dream, once, twice, three times, memorizing the details. I keep shaking my head. It doesn't make sense. Steve was the one who rescued me from the Dumpster, wasn't he? He wouldn't cause me to get tossed into it . . . would he?

"Only a dream, only a dream," I mutter. *Must be imagining things, Wentworth.* Why would Steve want thugs to scare me? I look around. And where the hell is Steve?

My synapses fire at random until a concrete memory emerges. He said something about organizing his notes. I slide off the couch and shuffle to the den. No Steve. I call his name. Nothing.

My bladder is screaming so I head to the bathroom, take a leak, and flush. I wash my hands and glance at the mirror. A battered face with a scraggly beard looks back. *What the hell?* I raise my hand and am about to touch my oily, matted hair when my whole body shudders. I turn away.

I march to the kitchen. There's a note on the fridge:

> *Be back later. Spaghetti Factory today? Up to you.*

What the hell does 'later' mean? What time is it anyway? The clock on the stove reads 2:21. I look toward the window. Daylight. How can that be? Have I been asleep since yesterday afternoon? On the freaking couch? What time was it when we finished talking? Three? Four? Six, at the latest. Must have slept a whole day away. Damn.

My stomach growls but I ignore it. Don't care about food. My brain returns to the dream, fixates on the dream. What the hell was that about? Steve? The thugs? The Dumpster? He couldn't have been involved in that. The images replay on a loop in my mind. Over and over and over.

I pace the hallway. Back and forth. Back and forth. I need something. I need a drink. Now. Anything to still my racing thoughts.

Thugs. Dumpster. Fist. Steve.

I stop walking and run my hands through my hair. *It was a dream, only a dream.* I'm losing my grip; got to get some traction here.

Dumpster. Fist. Thugs. Steve.

My brain's running at warp speed and my limbs are quivering like leaves on an aspen. My mouth is dry. I need. I want. Booze. Now. Anything to shut down my brain. Fuck the idea of getting traction. I'm getting drunk.

I still have money, don't I? I shove my hand toward my pocket. I'm quaking so much that I miss on the first try. I try again, locate the pocket, and pull out a twenty along with some change. Yep. I still have money. Need more. Need to lay in a supply of booze. Money, money, money. I will sit on the street and beg if I have to, but . . . wait a minute. Marshmallow Man has a recycle bin, full of bottles and cans. I rush to the kitchen, hoping like hell that Steve hasn't returned the containers already. As soon as I see the familiar blue bin, I relax. A wide grin spreads across my face.

The recycle bin is overflowing with bounty; next to it is a green garbage bag which is filled with large bottles—the twenty-cent-refund variety. I rub my hands together and then rummage until I find another bag to empty the bin into. Before long, I'm on my way to Davie Street.

First stop: grocery store. I unload my treasure. Next stop: the liquor store. I load up with greater treasure.

Before long, I'm back in the condo, safe and sound, with three bottles of twist-off cap white wine. I stash two bottles under the bed in my room, and take the already half-empty third to the den, intending to polish it off while I play with Marshmallow Man's computer.

Of course, that idea doesn't come to fruition, because there is no computer. Marshmallow Man has a laptop; guess he took it with him. Damn. I park my butt in Steve's swivel chair anyway and spin around. Now I'm trying to remember why I wanted to log on in the first place. What am I looking for? I snap my fingers. Oh, yeah. Got to check Marshmallow Man's story. Says he is writing about the homeless. I wonder if he hires thugs to beat up homeless people. I shake my head and laugh out loud. Nah. I can't be playing with a full deck here. But still, it might be interesting to Google "Steve Jameson, Vancouver." But how the hell can I do that if there is no computer? Huh. Guess I can always go to the library. Internet access there.

The thought makes me shudder. I've never been comfortable in a library. Mom was always dragging me there when I was kid . . . and I was always kicking and screaming at the idea. Preferred playing to reading. Libraries were fine for hanging out when I was in college. Or for last minute essay stuff. But that was a long time ago. Libraries were Sarah's thing, not mine. In my current life, libraries are shelter. Guess I could manage to use a computer there, though, if I wanted. Do I need a library card for that? Don't have a clue.

At the moment, I don't care. The booze is taking over, and my interest in Steve's agenda, real or imagined, is waning. I spin in the chair, grinning like a kid in a Disneyland teacup. When the ficus tree whirls into view, I plant my feet, causing the chair to jerk to a halt.

At first, I just stare at the tree. After a few minutes, I put the bottle on the desk and go to it. Methodically, carefully, I remove dead leaves and drop them into the wastebasket nearby. Then I retrieve my wine bottle and polish off its contents.

Now what? Rinse the bottle and hide the evidence, that's what.

Once the bottle is thoroughly clean, I take it to my room, open the closet, drop to the floor, and root around like a frightened rodent seeking shelter. *Got to hide the bottle.* No crannies or niches available, so I stash the bottle in the corner and conceal it with pillows. Wait a minute . . . what about the two full bottles? I grab them from under the bed and squirrel them away in the same closet corner.

Confident that I have found a good hiding place, happy that I have emergency reserves, I return to the den—Steve's mini-mancave. Time to do some spelunking. Maybe there is something else here that will tell me more about Marshmallow Man. Only problem is that, at the moment, I can't remember why I wanted to find out more about him in the first place.

I'm standing there scratching my head when a sudden noise—the sound of keys jangling—makes me jump. I hightail it out of the den and, by the time Steve enters, I'm on the couch. My breathing is coming in short spurts. Better calm down. I take deep breaths. Inhale. Exhale. Inhale. Exhale.

Steve approaches. "Yo, Justin. You awake?"

I fake a moan and roll over. Mistake. It hurts like hell. I moan for real this time.

"You okay, Justin? Need anything?"

Steve is standing over me now. My eyes are closed, but I can still feel his gaze piercing me. In a flash, I'm reliving the Dumpster dream. My heart pumps furiously, powering blood to my legs, preparing them for flight.

Run away. Run away. Run away.

No. Damn it. Not running. *No.* I tighten every muscle in my body. I don't know what's going on. Don't know *if* anything is going on. Maybe I'm just paranoid. It's easy to get that way, living in the street where every sound, every thought, every look is potential danger. Scared or not, I'm staying.

Am I scared? Scared of Steve. Nah, not really. I figure that if he wanted me dead he would have done that or arranged that by now. Besides, he's a born-again, isn't he? I don't think that murder is allowed. I stifle a laugh. Many religious sects are guilty of mass murder. The corner of my mouth twitches. Steve a murderer? I don't think so. I sure as hell hope not. But what does he want with me? Don't know. Regardless, I'm not going anywhere. I need help. Have to get my Sarah and Bobby back. I can't do it on my own and I sure as hell can't do it from the street. My hope is Steve Jameson. I need him to be who he says he is.

Me and Steve. Steve and me.

Stuck.

19

TRUST FUND LIVING

It's time to perform my pretend wake up. I stretch, yawn, and look at my savior with my one good eye. Actually notice that my other eye is opening up a bit. Steve notices, too.

"Hey! Your eye is getting better. It's open. Can you see through it?"

I squeeze my good eye shut. "Got your marshmallow jacket dry-cleaned, I see."

"That's a relief. You *can* still see through that eye. 'Marshmallow jacket' . . . that's funny." Steve grins. "I didn't get the jacket cleaned though. I had no more use for it, so I just threw it out and bought a new one. Here!" He tosses me a Subway sandwich. "You been sleeping for so long, I figured you'd be too weak to go to the Spaghetti Factory, so I brought you something to eat."

"Thanks. " I take the sandwich and peel back the wrapper. I am aware of something nagging at me, but I'm not sure what. Don't want to go to the Spaghetti Factory—Steve's right about that—but that's not what's gnawing my insides. I give Steve's new jacket the once-over and slide my butt to the edge of the couch. There I pause, shrug, and look around. "This is a pretty fancy place for a student. Two-bedroom, two-bath condo. Thirteen hundred square feet. Three blocks from English Bay. Worth a mint."

"You sound like a real estate agent." Steve grins.

"I used to be." Damn. Me and my big mouth. I'm not in the mood to give Steve information today. His new jacket . . . that's what's bothering me, but I don't know why.

"Did you sell West End property?"

"Yeah, yeah. West End, high end. Whatever. Like I said, this is an expensive condo. How does a grad student afford it?"

Steve shrugs. "My parents made a lot of money in the last few years. They set up a trust fund for me. No big deal. Never want for anything. They give me lots of stuff."

My jaw tightens. I drop my sandwich onto the coffee table and jump to my feet, fists raised, heart pounding. "Yeah. Easy as hell when they give you whatever you want and promise they'll always be there. Then they leave. No warning. You turn around and they're gone. Just like that. No family. No home. Not a fucking penny to your name."

Steve recoils. "Whoa . . . take it easy, Justin." He extends both arms, palms out, preparing to ward off an attack. "Not my fault, bud. Don't take it out on me." His voice ripples.

Jesus! Was worried about him hurting me, and now I'm scaring the hell out of him. My rage disappears as quickly as it showed up. I drop to the couch and lower my head. "Sorry."

When Steve speaks again, his voice is calm, monotone. "Do you want to talk about it, Justin?"

"Not really."

"You sure?"

I stare at the carpet.

"Okay then." Steve moves closer and plops into the chair across from me.

My heart still hammers. I take deep, slow breaths. Out of the corner of my eye, I see Steve's foot tapping, padding noiselessly on the carpet. He's going to ask something else, I just know it. *Tread lightly,* bud.

"What about real estate?" Steve's voice still wavers slightly. "Sure picked a heck of a time to get into that, didn't you?"

"Yeah, well . . . " Damn. Don't want to talk about this either. *Leave me alone,* bud.

"Guess you didn't see the warning signs. When did you start selling real estate anyway?"

"Not now, Steve." I get up, turn away. "Maybe we'll go to the Spaghetti Factory tomorrow. Tired. Sore. Need more sleep."

"Ah, come on, bud. It'll help if you talk about it. At least, sit here and finish your sandwich. You won't regain your strength if you don't eat."

I look back, staring first at him and then at the abandoned sandwich. He's right. If I want my life back, if I am to have any chance with Sarah and Bobby, I need to get healthy. I go to the couch, sit, and pick up the sandwich. Without a word, I nibble, bit by bit, mouse-sized bites, until there is nothing left. I stand and walk away.

"One more thing, bud."

I stop.

"No offense, but if you are going to stay here, you've got to hit the shower. You're pretty ripe. I left towels and clean clothes in your bathroom."

I nod and continue walking.

Soon I'm in the shower, reveling in the hot water that prickles my scalp and rains down my shoulders. A simple thing—a shower. Yet a luxury. No such luxury during the months that I lived in the street. Now, as I stand there, tears surge, and I swallow the urge to cry. There is no pain here, only gratitude. A shower—something that I took for granted my whole life—is a privilege. The water pounds me, massages my beaten body. I reach for the shampoo and squeeze a glob into my hand. As I knead it into my scalp, my tears do flow. They mix with the droplets from the shower and siphon away. I don't realize that I am sobbing until I hear Steve banging on the door.

"Are you okay in there? You need anything?"

"I'm fine, just fine," my voice croaks. I clear my throat. "Be out in a minute."

But I take much longer than a minute. I stay in the shower until the water turns cold. Even then I linger, invigorated by the sensation of tiny icicles stinging my face and body.

By the time I towel off and haul on cargo shorts and a t-shirt—clean clothes left by my host—I am sober. I no longer have a desire to drown reality with booze. Not now. I head to my room, pull back the bed covers, and plop down. Soft, warm, and comfortable, this bed. Love having this bed. Love being clean.

Gratitude penetrates my brain and filters its way through my body. An alien feeling—gratitude. I've always known the definition of the *word*, but this is undoubtedly the first time I have actually felt it. Gratitude. And it's not for a big house or an expensive car. It's for food and shelter and warmth. *Thanks, Steve.*

The instant Steve's name crosses my mind, gratitude seeps out and suspicion creeps in. Would Steve really hire thugs to hurt me? Maybe. But maybe my screwed-up head is just playing tricks on me. *Maybe* I should go to the living room and ask him outright. I drop one leg over the side of the bed, let it dangle for a minute, and then retrieve it.

My body is calm and my brain is quiet. I like this stillness, and I don't want to pierce it with pain. Questions do that, stab at your brain and make memories bleed to the surface. My mind is resting now; this is not the time for a question period with Steve. Maybe tomorrow I'll talk to him. Yes, tomorrow.

As I'm drifting off, my mind wanders back to Bobby. I remember sitting on his bed, reading to him. Dory and Nemo. I smile. I remember kissing him goodnight, going to the master bedroom and crawling into bed. Not sleeping, feeling incomplete, unbalanced, like a bicycle with a wheel missing, waiting for Sarah to return from class, or from the library. Waiting for Sarah.

I am aware of a door opening, someone approaching, blankets falling over me. A slight chill as air stirs around me. Then . . . just the stillness. "Sarah?" I whisper.

"Sorry, bud, it's only Steve. Good night, Justin."

I let out a long sigh.

20

SEESAW

I awake the next morning, cloaked in comfort. I inhale. Fabric softener . . . vanilla, I think. A pleasant smell. My nose twitches and my body buries deeper into the blankets. Nothing like clean sheets and a soft mattress. My lips curve into a smile.

Memory intrudes: *dream, Steve, thugs, fists.* My smile evaporates. Damn. I can't think about that. Damn again. Too late. Already there.

I sigh and uncurl my body—the start of a whole-body stretch. Extending my arms over my head, I push, push, push against the wall behind the bed. I straighten my legs and flex my ankles. Then I grab a fistful of blankets and fling them. I have no desire to get up yet, so I just lie on my back, arms crossed behind head, staring at the ceiling. *Should I confront Steve? Should I just ignore the dream?* I blink, seesawing between the two.

The screech of a siren severs both silence and sluggishness. Completely alert, I jump from the bed and charge across the room, heart racing. I peer through a crack in the blinds. Nothing there. The wail persists, escalating, cresting, abating. Silence returns. I take a deep breath and lean against the window ledge, heart hammering. Damn. I'm not even on the street and still the sound of a siren scares me half to death. That does it. Decision made. I am not confronting Steve. He could toss me to the curb. Can't let that happen. Not now, anyway. *Keep your mouth shut, Wentworth.* Yeah, good idea . . . for now. New resolve: mouth shut, eyes open.

For a few days, I am a silent observer. I ask no questions and, gratefully, Steve initiates no interviews.

A routine emerges. In the morning, I make coffee. I putter around. I have to keep moving, for mornings are rife with sobriety, a.k.a. hell. Since my body squirms and wriggles and refuses to sit still anyway, I give in to it by tidying the kitchen and emptying waste baskets. I pace the hallway, pushing the Swiffer mop or vacuuming the carpet runner. I dust. When that's done, I tend to the ficus tree . . . removing leaves, snipping branches, adding water.

Steve gets up later than me and joins me for coffee. We chat; actually, *he* chats. I sit soundless, sipping. Yeah, sometimes his yammering bugs the hell out of me. But Steve gives me food, money, even a bus pass. The least I can do in the morning is pay attention while he recounts his activities. That's what I tell myself. That's what I want to believe. But a thunderhead of suspicion hovers relentlessly, reminding me to listen and learn. *Who is this Good Samaritan? What does he want with me?*

Maybe I'm wasting my time, worrying. Sure hope so. Maybe there's nothing to figure out. To this point, all I have learned is that Steve is a busy guy: Bible group and study group and choir practice and Church on Sunday. Not a thing about hiring thugs. No. Not a damn thing. I'm grateful for that. The truth is, I like it here. More than that, I *need* to be here. I need Steve's help. Gotta heal. Gotta get off the booze.

Booze. Damn. I start every day, determined not to imbibe, and do fine as long as I keep busy. In the mornings. But by midday, my resolve wanes and by afternoons? Well, consuming booze is how I spend my afternoons . . . and evenings.

Physically, I'm feeling a bit better. My ribs don't hurt as much. Facial bruises have changed from purple to pink, yellow in some places. I'm gaining weight. Can barely fit into my ragged jeans. But they feel good anyway because they are clean. Thanks to Steve. Yep, Marshmallow Man even launders my clothes.

I'm mopping the kitchen early one afternoon, contemplating my first drink of the day, when Steve shows up, fresh from Bible Study, and plops down at the kitchen table. He looks around and nods.

"Don't need a maid service, long as I got you, bud."

"Least I can do."

"Kitchen looks great. You're looking better, too, come to think of it."

"Thanks."

"Ready to talk some more?"

Silence falls. I wait, expecting my body to stiffen in resistance to Steve's question, but it doesn't. Huh. I shrug. "Talk about what?"

"Never did tell me about the real estate thing. When did you start selling real estate?"

I return the mop to its alcove and turn to face Steve. "Guess I can talk about that." I maneuver my way into a chair across from him. "Probably was a good thing, you leaving me alone for a few days . . . especially after I blew my stack about my parents, I mean."

Steve sniffs as he pulls a notebook and pen from his backpack. "Scared the heck out of me."

"Yeah, I know. Didn't mean to. Just erupted, you know?"

Steve nods.

I wait for the next question, but it doesn't come. I look at him, raise an eyebrow.

Nothing.

Okay. Guess he wants me to choose the direction of the conversation. Good enough. "The death of my parents bulldozed me." The instant those words fall out of my mouth, I wince, anticipating pain. None comes. I shrug and keep going. "I felt nothing for days, weeks after they died. Then, guilt showed up and set in deep. I just couldn't fathom it: why *them* and not *me*? I thought I was going to drown in guilt." I lick my lips. Thirsty. Craving.

"I think guilt's a pretty normal reaction, bud."

"Yeah, so I was told." A wave of anxiety sweeps through me. I jerk to my feet and stride to the fridge. I open the door, close the door, and return to my chair.

Steve says nothing. His eyes flicker. Fear? Maybe.

"No worries, bud. Just anxious, that's all." Huh. *No worries.* My dad used to say that all the time. My hands are suddenly frigid. I rub them together and cross my arms, burying my hands in my armpits. "Where was I? Oh, yeah. Next thing I know, the guilt's gone. No guilt, but I'm mad as hell . . . mad at my parents for leaving and for leaving me penniless. I figured the rage would drain away eventually, that I'd feel normal again. But I kind of got stuck."

"Must have been tough."

"Understatement."

Steve nods. "But, even though they left you broke, you earned a lot of money, didn't you?"

"Yeah. Megabucks. Spent it all . . . and then some."

"You think the spending was related to the anger?"

I tilt my head. "Huh. Never thought of it that way. Maybe. I told myself I deserved to have everything." I shrug. "But maybe I felt I didn't deserve anything. After all, they left me nothing. And that's how I ended up . . . with nothing."

"You really think things would have been different if your parents had left you money?"

I unfold my arms and throw my hands into the air. "Don't know. What I do know is that, every time I slapped down a credit card, I was trying to fill a hole, or make up for something that was missing."

"How about the drinking? How did that figure into it?"

I shake my head. "Not sure. Guess it started with trying to keep the memory of my parents' death buried. Huh. That must've worked . . . still don't remember a thing about the accident. Then, I guess it was about money . . . I'd spend too much, feel guilty, cover the guilt with booze. A cycle." My body squirms, and I jump to my feet again. I lurch into motion and pace the kitchen floor—four steps forward, sharp turn, four steps back—repeatedly, like a tin duck in a shooting gallery. As I make a one-eighty, I catch a glimpse of Steve: back rigid, pen frozen in midair.

"You sure you're not about to erupt again, bud?" His voice is high-pitched, reedy.

I wave my hand through the air and keep walking. "Don't worry. You're safe, but Jesus, dude! I don't get it. Why does part of me still blame my parents? Maybe, just maybe, if they had left me with some financial support, I would have been more responsible with my own family. Maybe." I come to a standstill. "But sometimes I think there's more. Like I'm missing something.

Don't know what. Maybe I'm just looking for excuses for being a screw up." I go back to my chair and drop down again.

Steve lets out a deep breath and lowers his gaze. "You think that the 'something' is related to the accident?" He's doodling on the notepad now. Drawing concentric circles. "Do you *want* to remember the accident?"

My heart pounds. "Hell, no!"

Steve's head pops up and he stares me right in the eyes.

"Why would I want to be tormented by that? All I want is . . . " I pause, knowing that Sarah and Bobby are the only words that fit at the end of that sentence. I clear my throat and start again. "All I want is . . . a second chance. I've got to get a handle on the anger. That and the money and the drinking." I shudder. "Hard to deal with, all at once. First, I need to let my body heal."

"Lots of time, bud. You can stay here as long as you need. No problem."

"Thanks." *Why the hell are you doing this for me?* I open my mouth to ask but another thought intervenes. *Damn cold on the sidewalk, Wentworth.* Panic rips through me. I clamp my lips tight, praying that Steve doesn't see my hands tremble.

Maybe he does, but he doesn't say. He just waves off my weak "thanks," gnaws his lower lip, and toys with his pen. Then, slowly, he says, "I bet your parents never intended to leave you broke. I bet there is a reason . . . "

I raise both hands, palms toward him. "Whatever. Not a thing I can do about it now, right?" I cross my arms and let out a sigh. "You want to know about real estate? I'll tell you about that . . . as long as you stop clicking that damn pen."

Instant stillness. Steve takes a deep breath. "Okay, okay . . . When did you start selling?"

"As soon as we moved to Vancouver. Seemed like easy money. And, for a while, it was. Made lots." I smirk. "Was bursting with pride the first time I got a big paycheck. I headed straight for home . . . couldn't wait to impress Sarah." I suddenly frown. "I remember wishing Mom and Dad were there to see it, too. I remember that the thought of them put a damper on everything. I tried to shake off the sadness. Next thing I knew, the car was parked in front of a jewelry store on West Georgia. I got out of the car and went inside."

Steve leans back in his chair. "Ahhh. The Rolex?"

I crease my brow. Did I tell him about that? Must have. I sigh. "Yeah, the Rolex."

21

PAUPER TO PRINCE

May, 1997

H ey, Sarah! I'm home." Where the hell is she? "Sarah!" I toss my jacket onto the couch.

"Out here. On the balcony."

I roll up my shirt sleeves and charge toward the sliding door. In the process, I almost smack into the ficus that has recently taken up residence in the living room. I manage to sidestep that and then blast off again. *Bang!* I slam right into the partly-open balcony door. "Damn!" I sweep the door along its track, jump over the pint-sized ledge, and stand there, arms extended. My brand new Rolex sparkles in the sun.

Sarah unfolds from her crouched position and wipes her face with the back of her gardening glove, creating a smudge from nose to hairline. Cute as hell. Want to take her right this second.

She tilts her head like a curious puppy. "You're looking pretty pleased with yourself, Mr. Wentworth. What's up?" Her eyes lock on the glistening watch. Her shoulders droop. "Damn it all, Justin . . . "

Alarm bells blare in my head. *Distract, distract, distract.* I yank out my wallet and fumble through it. "Just bringing home the bacon." Retrieving my monster paycheck, I thrust it right under her nose. Pride bursts inside me. Suddenly I'm an air cadet again, standing at attention, waiting for inspection. Knowing that the report will be glowing. Knowing that she'll forget about the watch.

Sarah does not disappoint. She drops her trowel and jumps into my arms. "Justin! I'm so proud of you. You promised me you could do this!"

My shining moment. Exactly what I wanted. Exactly what I needed.

But Sarah pulls back and slips out of my arms. Her face darkens. "I see you've been celebrating without me." She grabs my wrist, raises it to get a closer look. "How much did this set us back?"

Not what I want to hear. "What difference does it make? Didn't you see the paycheck?"

"How much?" She drops my arm and steps back, hands on hips.

I sigh. "Three or four thousand. But it's no big deal, Sarah. I just brought home twice that."

"Give me the watch. Give me the receipt."

"What for?"

"I'm taking it back."

My heart speeds up. "You can't do that."

"Oh, yes I can. I'm doing it right now."

"No way. I worked hard for this. I deserve it."

"We owe too much. *Visa. MasterCard. American Express.* When does it end?" She removes one glove and holds out her hand. "Pass it over. I'm taking it back *right now.*

"Right now." *Distract. Distract. Distract.* "What about those geraniums you're potting?"

"Nice try. The geraniums can wait."

"But I'm making all kinds of money, Sarah. The real estate market is booming and I need this watch. I have to present a certain image." I look into her eyes to determine if that explanation has impact.

She glares.

Damn. I step close, reach out, cradle her face in my hands. "Look, Sarah, you just wait . . . someday I'm going to buy you a mansion with a big yard where you can spend hours nurturing all kinds of exotic trees and flowers."

She pulls away from me. "Uh uh. Not a chance. You're not going to distract me with fantasies." She grasps my wrist again and pulls at the expandable watch band. "I'm working my butt off too, you know. Trying to get a master's degree *and* slaving away in that dusty bookshop. Not putting up with this." She yanks the watch off and slides it into her pocket.

"Damn it all, Sarah . . . "

"Receipt, please."

I grope through the wallet, find the requested piece of paper, and hold it out. Sarah reaches for it. My fingers won't release it. She tugs. I still grip. Sarah removes my fingers, one at a time, until the receipt is in her hand. She sighs.

"Thanks, Justin," she says. "Maybe we can return it together, and then go to dinner. That would be a cheaper way to celebrate the big payday, don't you think?"

I drop my head, turn, and slink away like a wounded animal. The hurt morphs into anger as I step from the balcony to the living room. Grabbing my jacket, I stomp through the apartment, out the door, down the hall, to the exit. I know I'm being childish, but I don't care. I wanted that watch. I needed it. *Damn it all, Wentworth, does that even make sense?*

I pound the pavement to Davie Street and pause there, scanning, looking for a place to get a drink. Easily spot a couple of pubs. I walk into the nearer one, park my butt at the bar, and drink until my brain is in a haze.

It must be hours later when I return. I'm no longer feeling wounded or angry. Just numb, comfortably numb.

Sarah greets me at the apartment door.

I open my mouth to argue my actions. I stop. She's smiling, for Christ's sake. Sarah's smiling. Completely flabbergasted, I just stand there with my mouth agape.

Sarah grabs my arm and pulls me in. Her lips curve downward when she catches a whiff of the booze, and I figure her rage was just delayed. I brace myself. But she simply rolls her eyes and turns away to close the door. When she looks at me again, her smile is back. Huh. Amazing. She really is *not* angry.

"Stay there, Justin Wentworth." She props me up against the wall. "Head down, please."

I look down and see her feet. Bare. A blur of cherry-red toenail polish. I blink, but my vision is still fuzzy. Two paw prints dance on the top of her left foot. Her *forever* tattoo.

"And close your eyes."

I squint.

"All the way closed, please."

"What's going on, Sarah?"

Her feet scamper along the carpet to the bedroom. Drawers slam. Paper rustles. Footsteps scurry back. Again, she's standing in front of me. She moves closer until her torso touches mine. Her body vibrates with excitement, sending shivers through me. The scent of her hair—strawberries and vanilla—fills my nostrils.

"Open your eyes."

A shiny object floats in front of my face. It glistens and sparkles.

Sarah is babbling. "I know you wanted it, but it is so expensive, and I really wanted to take it back. But you were so upset. I couldn't return it, Justin, I just couldn't. You did work hard and you do deserve it. I got it engraved, so now we *can't* return it. Look at the back." She stops. Her eyes are gleaming with hope as she awaits my response.

I take the watch from her trembling hand, hold it out to the side and flip it over.

> *Once a Pauper, now a Prince.*
> *My Prince.*
> *Forever,*
> *Sarah.*

I smile. I put the watch on my wrist. It belongs there. I deserve it. I embrace my wife.

22

PIED PIPER

January, 2010

Was that the watch the thugs took?”

I frown. “Don’t remember telling you that.”

“You did. Probably forgot. Alcohol will do that to you.”

I shake my head. “But I’m not drinking . . . ”

Steve smirks. “Yeah, right.” He gets up and walks to the kitchen counter. “You want coffee?”

“Uh uh.” My neck aches. I reach up to rub it.

Steve pours a coffee for himself and returns to the table. “I’m not an idiot, Justin.”

My body stiffens.

“You don’t have to steal the stuff in the recycle bin to buy booze, bud. I’ll give you money.”

“For booze? *Sure* you will.”

Steve jumps up, marches to the sink and dumps his coffee down the drain. “Let’s go.”

“Go where?”

“Your choice. Liquor store or AA."

“Don’t need AA.”

"Are you sure? There are lots . . . "

"You heard me the first time, *bud.*"

"Okay. I guess it's the liquor store, then."

I stare at him in disbelief, but he's heading to the door. I'm not about give up an opportunity like this, so I get up and plod along after him. For some reason, *The Pied Piper* story crosses my mind. Huh. Interesting. I shrug. Whatever.

About two blocks from the condo, Steve starts in: "*If* you ever think you need AA, let me know."

I bite back the urge to swear at him. "Don't need AA." The ache in my neck is getting worse.

"Maybe you think that *now.*" He raises his arms in conductor mode.

Damn. I've seen this before. He'll never shut up.

"Maybe you'll change your mind," says Maestro Steve. "Maybe the twelve-step program . . . "

"*Maybe* we should go to the Spaghetti Factory later today." Did that do it? I hold my breath.

Steve sighs and drops his arms. "Sure, we can do that."

Success. Symphony interrupted. The ache leaves my neck and I exhale, long and slow. "When we get back to the condo, I'll have a shower." Showers are my favorite thing now. Next to cheap wine.

"No problem."

We walk the rest of the way in silence. Into the store, buy two bottles of wine, out of the store. Not another word about AA. About anything. When we get back to Steve's, he shrugs off his jacket and tosses it onto a chair. "I'll get you some clean towels." He heads down the hallway, bouncing along and whistling a Disney tune. I grin. Steve's Goody Two-shoes attitude is an affirmation. I choose to think he's a good guy . . . for now, anyway.

"Take your time," says Steve as he passes me the towels. "Oh, by the way, I bought some new clothes for you earlier today . . . I'll leave them outside the door."

"Thanks."

I ease into the shower. Yeah, the experience is becoming familiar now, but I still derive pleasure from every bead of water. I squeeze a glob of shampoo onto my hair and catch myself humming the same melody that Steve was whistling: "Heigh Ho" from *Snow White and the Seven Dwarfs.*

Huh. Disney. Steve. Steve. Disney. Both words create the same sensation in me for, being clean and fed, I am excited, content, like a kid in the Magic Kingdom. A temporary feeling? No doubt. Visits to Disneyland are short hops into fantasy.

My face splits into a grin as memories of Disneyland bubble up: Bobby hugging Donald Duck, Sarah and Bobby sporting mouse ears, Sarah and Bobby and me whirling and twirling in a giant teacup. I close my eyes, clinging to memories, letting their warmth course through me while hot water flows over me. I suck in a deep breath and slide it out. I rinse my hair, soap and soak my body . . . twice.

Still smiling, I rotate the shower lever, choking off the flow. An instant chill hits and I stand there as my body weeps water . . . and memories. I lean into the shower wall, eyes closed, struggling to hold onto the image of Sarah and Bobby and me, but it slips away. New pictures slide in. Images of credit cards bills and overdue notices. I cringe and choke back a sob.

What was I thinking? Taking my family to Hawaii *and* Europe on the heels of the Disneyland trip? *Idiot.* All first class vacations. All my idea. I wanted to give Sarah everything. I was determined to give Bobby everything, just like my parents did for me. I thump my head against the tile, over and over. *Just like my parents . . .*

Sarah tried, damn it, she tried to convince me to stop spending, even hired a financial consultant once. But I was having none of it. Couldn't stop. Didn't know why. Just knew that there was a whopping, black crater inside me, and I kept shoveling stuff into it. God, I'd kill or die for Sarah. But I couldn't stop spending. And then the drinking . . .

Enough! I push away from the shower wall and shake my head. *Got to stop torturing myself.* I reach for a towel and wrap it around my waist.

Body trembling, breathing erratic, I exit the shower. I stumble to the bathroom door, open it a crack, and retrieve the blue plastic bag Steve has deposited there. I dump the contents onto the floor. Shirts, jeans, underwear, jacket . . . all with price tags. I drop the plastic bag. White letters glare up at me—Sears. My legs turn to rubber and I slump to my knees. My head spins. Sears. I need a drink. Sears. Sears . . . and Sarah.

23

DAY BECOMES NIGHT

December, 2000

I rush from the hardware department at Sears and search the crowd. Where the heck is Sarah? My eyes finally land on her, in the center aisle, still as a mannequin. *What is she staring at?* I ease up to her and align my vision with hers. Suddenly, I'm looking at the toy department, specifically at three toddlers engaged in a group hug with a giant teddy bear. *Uh oh.* Beads of sweat form on my brow.

Sarah's head turns slowly toward me. "What do you think about the idea of having a . . . "

I flinch. "Don't even say it. You told me years ago that you didn't want to have children. That kids lead to complications, trouble, pain. You didn't want a child of yours to experience what you . . ."

Sarah shrivels and the light in her eyes vanishes.

I slam my lips together. Damn it all. I have crushed her. Guilt stabs my gut. Guilt and craving. Alcohol. More guilt. She doesn't know that I am drinking almost daily now. She doesn't know the things I do to keep her from finding out about the money, the booze. She doesn't know that if I want something, I buy it. Why shouldn't I? I'm selling real estate and the market is booming. I'm making lots of dough. Saving none, but intend to buy a house soon. Lots of houses available with no money down. Yep, I'm enjoying myself. No need to make changes. No babies, that's for sure. I open my mouth to deflect, redirect. I'm a salesman; that's what I do. But Sarah speaks before I do.

"Justin, I'm sorry," she says, her eyes cast downward. "Yes, we did have an agreement. And yes, I did spring this on you. But it has been nearly a decade since we met. I am not that bright-eyed kid anymore. It came as a complete surprise to me . . . " She shrugs and begins digging at the floor with the toe of her sneaker.

"But we have plans remember? Buying a house? Finishing your degree?" I wrap my arms around her.

"I'm sure I am not the first woman in the world that this has happened to."

"Of course not. But we have plans, remember?" *Damn.* I'm repeating myself.

"Yeah, I remember. And university is great . . . I really want to finish my master's degree." She looks up at me, her eyes shimmering with tears. "I didn't mean for this to happen," she whispers. "I guess I have been studying so hard—the Shakespeare course alone is enough to distract anyone. I get lost in the books, Justin, and I forget everything. Day becomes night, night becomes day, sometimes I even forget to eat. And I guess I forgot to take the pill."

The meaning of her words seeps into my brain and I nod, take her hand, and pull her away from the toy department. Can't comment. Maybe later, when my heart stops pounding. Yes, later, because now I am a derailed train that needs to get back on its tracks and keep chugging, keep going in the direction it was heading. Where? I don't know. *Clickety-clack, clickety-clack, clickety-clack.*

We say nothing as we stumble our way to the car and head for home. We say nothing as we enter the apartment. I drop the keys on the hallstand and go to the living room. I sit. Sarah doesn't join me. She dashes to the bedroom and slams the door. I head in that direction, but when I hear her sobbing, I turn away.

I want a drink. No, I *need* a drink. When did wanting become needing? I don't know and don't care. With the stealth of a coyote, I pad my way to the door, reclaim my keys, and escape to the nearest bar.

24

GOT ANY KIDS?

January, 2010

I crumple the Sears bag, destroy the price tags, and deposit everything into the wastebasket. Then I pick up the new clothes and run my hands over them. Cotton and wool and denim. Damn. Steve must have spent a fortune. Whatever. My mood brightens. This is Christmas, and I am a kid again.

I put on the underwear and adjust myself. Who'd have thought that new briefs would feel so good? I pull the jeans over them. Perfect fit. I grab a towel, wipe the steam from the mirror and peer into it. My body winces at the sight of the weathered face that stares back at me. I gulp back tears. Damn . . . I'm as emotional as a pregnant woman, just like Sarah before Bobby was born.

I rub my good eye with the heel of my hand, yank open a drawer, and pull out the hair dryer. Jamming the plug into the outlet, I turn the dryer on HOT and HIGH. Amazing difference between stringy, dirty hair of the street and the soft, flowing, locks of the now. Yeah, I need a haircut, but for the time being, I'll keep the hair below my ears and over my eye. At least until the damage heals. I comb my hair into position, pull on a T-shirt and use the comb again. After tossing the towels into a nearby wicker hamper, I put on a long sleeve shirt—blue, my favorite color—grab my new jacket—also blue. What's with this guy and puffy jackets anyway? Jacket in hand, shoulders pulled back, I open the door and march into the living room.

Steve is sitting there, iPhone in hand, texting like crazy. When he hears me, he stops, abruptly—like a burglar interrupted—and shoves his phone into the holder attached to his belt. He looks up.

"You clean up good, bud . . . I mean, Justin."

"Thanks." I stand there, gazing at his phone. Huh. Sure got off the phone quick.

He stares.

"Old Spaghetti Factory?" I remind him.

"Oh, yeah, right!" Steve jumps up and grabs his jacket and keys. "It's really not all that far, but I don't think you are up for walking yet, are you? Bus okay? We can take the BMW if you want."

BMW. *Nice.* Interest stirred, I lick my lips like I'm anticipating a major purchase. But a snapshot image—the repo man hauling away my Lexus—flashes before me, sending anticipation to the graveyard. *Damn. Talk about a reality check.* I take a deep breath and turn toward Steve. "Bus is fine."

He stares for a few seconds, eyebrows raised. Then he shrugs. "Good enough." He heads for the door.

"Thanks for the clothes, Steve," I say to his back.

"You're welcome," he replies and begins whistling Disney again.

I follow, grinning. No murderer, here, I am sure of it. Something niggles at me. I remember his thumbs hammering his iPhone. *So, who were you texting, bud?*

As soon as we enter the Old Spaghetti Factory, the aroma of pasta and bread wafts up my nose. Memories stab at me: Sarah and me, seated in the railway car in the center of the restaurant. I am relieved when the waiter bypasses the railway car and seats us at the back. We place our orders: spaghetti with meat sauce and meatballs. Wine for me. Coke for Steve.

Shortly after the waiter zooms off, Steve pulls out his notebook and starts in. "Got any kids, Justin?"

I cough, wipe my mouth with my sleeve, and cough again. The waiter delivers our beverages; I down my wine and ask for another.

Steve leans back in his chair. "So . . . you do have kids. How many? Male or female?"

I swallow and clutch my empty wine glass. "Just one. A boy—name's Bobby."

"Got a picture?"

I sniff. "Yeah, right."

"Okay, okay. How old is Bobby?"

"Nine, almost nine." A sigh escapes me. I shove my hand into my pocket and find the castle. I latch onto it, pull it out and stare at it.

"You gonna tell me what's so special about that castle?"

The waiter shows up and replaces my empty glass with a full one. "I'll be right back with your meals."

I ignore him, thrust the castle back into my pocket, and pick up the glass. The waiter shrugs and ambles away.

"Thanks," calls Steve who then turns back to me. "So, Bobby's nine, huh? Born in 2001." Steve raises his eyebrows. "Before or after Nine/eleven?"

"Before." I gulp the wine, all of it. "In April."

Steve leans forward and taps his pen on the table. "Must have been scary—I mean, we were all scared when the twin towers went down, but, with a young child, you must have been petrified."

"Understatement."

The waiter delivers on his promise, planking down two steaming plates of spaghetti and meat balls. "Would you like parmesan cheese? Cracked pepper?"

Steve shakes his head. I sense his impatience: he wants answers. But I don't care. I nod my head to the waiter and sit silently while grated parmesan snows onto my plate. I refuse the cracked pepper but order a third glass of wine. All the while, in the background, a steady percussion: Steve's pen—*tap, tap, tap* . . .

The waiter leaves. The drumming stops. "Well?" asks Steve.

"Well, what?"

"Tell me about Nine/eleven, about how scared you were."

"Oh, I was scared, but the whole situation actually helped me."

Steve recoils. "Excuse me?" He drops his pen and his jaw.

Can't blame Steve for his reaction. Moronic thing to say. *You're an ass, Wentworth. An absolute ass.* A stiletto of self-hatred stabs my gut and I choke back the urge to yelp. I suck in a deep breath, hold it, and release it in a hydraulic hiss. A shudder runs through me and I seek comfort in my wine glass. Damn it. Where the hell is my third glass? I glance around, spot the waiter, and wave my empty glass at him. He nods and scurries off. I take another breath and look back at Steve whose mouth is still hanging open.

I pick up my fork and begin twirling spaghetti. Sighing, Steve mirrors my action. We eat in silence. The wine appears and, this time, I sip. Near the end of the meal, I lean back. "Nine/eleven scared the hell out of me . . . and Sarah."

25

TINY WOMAN, INFANT CHILD

September, 2001

arah is sitting cross-legged on our king-sized bed, holding our five-month-old Bobby. I watch their reflection in the dresser mirror as I button my shirt. I smile a spontaneous smile.

Surprises me how much having that little man in my life changes things. Not drinking now. Working harder. I'm sorry that Sarah gave up school, but she'll go back, I'm sure. Right now, her whole life is her son. I pause. Huh. Appropriate that my shirt is green. I'm jealous, for Christ's sake. What the hell is that all about? I rush to the closet and grab my jacket.

"I'm off to work. Love you both." I embrace my family and plant kisses on their faces.

Once in the car, I sit and stare into the darkness of the parking garage. Maybe I should just forget work today, just do a little something for myself for a change. Haven't missed a day since Bobby was born. Haven't even had a drink. I definitely need some "me" time. I'll just spend a couple of hours at the office and then leave for the day. I grin. I do love the flexibility of real estate work. Maybe I'll go to a movie or stop at the pub. I start the Lexus and pull out of the garage. Once in the street, I flip on the radio to catch the news.

" . . . airplane crashed into one of the twin towers in New York City . . . " The announcer's voice is shaking violently, uncontrollably—a vocal earthquake.

I immediately push a button to access another station. It echoes the first. My heart races.

"What the hell . . . ? Is this a hoax?" I press another button, searching for some happy morning talk show, upbeat music, anything to get from bizarre to norm. Over and over and over, I change stations. A useless endeavor; they're all the same.

By the time I pull into the parking lot at work, the radio report has been amended: two airplanes, not one; two towers, not one.

I sprint into the real estate office. The cubicles are empty. The door to the board room is slightly ajar and a garbled stream of TV voices slithers through the crack. I edge up to the door and push it wide open. Staff members huddle inside, motionless, staring blankly at the small screen. Mannequins watching TV. I turn my head toward the screen and become one with them— the mute, frozen spectators. Minutes pass before anyone speaks. Then one, singular "Oh my God!" erupts, and a glut of voices follows, peppering the room, firing staccato phrases of disbelief.

I remain mute. No words. And no thoughts but one—my family.

I do an about-face and flee.

As I am driving home, I question what we have done by bringing a child into this world. I never gave terrorism a second thought when the threat was in a distant land, but it is here, now . . . imminent. What will become of our world and my Bobby? My son. Guilt stabs me as I recall the envy I felt as I left home this morning. How could I be jealous of such a gift as a child? *Grow the fuck up, Wentworth!* I ram the accelerator to the floor and leave it there until I reach the parking garage where narrow passageways force me to slow down. By the time I pull into my parking space, my body is raining sweat. The seat belt buckle is slippery in my fingers, but I manage to release it. I race to the elevator and push the button for the third floor. Damn! This elevator is so fucking slow. Can't wait. I take the stairs. Up three flights. Charge into the hallway. Race to our door. I shove the key in the lock and barrel into the living room.

Sarah is huddled on the sofa with the sleeping Bobby in her arms. One look at her face and I know that she has heard. I rush over, drop to my knees, place my head on Sarah's lap and wrap my arms around both of them.

"I had to turn off the radio," Sarah whispers. "When I heard the news, I was so scared that Bobby felt my fear. He cried and cried; I had to calm myself in order to calm him."

I heed her cue and take a few deep breaths. Gradually, my breathing and heart rate slow down.

"Is it all really true, Justin?"

"Yes. I saw the television reports at work. It's true. I came right home to be with you. You and Bobby. I need to be here, with you." I pull myself up from the floor and slide onto the sofa.

For a long time, we sit there. For the first time, I know the true meaning of family. They—a tiny woman and an infant child—are my rock. My strength grows in their presence. For them I can, and will, do anything.

26

WHERE ARE THEY NOW?

January, 2010

S o where are they now?"

"Huh?"

"Sarah and Bobby? You just said you'd do anything for them. Where are they . . . at her mother's? In Ajax, Ontario?"

I frown. "Don't remember telling you Sarah was from Ajax."

He rolls his eyes and lets out a swift breath. "Well, you did. *And* you said she would never go back there." He leans forward and narrows his gaze. "Did she change her mind, Justin?"

I gulp and rub the back of my neck.

"I take it that's a *yes*?"

I say nothing.

"Definitely a *yes*. But why? You just told me you'd do anything for them, didn't you? That they are your rock?" His voice drops to a whisper. "Okay, so money and booze were problems, but there must have been a catalyst. What was it? Why did Sarah leave? Did you do something that triggered it? She wanted the whole *forever* thing, didn't she? So you must have . . . "

"Would you like dessert?" interrupts the waiter as he collects our empty plates.

Steve leans back in his chair and glares at him. "Just the bill, please."

Nodding, the waiter deposits the bill on the table. Steve drops his pen and yanks his credit card from his wallet.

As the waiter scoops up the Visa and whisks it away, I shoot him a grateful look. He doesn't notice, but I don't mind. A smile tugs at the corners of my mouth. Impeccable timing, that waiter. *Tough luck, Steve.* Relaxed, ready to go, I zip my jacket, plant both hands on the table, and struggle to my feet.

Steve's hand flies from nowhere and grabs my arm. Blindsided, locked in position, I meet his gaze.

His eyes burn with purpose. "Why?" he fires, voice intense as a line drive. "Why did Sarah leave?"

My smile disintegrates. I grit my teeth and attempt to stiffen my body, but it's too late. The blow has landed, knocking open the door to my past, knocking me back into my chair. Memory simmers, bubbles, erupts. My Sarah, fists raised, voice shrill with rage. *Damn, damn, damn.* I shake my head, but the image remains. Sweat pours off my brow.

Steve waits, clamping his lips tight. He releases my arm and his fingers begin a slow drum roll on the table. Faster and faster they go, and then, abruptly, stop. Something about that action niggles at me, but I'm in too deep a hole to care.

Steve sighs now, a lament. "Sorry, Justin." His voice has dropped to a whisper.

I take a deep breath. *Thank God, he's done.*

But Steve presses the issue. "At some point you have to let it out. Might as well tell me. Please give me some kind of answer . . . why would Sarah, your *forever* Sarah, just up and leave?"

"Damn it all, just shut up, will you?" My words explode through the restaurant clatter, stopping it dead. I look around. There are many eyes, questioning, judging, burning through me. I lower my head until the heat in my face abates, until restaurant sounds resume. Then I glance up and meet Steve's gaze. No judgment there, just the question . . . and patience. I lock my eyes with his, determined to stare him down.

Steve does not falter.

I sigh, long and slow. "Sarah left because . . . " My voice is hoarse so I clear my throat and start again. "She left because my drinking eclipsed my judgment and Bobby got hurt, a minor accident."

"Oh," says Steve. He nods slowly. "Oh," he repeats.

I hold my breath, waiting for . . . what? Reproach? Sympathy? I don't know. He merely continues to nod, his eyes flickering. I am rigid, watching, while he sifts through my response until it seeps into his countenance like water into sand. Soon the question marks in his eyes vanish, replaced by . . . what?

I scrutinize his face. Nothing.

"I see," he says.

That's it? *I see.* No judgment? No recrimination? Huh. I exhale and wipe my sweaty palms on my lap. Then I allow my body to melt into the chair. Strange, the sensation of relief that fills me now. Unexpected. Maybe I needed to tell someone? I nod. Yeah, that's it. A good feeling, letting it out.

"Are we done for today?" asks Steve.

I manage a weak smile. "Pretty much."

"Ready to go?"

"No hurry." Huh. Surprising. Couldn't wait to get out of here a few seconds ago. But now? Truth about Sarah and Bobby is out there. I feel at ease, muscles slack, limbs loose. I lean back and hook one arm over the back of my chair.

"Well . . . " Steve looks around for the waiter. No sign of him. "I have to hang around until the credit card receipt shows up."

"No problem."

He picks up his pen and flips through his notebook to a clean page. "Up for more questions?"

"Fire away."

"Great. So, you want to tell me how the events of Nine/eleven actually helped you?"

I nod, slowly, repeatedly. "Helped because I grew up a bit. I was doing okay when Bobby was born, but after a few months . . . well, old habits die hard. On the very morning of Nine/eleven, I was about to blow off work. Maybe hit a movie, or a bar. Then, when I turned on the car radio . . . " I throw my hands in the air. "The tragedy shocked me, stopped me. For a while, anyway. I worked hard. I hated going to work most days though. Bobby was growing so fast I was afraid I'd miss something." I pause and smile. "Got a video camera, just so Sarah could record Bobby during the day. His first steps, his first words—the stuff I missed while I was at work. We'd watch it together every night. Filmed lots of stuff myself, too, like the first time he saw a dog on the seawall in Stanley Park."

The waiter intervenes, dropping off the credit card receipt. Steve scrutinizes it, line by line, all the while gnawing on his pen.

I lean forward, extract the castle from my pocket, and stare at it.

27

BOBBY'S CASTLE

July, 2002

Bow wow, Mommy, bow wow!" Bobby points at an approaching golden retriever.

Sarah's laughter rings through the breeze. She grips my arm, pops up onto her toes, and plants a kiss on my cheek. "Love seeing you so happy, Justin."

Smiling, I raise the video camera.

Bobby giggles with glee and pounds his chubby fists on the arms of the stroller.

"Have to get that boy a dog," comments the dog's owner who stops to allow Bobby to pet the "bow wow."

"Oh, we will . . . someday," I reply. "He's a bit young yet."

After the stranger passes, I turn to Sarah. "Sorry, Sarah. Maybe I jumped the gun on that one. What do *you* think about getting a dog for Bobby?"

"Need you even ask?" Sarah pulls off a flip-flop and points at her paw print tattoo. " 'A heartbeat at my feet,' " she says. "Hmmm . . . who said that? Edith Wharton, I think." She shakes her head. "Doesn't matter. Point is . . . of course, Bobby should have a dog!" She drops her flip-flop and slides her foot back into it. "But you are right about the 'someday' part. *When* we can afford a decent house, one with a proper back yard, *then* we can get a dog."

I nod. "Guess we'll just have to get that house then." As we continue along the seawall, I busy my brain trying to think up a way to get a house *now*. It occurs to me that I always want everything *now*. Instant gratification. Wonder if I'll ever get over that. Maybe I don't have to. Maybe I'll just figure out a way to get a house, a big house, regardless of the cost. I'm in the real estate business, for Christ's sake. I know all the ins and outs. Do the risks really apply?

Out of the corner of my eye, I spot a shopping cart under Lumberman's Arch, an overloaded shopping cart. I stare at it. A grubby man in a tattered coat sidles up to the cart and grasps its handle. He snaps his head in my direction, returns my stare with a look of defiance. I hold the look briefly, but anxiety courses through me, and I turn away like a beta dog conceding to its alpha counterpart. I have no idea why the very sight of him scares me. My heart pounds, my legs move faster. With a start, I realize that Sarah is struggling to keep up with me. I slow my pace.

"Sorry, am I going too fast for you? Oh my God, Bobby is sound asleep. Maybe we have had enough for the day. Should we turn back?"

Sarah nods and tucks a blanket around Bobby. "He's done in, poor little tyke. He'll probably sleep until tomorrow, and I'm sure I'll be out as soon as my head hits the pillow tonight." She heaves a deep, contented sigh and stares up at me. "It's been a wonderful day, Justin. As tired as I am, I hate to see it end."

"We'll have lots of wonderful days, Sarah." I hug her close. We retrace our steps. When we pass Lumberman's Arch, I don't turn my head, but I am sure that the eyes of the homeless man are locked on me. A chill creeps across my back. My right hand reaches up and brushes my shoulder like I'm sweeping off a spider, and my thoughts slip back to real estate.

"So, Sarah, a big back yard for Bobby and his dog to run and play in . . . What else is on your wish list for our house?"

"Nothing."

"What do you mean, 'nothing'?"

"Nothing." She reaches for my arm and squeezes. "Told you before . . . I'd live in a garage just to be with you. All I want is what I've got. You and Bobby. Forever." She lets out a relaxed sigh.

A garage? She's got to be kidding. "Get real, Sarah. You want a house as much as I do. We should . . . "

Sarah shakes her head. "Nooooooo way, dude. No way. You are not going to talk me into a house now. We have enough expenses with the rent and with Bobby. I'm not working now and, when Bobby's older, I want to finish my master's. A house will just lock us into debt." Sarah is the one who speeds up now, making me move faster.

"I know how you feel about debt, Sarah. But I'm telling you, real estate is my business. I know what's going on. The market is going to start jumping very soon. We need to get in on the ground floor and I have been . . . "

"Not a chance. You always want everything right away. Knowing you, you don't want a house, you want a castle. So what if the market soars . . . you know what they say about what goes up. Gravity, Justin. And I'm not just referring to Newton's Law. Gravity . . . as in 'get serious!' "

"But . . . "

"Nope."

I sigh. "Okay. You're right. We shouldn't get a house . . . not yet anyway. Sorry, Sarah."

She nods. Keeps going. Keeps setting the pace: quick, determined. Feel like I'm competing in a race. For a half hour, we walk. Parallel. Silent.

Finally, her tempo slows. She reaches for my hand as we exit Stanley Park and turn onto the sidewalk at West Georgia.

"Feel better, Sarah? No house. For now anyway." I need to make her smile again. We pass a small pet shop on a corner and, in the window, I spy a castle, an aquarium castle. "Hey! There it is! My castle. You are right. I want a castle. I *am* a prince you know . . . says so on my watch!"

Sarah looks in the window and begins to laugh. *I've got her.* I continue walking now, content.

"Where are you going, Justin Wentworth?"

"Huh?"

"Get in there and buy that darn castle! That's what you want, isn't it?" She takes off her sunglasses and I see a spark of amusement in her eyes.

I grin. "Darn right!"

"Great! Maybe you can start up an aquarium in Bobby's room."

Into the store we go and when we come out, the tiny castle is stuffed into my pocket and a starter aquarium kit sits on the rack at the bottom of Bobby's stroller.

As soon as we get home, Sarah puts the sleeping Bobby into his crib and I start setting up the aquarium on his dresser.

Sarah slides up beside me. "Aren't you afraid you'll wake him up?" she whispers.

I glance at my son. "Don't think I need to worry about that. He's out like a light."

Sarah nods. "Do you know anything about fish?"

I turn to her and grin widely. "Call me Ishmael."

Her eyes pop wide with delight. "You actually read *Moby Dick*?"

I shrug. "Naw . . . just saw the movie."

She puts her hand over her mouth to stifle a laugh. "Have fun," she whispers as she tiptoes out of the room.

I continue with the set up. Before I know it, I'm talking away, telling Bobby about it. "We'll put this castle in tomorrow, son . . . when the water is ready. Then we'll buy a goldfish or two. What do you think?" I hold the castle up as I turn and look at him. He is still sleeping, soundly, peacefully. I smile, examine the castle, and sigh. *This will do, for now.*

I wait a few months before I broach the topic of buying a house again.

28

HIGH-END HOUSES

January, 2010

N o. No house-buying talk for a while after that," I mutter, still staring at the castle.

"What?" asks Steve.

My memory pops like a pierced balloon, and I fall back to the reality of my wooden chair, here, in the Old Spaghetti Factory with Steve. No Sarah. No Bobby. My shoulders sag until my spine is as curved as a comma.

"What did you just say about buying a house?" Steve asks again.

"Oh. Nothing. Just thinking about real estate stuff."

"Oh, that." Steve sits back in his chair. "Tell me . . . did you like the work?"

I busy myself with reading the newsprint placemat: "*Welcome to the Original Old Spaghetti Factory. In March of 1970, the . . .* "

"Real estate? Did you like it?"

I sigh, slowly, like I'm pressing a valve on a bike tire and letting the air slide out. What the hell. Going to tell him eventually anyway. "It was okay." I straighten my back. "Guess the best part—next to the big paydays—was being inside all those high-end houses. Great places to hang out, especially on rainy days when no clients showed up. Lots of things to do . . . lots of stuff to look at."

"Like what?"

"Hmmm . . . you know, leather recliners, big screen TV's, video games, pool tables, stained glass windows . . . all that."

"Bet you found where the liquor was located."

"Ouch!"

"Sorry. Nasty comment. But, since it's out there . . . am I right?"

"Pretty much."

"I take it you wanted one of those big houses for yourself?"

I shrug.

"Ever get it?"

Another shrug.

"Enough." Steve claps his hands together. "Enough with the questions. Sorry if I've pushed too hard. You've gone above and beyond. Thanks, Justin." He extends his hand.

I transfer the castle to my left hand and reach across the table. An automatic response. A firm handshake. A quick release.

"Okay, so put away that darn castle and let's get a move on." Steve takes a final swig of Coke and plunks the glass down.

I shove the castle into my pocket and polish off my wine. No wine for Steve. Nope . . . no wine, no swearing—at least not without encouragement from me— no . . . ? What else? Did he tip the waiter? Don't think so. I've been so absorbed in myself that I don't know. What happened to my resolve? My "mouth-shut, eyes-open" approach? I have to pay more attention.

We exit the restaurant and head to the bus stop. On the way, we pass a homeless woman selling maps.

Steve stops and chats, notebook in hand.

I wait while he buys a map that he doesn't need.

We move on.

Farther along, a man sits on a corner. Taped to an empty bucket beside him is a sign—black letters scrawled across corrugated cardboard: HIV AND HOMELESS.

Steve stops. "You want to go to a shelter, sir?"

The man shakes his head and turns away.

Steve drops some change into the bucket. "Good luck to you."

I shift my weight from one foot to the other.

We move again. Now I'm walking slightly faster than Steve.

On a street corner stands another of the dispossessed, this one wearing a long, black coat and orating to a non-existent audience: "One always works so hard," he says. "There have to be sacrifices; there have to be many sacrifices." Passersby lower their heads and give him a wide berth.

Not so Steve. He stops again. "Do you want to go to a shelter, sir?"

"The open air is my shelter. The sun and rain cleanse me."

"Do you need some money, sir?"

I wait. My skin is crawling. My breathing is labored.

The man ignores Steve's question and goes back to his speech. "One always works so hard . . . "

Jesus! That guy gives me the creeps. All these societal rejects irritate me. Most of them will never make it off the street. *Them*. Not me. *Them*. Oh, God, *not me*.

My heart beats faster. Faces, desperate faces, strobe in my brain. I cover my ears to mute roars from engines and blasts from car horns. The stench of gas fumes invades my nostrils and churns my gut. *Got to get off the damn street. Got to stay off the damn street.* I race ahead of Steve to the bus stop.

"Justin! What the heck is the matter with you? Can't you wait for a few seconds while I talk to . . . " Steve catches up with me and peers into my face. He sighs. "I'm sorry. I didn't realize . . . it must be hard for you to . . . "

"Let's just get the hell out of here!"

"Yeah, yeah." Steve pats me on the back.

We stroll up to the stop and board the first bus. I sit near the front and Steve drops into the seat next to me. He doesn't say anything, just sits there.

I stare out the side window, thinking about what I have just witnessed: Steve ministering to the masses. It certainly appears that he lives to serve. No evidence to the contrary. Why did I, *do* I, suspect this man of hiring thugs to rough me up? He assists people, lots of people. I can't help but wonder though . . . if he's interviewing and helping *everyone* he meets on the street, why did he pick *me* to take home? Why me? Why not the woman with the maps or the HIV guy or the orator with the imaginary audience?

I turn to him. "Why do you keep doing that?"

"Doing what?"

"Talking to vagrants. Taking notes. Giving them money. You *were* giving them money, weren't you?"

"Yeah. Not much, but yeah."

"They're only going to use it for booze or drugs, you know."

"Yeah." Steve shrugs. 'Don't really care. I promised my grandfather . . . "

"What's your grandfather got to do with it?"

"Just promised him, that's all."

The bus jolts to a halt. Steve looks up. An elderly lady boards. After a few seconds, Steve speaks again, but not to me. "Would you like to have my seat, madam?"

"Thank you, young man."

Steve rises and the grey-haired lady with a cane slips into his seat.

I don't get it. Over and over, I am witness to Steve's . . . what would Oprah call it . . . random acts of kindness? Yeah, that's it . . . random acts of kindness. Over and over. Is *anybody* really that nice? I doubt it. "Promised his grandfather," he said. What the hell was that about? A condition of his trust fund? No, can't be that. The trust fund is from his parents, isn't it? What does his grandfather have to do with it?

Steve stands across the aisle now, one hand on the overhead pole, balancing, swaying, a look of contentment on his face.

I glance up, lock my eyes on the cell phone attached to Steve's belt next to the *Jesus Saves* buckle. I sigh. Maybe Steve had nothing to do with the thugs. Maybe it was all a dream, nothing more. I thought I had come to terms with all this. Why can't I let this go? Don't know, but maybe I should have a look at that cell phone.

As our bus rounds the corner onto Davie Street, Steve pulls out his phone and begins texting. Shortly, the bus rumbles to our stop and the doors swing wide. "Steve, are we going?" I say, pointing to the open door.

Steve looks up, surprised. He nods and returns his phone to his belt.

29

AS BIG AS A CASTLE

May, 2005

D addy, are we going?" Bobby tugs at my sleeve.

"In a minute, Bobby. I'm on the phone."

"But you said Stanley Park . . . I'm moving out of patience, Daddy."

I turn and see that my four-year-old son is standing with his hands on his hips. My grin is spontaneous. "I'll call back later," I say to the agent and flip the phone shut.

"Indeed I did say Stanley Park. Sometimes I have to take a phone call. And I get that you are *running* out of patience. Sometimes Mommy and I *run* out of patience, too."

"I know." Bobby nods solemnly. "I am very quiet when you and Mommy run out of patience." His eyes are wide and sincere, overflowing with trust and innocence.

My mother's face flashes before me; her voice echoes inside me. '*S-o-n and s-u-n.*'

Damn. *I get it, Mom.* I reach to hug Bobby but he sidesteps.

"Stanley Park, Daddy!"

"Okay, okay, let's go!" I throw my arms out again and scoop him up. He squeals with laughter as I cart him to the car and plop him into his car seat.

"When do I get to ride in the front, Daddy? I'm a big boy now!"

"Not yet. Back seat is still safer. You may be a big boy, but I'm the daddy. It's my job to take care of you. You have to sit in a car seat because you are . . ."

"I know. I know. Precious cargo."

"That's right. You are definitely precious cargo." I plant a kiss on his head, shut the door and get into the front, expecting him to argue the point further. However, Bobby says nothing as I pull out of the parking garage and into the street.

"What's that thing up there?"

I look into the rearview mirror and then into the direction that Bobby is pointing. I grin. Bobby has forgotten about the front seat already. It's time for the typical, four-year-old question period.

"Oh, that's a crane. It lifts things that are too heavy for people to lift."

"Oh. What's that?" Once again, Bobby is pointing. Before I can figure out what the object of his curiosity is, he has moved on. "Oh, a kite, Daddy, a kite!"

Sure enough, people are flying kites on the beach. At this point, I just let Bobby chatter away; I can't keep up with him anyway. He moves from one thing to another so darn fast that I might as well be a snail trying to race with a stallion. Just like his mom. They're both smarter than me, I'm sure of that.

Our first stop in Stanley Park is the aquarium—a mandatory part of every visit since the *Finding Nemo* movie hit theaters. Then we take to the seawall. From there we veer off onto a trail. Bobby is bursting with energy and running back and forth along the path, away from me and back again, never out of sight. As soon as he tires of the game, I swing him up, onto my shoulders. Now he is in the crow's nest on a pirate ship, searching for treasure. Through his pretend telescope, he spots a giant, hollow tree.

"Down, Daddy, down!"

I oblige and he scampers to the tree. I join him, and together we walk all around the outside. Then we crawl in and explore every nook and cranny. Bobby sits cross-legged and I copy him.

"It's as big as a castle, Daddy." His eyes are wide. "I want a castle, Daddy. Can we have a castle?"

Someday, son, someday," I reply. As I stare into his eyes, a warm glow filters through me. I want to give him the world. *Bobby*. It occurs to me that our decision to buy a house should be centered on Bobby. We should move to a big house so Bobby can have more room to grow. We should move to a big house with a big yard so Bobby can have his dog. We should move before Bobby starts school, so he won't have to change schools in kindergarten or first grade. Yes, we should definitely move before Bobby starts school.

A razor-sharp jolt of memory assails me: being forced to sell my parents' home. On its heels comes Mr. Cormier's warning . . . *Be master, not slave, to the money, Justin.* I banish both thoughts. My parents' issues, not mine. It's time for Sarah and me to buy a house. My son wants a castle. My son will have it. Big mortgage, but so what? Business is good. I can handle it.

Now I just have to talk to Sarah.

30

CAN'T GO BACK THERE

January, 2010

Steve and I step off the bus into darkness and I instinctively do a three-sixty, checking for potential danger. Then I scramble to catch up to Steve—safety in numbers. We trudge in unison along Davie and down Nicola Street to his place.

No words pass between us now. There are only the sounds of the city, accompanied by the jangle of Steve's keys as he unlocks the exterior door. I smile as it occurs to me that the same keys which had startled me earlier today are now a comfort; they represent home. A temporary home, yes, but a home nonetheless. I inhale deeply and let out a relaxed sigh.

My eyes fall on the flash drive attached to his key ring.

Huh. Interesting. Never noticed the flash drive there before. Wonder what he's storing on it? Assignments, maybe. Research. Maybe an angle on my story or a class schedule. Come to think of it, Steve didn't go to any classes today. Or yesterday. Never mentions university other than in reference to me. Facebook, cell phone, flash drive . . . lots of things around that could give clues to Steve's agenda. Maybe he doesn't have an agenda. Maybe he is who he says . . . just a guy doing research on the homeless. It certainly seems that way.

The building is silent as we enter. Beige walls, beige tile, everything hushed. Steve unlocks the entry to the stairwell. I trail along, savoring the sense of security that filters through me when the automatic door slams, and locks, behind me. Security? Huh. Is anything really secure? Should I trust anyone?

I put my hand on the metal banister and begin the slow, systematic climb. Maybe I should just trust Steve. Maybe not. I trusted my parents, didn't I? Jesus. Betrayed by my own parents. It still doesn't make sense to me, even after all this time. The accident alone was hard enough. But the poverty, the betrayal, that followed? *What kind of parent doesn't plan for his family?*

I freeze in place as a thunderclap of truth hits me. *Did I plan for my wife and son?* I sway and grip the stair rail, my heart hammering against my ribcage. Damn. Steve trudges on ahead. I jerk back to the moment, to movement, before he has a chance to question my sudden halt. I catch up, trying to breathe slowly.

"You okay, bud?" he asks as we reach the second floor and exit the stairwell.

"Fine." He looks like he's about to ask again, so I distract. "You going to class tomorrow?"

"Yep. I have a couple of classes. Why? You wanna come?"

"Sure."

Steve freezes. "What?"

"Just kidding. Not really interested. I've done my time in school."

Obviously relieved, Steve continues down the hall. "What do you plan to do all day?"

I shrug. "Probably rest. Watch TV. I'm still healing, you know."

Steve stops at the door to his condo and turns to stare at me. Curiosity creases his brow. Then he shrugs. "Yeah. I guess you are. That eye of yours will be fully functional in a few days. The bruising will take a while to disappear though. Your insides will take longer to heal. It's probably best if you just stay around here." He enters the condo.

I stroll in behind him and head directly to my room.

"Hey, you want to hang out for a while in the living room? We can talk some more."

I wave him off. "Nah. Good night, Steve."

"You going to sleep . . . *again*? Planning to sleep your life away?"

"Good night, Steve."

"Night . . . it's only five-thirty, for heaven's sake!"

"Time don't make no never mind to me, Steve. One day, the next day, one hour, the next one . . . all the same."

"Fair enough. Night, bud!"

I stop and glare.

He doesn't correct himself. "I don't mean anything derogatory, really, Justin. It's just my way."

"Still don't like it."

"Deal with it."

I trudge down the hallway, enter my room and close the door. I pad across the floor to the window and peer out into the alley below. I don't want to see the Dumpster there, but I force myself to look at it, to lock on it, anyway. It reminds me how close I am to the street. *Can't go back there. I'll never be ready to go back.*

Maybe I should have taken better care when I had the opportunity. I shove my hands into my pockets and slouch against the window frame. What an arrogant, selfish ass I was . . . rushing my family into that big house near Douglas Park. Tears cloud my vision and the Dumpster swimming in front of my eyes morphs into a house, *the* house.

31

NO MONEY DOWN

June, 2005

Here we are, approaching our fourth open house today. It feels like I've been carrying the sleeping Bobby for hours. He may be little, but my arms throb under the dead weight of his body. I'm not complaining though, because my Sarah's smiling. *She likes this house already.* Emboldened, I dash toward the steps. Sarah's stiletto heels click on the walk behind me.

"Just because we're going to open houses doesn't mean we have to buy anything," I had said that morning. I know she wasn't convinced, but she agreed to this outing because Bobby is four and will be starting school soon. Our goals are the same for Bobby: a good school in a family-oriented neighborhood. No jumping from school to school for our son. We want consistency in education and permanence in a home. *A forever home that no one can take away.* A picture of my parents' home jumps into my head. I blink, dismissing it. Yes, I want a *forever* home. Sarah wants *forever*, too. Maybe this heritage craftsman home with its porch, swing and backyard is one we can agree on. I nod. Maybe.

The instant we set foot on the porch, Bobby's eyes pop open. "A swing, Daddy, a swing!" He wiggles out of my arms and scampers to the swing. "Push me, Daddy!"

"Maybe later, son." I smile at Sarah.

"Come on, Bobby," says Sarah, "we can't play on the swing. This is not our house. We are just shopping today. This is like when we are in the toy store and we look at all the toys, but we can't buy everything, and we can't play with everything."

"Ah, gee, Mommy," Bobby grumbles, but immediately abandons the swing and runs to the front door, which is slightly ajar. He pushes it and tumbles inside with Sarah and me at his heels.

"This is as big as a castle," exclaims Bobby, holding his arms wide. "Just like the big tree in Stanley Park . . . remember, Daddy?"

"I remember, son. I remember." My eyes are immediately drawn to the nine-foot, tray ceiling. "Wow, Sarah, just look at that!"

"I just love the colors of the light . . . it's magical, like a rainbow!"

I turn, puzzled, and realize that she is gazing at the stained glass window high on the right. I grin as I watch her follow the colored light to the oak hardwood flooring and past that to the hall stairs.

Bobby bursts toward the stairs and begins clambering up them, grabbing first the mahogany newel post and then each hand-carved baluster. He is halfway up before Sarah and I are jolted into action.

"Bobby!" Sarah calls. Bobby picks up speed.

"Bobby!" I'm trying to sound like the scolding father. Truth is, I'm enjoying the hell out of this. Both my wife and my son love this house. And I know a secret. Buying a house is an emotional decision, and that decision is made in the first ten seconds. *Damn, I really want this house.* I catch up to Sarah and manage to slow her down. By the time we get to the second floor, Bobby is inside one of the bedrooms.

"*Nemo!* Mommy! Daddy! *Nemo!* And *Dory!*"

Sarah and I are caught up in his joy now and race in behind him. The wallpaper in the room is dancing with images from *Finding Nemo.*

Now I know Bobby is going to get his castle. He deserves the best and we deserve to have a permanent home. Tension slides out of my body. I hold back and let Sarah and Bobby explore. This room has more than ideal wallpaper; it has two closets with racks placed low so a child can reach *and* it has a built-in toy chest near the window.

"My room, my room! Let's go shopping in the other rooms, too, Mommy! Do we have to buy all the rooms, or can we just buy my room?" Bobby runs into the hallway.

"Looks like he's leading this tour." Sarah smiles at me.

I shrug. "I don't mind letting him be the real estate agent for a change."

"Mommy! Daddy! Here's your room!"

We rush across the hall toward the sound of Bobby's voice. As soon as we enter the master bedroom, Sarah gasps.

"We could fit two bedrooms suites in here!"

"Yes, I guess so." I congratulate myself on sounding nonchalant. "Or . . . you could have that quiet reading corner you have always wanted. Maybe over there by the bay window." I brush my arm through the air like I am opening a stage curtain. *Careful, idiot. Don't overdo it.*

"Yes, that would be lovely. Maybe a recliner and a standing lamp. One with a swinging arm. And, of course, a small bookcase to hold my treasures. A bookcase with glass doors." She hovers for a few seconds and I know she is lost in the same dream that I am . . . the dream of owning this house. Then she looks around and swerves toward me. "Where's Bobby?"

"I . . . he was here a minute ago."

"Bobby! Where are you?"

"In here, Mommy!"

Sarah and I sprint into the *en suite* bathroom and find our son standing in the claw-foot tub.

"We could go swimming in this tub!" Bobby leans forward, waving his arms in a breast stroke. "Do you like it, Mommy?"

"Yes, of course I like it, but you are not supposed to get into it with your shoes on." Sarah lifts Bobby out of the tub and plants him on the floor. "Darn!" She stares at her feet. "We all have our shoes on. Better take them off so we don't get anything dirty." She parks herself on the floor beside Bobby.

"Daddy has shoes, too!"

"Yes, he does, doesn't he?" Sarah glares up at me.

"Not for long." I pull off both shoes.

Sarah passes Bobby's shoes to me, removes her heels and stands. A sigh escapes her. "It sure would be nice to have this bathroom . . . it's like a spa."

"Lots of light in here, too." I point at the two windows, translucent for privacy. "And look at the size of the shower."

"Big enough for you and Mommy!" Bobby nods his head.

We laugh. I drop the shoes and scoop up my miniature real estate agent. "You would be great at selling, Bobby Wentworth."

"No sell, Daddy. Buy. This is my house. Mine! Mine! Mine!"

"You sound like the seagulls in *Finding Nemo*." I squeeze him tight, bear-hug tight.

"Have you seen the walk-in closet?" I beam at Sarah. Truth is, even I haven't seen it. But I have studied the floor plan so I know it is there. A walk-in closet is a punctuation mark—an exclamation point—in a sale, especially when trying to persuade a woman buyer. I put Bobby down and pick up our shoes. Then I lead my family toward the closet and use my elbow to nudge open the door. My mouth drops in amazement—a good sign; if I'm impressed, Sarah must be ecstatic. The closet is bigger than Bobby's current room. It has a tier of shoe racks, a full length mirror and, in the middle, a padded bench. Perfect. I grin. My job is done now. Time to shut up completely. *Never go past the close, Wentworth.*

From that point, Bobby and I follow Sarah around. To the guest room, another full bath, another bedroom and down the stairs. As we pass by the entrance, the door opens. More viewers. Damn. There are many pairs of shoes by the door already. As I place our shoes on the mat, a sharp pang enters my gut, a compulsion. We must hurry. This place won't be on the market for long.

Sarah and I hold Bobby's hands and guide him to the kitchen. There we have to wait for a crowd to move into the family room. Then, when we have a clear view of the whole kitchen, Sarah gasps. Note to self: second gasp from Sarah in one house. Another stab of urgency pierces my abdomen. *Make an offer. Make an offer. Sprint to the real estate agent and offer whatever it takes.* I know we could get caught in a bidding war here; God help us if we do. But I can't rush. I must wait. Let Sarah see everything.

The kitchen is open-concept. Sarah dashes to the sink and peers through the window above it. "A back yard! Bobby can play there and I can watch him." She swings around. "And look at all these cabinets! I love white cabinets! And a center island and stainless steel appliances!" She claps her hands together and then scurries toward the next room.

"Guess we better follow her." Smiling, I pick up Bobby again and join Sarah. We walk through the family room and living room and dining room, all of which have crown moldings and built-in cabinets with leaded-glass doors.

This house is twenty-five hundred square feet of perfection.

Our last stop on the tour is the back yard with the cedar fence, the pink rhododendrons, and the row of cherry blossom trees.

"A doggie, Daddy! A doggie! We can get a doggie! You said when we had a back yard, we could get a doggie!"

I raise an eyebrow at Sarah. She looks around.

Damn. She's nervous. *Keep your mouth shut, Wentworth. Wait it out.*

Finally, Sarah nods. I refrain myself from pumping my fist in triumph.

We walk back into the house, to the kitchen where I release Bobby to Sarah's care and pick up the agent's card from the table. I can't pronounce his last name, but his first name's Vladimir. Huh. Interesting. Never knew anyone with that name before.

Despite the crowd, it's not long before Vladimir makes his way to us. I know then that he is sharp—experienced enough to spot serious buyers. I flash my most charming smile and extend my hand. "Good morning, Vladimir. Interesting name you have. What does it mean?"

"Oh, that. Vladimir means 'renowned prince.' My mother's idea."

Prince. Huh. I like him already. I make a show of rolling up my shirt sleeve to expose my Rolex.

Vladimir's eyes glint. He bends and talks to my son. "And what is your name, little man?"

Sharp one, Vladimir. The way to a customer's heart is through his kid.

"I'm Bobby. And this is *my* house."

Vladimir laughs and straightens. His eyes are flashing neon now. Neon dollar signs. By the time we leave, we have made an offer on a million dollar home. No money down. I'm so proud.

32

BUILDING SANDCASTLES

January, 2010

No money down. I used every realtor trick in the book to accomplish that. I'm so ashamed.

Rain pelts against the window and sheets down, further blurring the image of the Dumpster in the alley. My brain flashes again on the house, the million dollar house, then back to the Dumpster.

It all seemed so sudden, the fall from good life to street life. Perched at the top of a mountain one minute, collapsed at the bottom the next.

Jesus. Who am I kidding? The mountain was an illusion. There was no mountain, only sand. I took the easy route. Plunging into debt. No backup plan. Hungering for the life I had as a boy, desperate to provide that life for Bobby. Wanting, no, *needing* him to love me the way I loved my mom and dad.

A spasm of wild grief hits and I double over. *Mom and Dad.* Twenty years and the wound is raw. No healing in sight. Damn. I tried to fill the gaping chasm left when they died. Buying that house, filling it to overflow: all part of it. As if that could bring them back.

I remain bent over for a few minutes. When the pain eases, I straighten up, blow out a sigh, and look back at the Dumpster.

Yeah, getting that house was easy, as easy as building sandcastles with Bobby. Stupid. The tide threatened. I ignored it. Drank to hide from it. It leveled me. Sarah left me. My forever Sarah. *Forever.* Yeah, right.

The window is foggy from my breath and I swish my sleeve over it. Once. Twice. Like a wiper blade. A bolt of lightning, as sudden as a camera flash, ignites the night sky. I blink and instantly picture myself driving. Me and Bobby. He is in the passenger seat and I turn to smile at him. Wait a minute . . . that didn't happen, did it? Bobby was too small for the passenger seat. I never let him sit there, did I? Of course not. I push away from the window ledge, head low. No I never did that but . . .

Memory comes crowding back, a hidden current, unleashed. I turn, sag against the window and slide down, down, down . . . until I collapse in a heap on the floor.

33

FALLOUT

August 2009

Bobby runs up the stairs and I turn to Sarah. Only then do I realize the extent of the fallout. She stands rigid, arms at her sides, eyes blank with shock. I reach out and touch her.

She instantly recoils. "What is Bobby talking about?"

Oh, God.

"What does he mean, Justin?"

I'm falling now. I grab the newel post.

"What did Bobby promise he wouldn't tell Mommy?"

"It's no big deal, Sarah."

"Out with it!"

My heart plummets and my body with it. I plop onto the bottom step of the staircase, lean over, and wrap my arms around my knees.

Sarah bends, latches onto my hair, yanks my head up. "Tell me!" she hisses. "Tell me now." She clenches her teeth. She waits.

I jerk my head to the side. "Okay, Okay."

She releases her grasp.

I take a deep breath and meet her gaze. "There was this accident."

Sarah folds her arms. "Keep going."

"I was driving Bobby home and I didn't see the garbage cans. Hit them. They went flying." I feign a smile. "Bobby thought it was exciting, like a bumper car ride."

Sarah steps back, staggers a little. "You had an accident with *my son* in the car and you didn't tell me?"

"Like I said, Sarah . . . it was no big deal."

Sarah blinks. "Is that how the car got dented, Justin? When you told me someone hit you in the parking lot, is that what really happened?"

I nod. "But like I said, it was no big deal." I'm repeating myself. Damn. She hasn't asked the big question. Maybe she won't ask. My hope soars.

"When was this?"

"Don't know. A couple of weeks ago, maybe."

"A couple of weeks." Sarah straightens, and paces. Back and forth. Back and forth. "A couple of weeks." She stops. Turns toward me. Narrows her eyes. "Wait a minute. A couple of weeks ago, Bobby came home with a big bump on his head. You told me he fell in the playground. At Douglas Park. Did he get hurt in that car accident, Justin?"

"Jesus, Sarah. Like I said, it was no big deal."

"No big deal! Our son got injured in a car accident and you lied about it? No big deal! What the hell were you thinking?"

"I didn't want to worry you, Sarah. He only had a little bump."

"Why would you hide it from me if it was such a little thing?" She freezes. "Oh, God. Oh, God. Oh God." She covers her face with her hands. "Were you drinking, Justin?" Her hands drop and her head snaps toward me. "Were you driving drunk with my son in the car?"

My eyes glaze over. The room is swimming, my son is wailing, and my Sarah . . .

"I'm done," she hisses. Her body brushes past me as she pounds her way up the stairs to Bobby.

34

EMOTIONAL TERMITE

January, 2010

I'm curled in a fetal position on the floor, engulfed in despair. There's nothing left: no family, no home, nothing . . . except the castle from Bobby's aquarium. Huh. Nothing but the castle. Damn. I even managed to lose my watch.

I balk at the memory of thugs probing, clawing, yanking the watch from my wrist. Sweat pours and my body shivers. I emit a low moan and begin rocking. It doesn't help; there's no comfort here. Now I'm back to the dream, the torture of the dream. *Thugs. Fists. Steve.*

Steve. My mind lingers on the name. *Steve.* It floats like a thick, low fog, blocking me from clarity. Clarity about what? Not a clue. I wait while my subconscious does a steady, slow burn. *Steve . . . Steve . . . Steve . . .*

The fog dissipates. Synapses fire. My body jumps.

The dream. Steve and the thugs. *If* Steve hired the thugs, *if* Steve is not trustworthy, then maybe he has my watch. He said *Rolex*, didn't he? Did I tell him the watch was a *Rolex*? Did I? *Son of a bitch!*

I scramble to my knees, rocket from the floor, and stomp to the door. I grab the doorknob. Twist it. *Click.* The sound tweaks another memory: the shoe boutique on Robson Street. *Click. Click. Click.* The sound of the door unlocking every morning. Sleeping on the sidewalk. Knives of cold shoot through me. *Damn cold on the sidewalk.*

I release the knob. Should I do this? I twist the knob again. *Click.* Release it again. Damn.

If Marshmallow Man has my watch, I'm getting it back. Another twist. *Click.* I pull the door open. Wait a minute. I close the door and lean on it. Wait. Wait 'til my heart stops pounding. *Slow down. Breathe. Inhale. Exhale. Inhale again.*

I have no proof that Steve is anything other than he says he is. Yet the idea that he hired the thugs is eating at me like an emotional termite. I tap my head against the door, creating a barely audible *thump, thump, thump.* It makes no sense . . . why can't I let go of the Steve/thug dream?

You're being an idiot, Wentworth. I sigh, stand straight, and release the doorknob.

Even if I'm right, confronting Steve *now* is not the answer. I could end up in the street *tonight,* for Christ's sake. I turn, shuffle to the bed and fall, prone, onto it.

Tomorrow. I will resolve this tomorrow. I have to put an end to this gnawing suspicion and I have to do it without alerting Steve. He will be gone all day, and I will comb every inch of this condo. Every nook and cranny. If my watch is here, I'll find it.

Content with the decision, I roll onto my back and contemplate sleep. A sudden thought propels me to a sitting position. *What if I get caught rooting around?* Huh. Easy. I'll just say I'm cleaning the place . . . *Just trying to pay you back for all you've done for me,* bud. Yeah, he'll buy that. Already said that he doesn't need a maid service with me around.

Smiling, I lie down again.

35

THE SEARCH

The next morning, after Steve leaves for the day, I stand in the living room, Swiffer duster at the ready. I'm staring at the focal wall with its hand-carved mantel, brass fireplace insert, wall-mounted, fifty-inch plasma TV, and built-in, floor to ceiling bookcases. Pretty impressive. In my real estate days, I would have killed to get a listing on a place like this. Lucky Steve.

The ceiling is nine feet high and, since I'm in no shape to climb a ladder—does Steve even have a ladder?—I am grateful for my six-foot frame. With only the kitchen step stool as an aid, I can explore the very top shelves, and that's where I start.

Books, books, books. All crammed tighter than Skytrain commuters at rush hour on a rainy day . . . no room to hide anything there, that's for sure. I decide to bypass dusting the top shelves. Short-ass Steve can't see the dust that high up anyway, so who cares?

I step off the stool and slide the duster across the rest of the shelves. More books. Lots of books: statistics and sociology and psychology. Okay, so Steve really *is* a student. Score one for Steve.

I step back and scan both bookcases. Any potential hiding places? Only two. In the form of lidded, hockey-puck containers which sit in front of the books. Both empty.

Finished with the shelves, I turn to the trunk which serves as a coffee table. Or is it a coffee table masquerading as a trunk? Must be the latter, since it has a sofa table and an end table to match. Huh. Pretty cool concept. The set is made of cherry wood. Strips of studded leather on the seams. Leather handles on every drawer, each of which I open, probe, and close—slick as a surgeon. Nothing but remote controls, CDs, DVDs, video games.

Next, the red and green couch. Piece of crap furniture in comparison to the adjacent, espresso-colored, leather recliner. Wonder why Steve keeps this couch? I toss the cushions on the floor and run my hands through every crevice. Nothing but coins, which I confiscate. Time to move on. I grab the stool.

The kitchen has high cupboards, but no gap between the top of them and the ceiling. Thank God. No climbing necessary.

I plop the stool onto the floor and step up to examine all the top cupboard shelves, which are lined with beer mugs. Lots of them—from Italy, Spain, France. Guess Steve is well-traveled. Huh. Beer mugs. Interesting souvenir for a non-drinker. Shrugging, I work my way down the shelves, to the counter, to the drawers, to the cupboard under the sink. More glasses, lots of Corelle dishes and stainless steel cutlery. Many small appliances: toaster, blender, food processor, kettle. A glut of cleaning products: Windex, Mr. Clean, SOS pads, Cascade, Vim.

No watch.

I examine the five tiers of shelves in the pantry, the freezer drawer in the fridge, even the storage drawer at the bottom of the shiny, stainless steel stove. Marshmallow Man's no cook, that's for sure. Has enough canned goods to supply a food bank for six months. Tons of frozen food, too. Some with freezer burn. A couple of frying pans. No sign of a broiling pan or roasting pan. Guess Steve eats out a lot. The entitled life of a trust fund baby. The entitled life that I expected to live.

Yep, Steve is living *my* life, that's for sure. Resentment surges, triggering a whirlwind of thoughts that twist and turn and nag: *Steve. Steve. Steve. Buys what he wants when he wants, uses people to get what he wants, tells people what they want to hear. No thought for anybody but himself.*

Huh. I know I'm not making sense here, but I don't give a damn. I let the thoughts spin . . .

We are not so different, Steve and I, and his actions were once my actions: I *spent money, I used people, I lied to everyone, including myself. Yet* he, *the trust fund baby whose source of support was not wrenched away, gets to have, gets to* keep, *this entitled life. And me? Fuck!* I rip open and slam every door and every drawer in every cupboard. *Fuck again!* Nothing here.

It kills me to admit it, but to this point, the word of Steve, the born-again, is absolute gospel. There is not a damn thing here that says he is anything other than what he claims to be, other than what I have witnessed him to be. But I'm spitting rage now. Logic be damned! I'm even more determined to uncover Steve's secrets. I head to the next room, and the next.

Four hours later, I am done . . . and done in. My fury has fizzled and I'm sitting in the den, in Steve's chair, staring blankly at the ficus and trying to decide which of us—me or the tree—is in a worse state. As if in an answer to my quandary, the ficus drops a leaf. I sigh, roll the chair close to the tree, and poke at the soil. Dry. Bone dry. I get up and ramble to the kitchen, returning with a jug of water which I pour into the pot. Then I plop back into the chair and swivel toward the blank space reserved for Steve's laptop.

Still wish I could check the web. Nothing else left. All I learned today is that Steve travels, eats out, and studies. He has two, no, *three* freaking Bibles, all well-thumbed. I feel like I'm missing something, some piece of information that is right in front of my face. But what? Don't know, but there's nothing else here to check. Do I want to do a computer search? Maybe.

Tomorrow, maybe, I'll go to the library. Maybe.

I return the water jug to the kitchen and pull the vacuum cleaner from the hall closet. Want to make sure the place looks neat when Steve comes home. Before I switch on the vacuum, I prod the bag inside, looking for oddly shaped objects. Nothing.

As I'm sliding the vacuum back and forth, back and forth, I make plans. Yep. The library. Downtown. Tomorrow. I will definitely go there tomorrow. May not find anything. But maybe Steve has published a university paper. Maybe his likes and dislikes are posted on Facebook. Want to continue searching for something, anything that will reveal the real Steve. Maybe the Steve I already know *is* the real Steve. Yep, maybe I'm wasting my time, but time is all I have. When I am certain that I have checked everything, then, and only then, can I let go of the idea about the whole Steve/thugs thing. Yep. Library tomorrow.

36

THE LIBRARY

When tomorrow comes, I'm standing statue-still, staring up . . . again. The focus is not bookshelves this time, but a whole freaking library. I'm on the corner of West Georgia and Homer, mouth gaping. Vancouver Central Library is huge—takes up a whole block. A monster. I look at the sidewalk and then up again. I rub the back of my neck and move from one foot to another. My heart races. Fear? For Christ's sake, it's just a library. A *big* library. And I've been here before. But then I was seeking shelter, not information. Never made it past the foyer.

Maybe I should go to the small library branch on Denman. The one near the first apartment Sarah and I had. A grunt escapes my throat. Yeah, right. Can't go there. I would probably run into some former acquaintance—a well-meaning inquisitor. The thought makes me shudder. Too bad, though. I sigh. Yep, too bad. Wouldn't mind that library. I used to walk past it every day and I often stopped and gazed through the long line of windows directly into the columns of books. Sometimes I stood outside waiting for Sarah, watching her as she sat, devouring books. I even imagined seeing her there after she left me. After she took Bobby and left me. Sarah loved libraries.

I'm still looking at the *big* library. Stalling.

What happened to yesterday's anger and determination? Vanished. Vacated. Gone on hiatus. Whatever. Maybe I shouldn't be here. Steve gives me food, shelter and transportation and I'm skulking around, investigating his motives. So much for gratitude.

Still stalling.

I pan the exterior of the building and catch sight of a guy sitting on the walkway, leaning on the wall. His laptop is plugged in to an exterior outlet and his fingers are flying across the keyboard. Is that legal? Using the library's power? Why would they put an outlet there anyway? Maybe I should borrow Steve's laptop. Huh. Like that's gonna happen; he never lets the darn thing out of his sight.

The electricity thief's head jerks up. "Hey. What are you staring at?" He's sitting bolt upright, clutching his laptop, glaring at me.

I step back, hands out, palms facing him. "Nothing. Not a darn thing." I turn my head and charge toward the entrance. After a few steps, I come to an abrupt halt and do a shoulder check. The laptop user is back to business, head down, typing away. I take a deep breath and refocus: the library.

Still stalling.

Do I really need to do this? What if I find out that my suspicions are right? I shudder. Right now I have a place to sleep and I'm terrified of losing it. I gaze at the sidewalk. The hard, unforgiving sidewalk. Freezing cold on the sidewalk.

Still stalling.

What are all these plaques on the walkway? Award-winning writers from British Columbia. Do you have to be born in BC or just reside here to get your name engraved? I wonder what Sarah thought of this, if she ever wanted her name on this Writer's Walk of Fame. I know she did some writing. I step from plaque to plaque, checking the names. The only one I know is W. P. Kinsella. I didn't read *Shoeless Joe* but I saw the movie: *Field of Dreams*, a story about a man who believes, and manifests, his dreams. Can I make my dream happen? That's why I'm here, isn't it? I let out a sigh. Might as well get on with it.

Pulling my shoulders back, I move toward the entrance. Concrete columns, tall like giant cedars, flank the curved walkway. I follow their arc, yank the door open, and stride through. After a few steps, I stop and look around.

The periphery is big, yeah, but the interior is immense. Brobdingnagian even. Huh. Brobdingnagian. I smile, picturing Sarah talking about *Gulliver's Travels*. She would be proud: I remembered. I remembered the word.

Soon the image of Sarah fades, taking my smile with it. Outside, I was hesitant, but I moved forward. Inside, I'm overwhelmed.

I'm familiar with this part of the building—the foyer—yet it feels different today. I glance upward and notice, as if for the first time, the tiers of glass walls. Must be eight or nine stories of glass. The sky-high ceiling serves as an echo chamber for the voices of passersby and the air is filled with swirling ghosts of indiscernible chatter . . . echoing, echoing, echoing. Gives me the creeps. Why the hell am I here?

"Hey! You're not supposed to be in here!" The voice, high-pitched and juvenile, slams me from the rear.

I swerve, heart racing.

A child, a boy, maybe four or five, is pointing at a lone pigeon on the floor behind me. The darn bird is strutting around like it owns the place.

"Mommy!" The boy scampers to his mother who is watching him from a nearby bench; he tugs at her coat, and stares up at her. "Mommy, that bird is supposed to be outside. On the street."

Despite myself, I start to laugh. "Hey, you get the door, and I'll try to shoo it out," I call to the boy and his mom.

The mother keeps a respectful distance, but nods. Standing, clutching her son's hand tightly, she goes to the door and holds it.

I crouch low and scoot around behind the bird, zigzagging, hoping the serpentine motion will help ease the bird forward, not startle it into flight. The plan has merit: the pigeon darts and skitters but does not take wing until it nears the exit. Then it flies through the door and lands on the sidewalk.

"Thanks, Mister," says the little boy.

He and his mom smile and wave and slide through the door. Gone.

Okay, that's done. The bird is on the sidewalk, where it belongs. Me? Maybe it's the image of mother and son that makes me turn back to the task at hand. Whatever. I can do this. I stride to the center of the foyer. Darn straight I can do this. I'm not stupid. I attended university, for Christ's sake. Yeah, right. I sniff. The whole academic thing never had any meaning for me. Damn. One negative thought and my body trembles. My lips are dry. I look around.

To my left are shops, coffee bars and a tavern. Saw the tavern there before and never questioned it. But now I wonder. A tavern? In a library? Not a bad idea, I guess. Even studious types like the occasional drink. Now there's an idea. A drink. That's what I need. A drink. I shove my hands into my pockets.

"Damn!" Empty . . . except for the few coins I found in the couch, stolen coins. Guilt stabs me. Maybe I should leave. Just stop all this nonsense, be grateful, and leave. I seesaw for a minute. Leave-stay, leave-stay. I picture the mother-son-pigeon scenario and my heart aches for Sarah and Bobby. I'm staying. My body jolts forward, past the tavern, past the shops.

I rush to the library doors and charge through.

I'm here: the inner sanctum. Known only to the card-carrying, book-loving Sarahs of the world. My breath whooshes out. Didn't realize I was holding it.

A couple of feet in, I stand, stare, then rotate like that stupid ballerina on Sarah's jewelry box. Which way? Have no idea where to go.

"Need any help, Mister?" A plump, brown-haired woman gazes up at me. Damn. *Run away. Run away. Run away.*

Blood pumps to my legs. I have to run before she kicks me out. But I don't move. Something—don't know what—pierces my fear. As I stare at the round, wrinkled face in front of me, my panic completely deflates. Why? What's different here?

Huh. Her face, that's what different. No contempt. No sneer. Just kindness. Concern. Like the nurse at St. Paul's, the one with the angel tattoo, this lady wants to help. I am so used to people looking down their noses at me. What the hell is going on?

I catch my reflection in a window behind her. My clothes are clean, new. My face is still mangled a bit, but shiny hair covers the damage. I take a deep breath. I'm normal. One of the regular people now. I straighten my back. "Huh? Oh, yes. Can I use the computer here?" Stupid question. Of course I can. Anybody can. I clear my throat and edit my request. "I mean, like . . . if I don't have . . . like . . . a library card or . . . anything?" *Jesus, Wentworth. You're squeaking like a mouse! Man up, for Christ's sake!*

The plump woman smiles. "Well, yes, you do need a library card. But that's not hard to get. Just show your ID and proof of residence. You can apply right over there." She points to the service desk.

My heart drops. My body shrivels. I have no ID. I have no home—not a permanent one anyway. I guess I'm not one of the regular people after all. Maybe not even a real person.

"Thanks." I walk toward the desk, and then check over my shoulder to see if she is watching. She's not. I turn left and come to a standstill in a section marked ZINE, whatever the hell that is.

No ID. No home. What now?

I scan the space and see a bank of computers near the glass wall that separates library from foyer. Eight computers in pairs, back-to-back. Eight users, engrossed in keyboards and screens. Huh. There has to be a way to . . . Then, I remember something Sarah said.

Sarah did this all the time . . . worked on computers in the library. Once, she left her library card at home. Needed to research something by Margaret somebody. Atwood or Laurence? Whatever. She didn't want to go all the way home, so she waited and watched as people left their computers. Eventually, she found one where someone forgot to log off. Huh. Smart cookie, my Sarah. Thanks, Sarah.

Now I have a plan. I amble toward the blue chairs that line the glass wall behind the computers and slide into a chair with curved, wooden arms that encircle my waist like an open handcuff on a thin wrist. Locking my eyes on the computers, I wait. When an anxious user turns and glares at me, I grab a discarded newspaper from the chair beside me and thumb through it until I land on the *Classifieds*. Maybe I can check out the job section. I smirk at the thought. Yeah, right. That's a *Catch-22*. Can't get a job without a home, can't get a home without a job. But I *can* pretend.

It's not long before someone walks away from a computer. Not long at all. I casually approach. No luck, so I return to my seat. I repeat the procedure three times. Pay dirt the last time. I refrain from pumping my fist into the air. Better just get on with it; don't know how much time I have. Google: S-t-e-v-e J-a-m-e-s-o-n, V-a-n-c-o-u-v-e-r.

Many hits. But only one of interest. An actual article written by Steve on homelessness in Vancouver.

A short time later, I'm back at the bus stop. I stand there in a daze.

"You getting in or what?"

My head pops up. There's my bus, parked right in front of me, door wide open. The bus driver is glaring at me, his fingers tapping the steering wheel.

"Yeah. Sorry." I climb aboard and flash my bus pass, which is a gift from Steve who has everything. Steve who is giving me shelter and food and transportation. And hope. He provided a break for me. Maybe I should just receive all Steve's gifts without question. Maybe Steve is exactly what he seems to be. Facebook says so. Likes: Gospel Singers and BMW's and Doing Research. Activities: Praising Jesus and Helping the Homeless. Dislikes: Taking the Bus.

Huh. He dislikes taking the bus, yet he has done so countless times with me. Maybe he is just a caring person who helps others . . . he *did* write a paper on the plight of the homeless. Maybe Steve is my route back to my family. Maybe I should just focus on getting my family back. If they are willing to come back. I have to quit drinking. That was the deal breaker, the drinking . . . and driving with Bobby in the car. Just a little accident. Not a big deal. Maybe Sarah will get over it.

I lumber down the aisle of the bus and plop into a seat. I toy with the bus pass that is dangling from a lanyard around my neck. A deep sigh escapes me. There is no maybe about Steve . . . Steve *is* my bridge to my family.

No more investigating. I'll just let my suspicions fall away. To hell with examining his cell phone and his flash drive and his laptop. To hell with my stupid dream. I will employ a new tactic. Good behavior. Total cooperation. Whatever it takes to get me back to my life and my family. I need to heal. Slowly. Very slowly. And I need Steve.

The bus turns onto Davie Street and stops near the liquor store. My body lurches. I can almost taste the alcohol. Easy to get off the bus, to beg on the street, to buy booze, to gulp it down. Yeah. Easy. I lean forward. I close my eyes and picture Sarah and Bobby . . . on the seawall, at Second Beach. Sarah's hair is blowing in the breeze. Bobby's little fists are packing sand into his green, plastic bucket. I pull back into my seat. No. No more booze. The bus door closes, punctuating my decision. I breathe deeply as the bus rumbles on.

37

NO WEDDING RING?

Remember the AA thing?" I ask Steve the next morning.

"Huh?"

"AA. You said something about a meeting."

Steve swings to face me, coffee pot in one hand, mug in the other.

"You serious, bud?"

"Dead serious."

Steve pours his coffee and puts the pot back on the stand. "So, what brought this on?"

"Just thinking."

"Thinking what?"

"Damn. You're not going to make this easy, are you?"

Steve pulls out a chair and sits beside me at the table. "Not about *easy*, bud. About research. Want to know what precipitated the change. You turned me down the first time . . . and the second, remember?"

I nod. "Yeah. Things are different now."

"How so?"

My hands tremble, signaling the beginning of withdrawal. Better get this out of my system before I cave. I reach into my pocket and latch onto the castle. Pull it out and set it on the table. "This was my son's. He loved *Finding Nemo* . . . you remember that movie?"

"Of course."

Bobby was crazy about Nemo and Dory. I must have watched that movie with him a thousand times." I smile. "Spent ages looking up clown fish and regal blue tangs on the internet, too."

The memory transports me to another time and I linger there, with Bobby. He is parked on my lap in front of the computer, waving his arms in excitement. My nostrils tingle as the scent of Johnson's baby shampoo filters through them.

"Sounds like you loved just being *Dad*."

Jolted back, I nod and choke on tears. I swallow and wipe my eyes. "It's been a long time since I've been called that. *Dad*." I shake my head. "We set up aquariums together, one fresh water, one salt. The salt water aquarium had its own Nemo and Dory. This castle . . . " I pick up the castle and turn it around and around in my fingers . . . "this castle was in both aquariums. It's all I have left."

"So you want to get sober for Bobby. Makes sense." Steve taps his fingers on his coffee mug. "Okay, bud, you want your son back. What about Sarah? I notice you're not carting around anything of hers."

"Not now. The thugs stole it. My watch was a gift from Sarah. Gone now." I catch myself looking at Steve's wrist. Huh. If he had it, he wouldn't be wearing it. *Let go of that damn dream, Wentworth.* Focus on Sarah and Bobby.

"A watch? Weren't you married? Where's the wedding ring?" He points at my left hand. "Not even a tan line there, bud."

My head pounds. "Had one. Lost it."

"Thugs steal that, too?"

"Lost it in a poker game."

Steve's eyes widen. "A poker game? You got to be kidding me! Didn't you have the watch then? Why didn't you just gamble the watch?"

Jesus. I'm gonna throw up any second. "Because I was an asshole and it was a Rolex. A fucking Rolex."

I jump up, knock over the chair and stumble to the bathroom. The heaving starts before I make it to the toilet. Vomit spews, covering everything that is white and clean and shiny. When I think I am done, my gut churns out more vomit and bile and self-hatred and rage. At the end, I am spent and lying in a rotting cesspool of brown and red and green. Jesus Christ. I'm indoors, inside Steve's shiny condo, and I'm still in the gutter.

Out of the corner of my eye, I see feet in the doorway and I know I'm done. Back to the street. Night is closing in.

Steve bends, places a bottle of Mr. Clean and two rolls of paper towels inside the door. He speaks. "Okay, bud. We'll go to a meeting."

His footsteps pad down the hallway. My arms reach up, grab the toilet bowl. I pull myself up and gag. Nothing comes out. Heave after heave. Nothing. I slide to the floor and into darkness.

38

AA MEETINGS

I don't talk much for the next few days. Not to Steve anyway. My body's needs come first. There are meetings, though. Lots of them.

Every time we—Steve and I—enter the monstrous old church for an AA meeting, I cringe. My heart pounds as we head down the stairs to a dank room in the basement. The smell of stale coffee abounds. My nose wrinkles in resistance. No aroma of Starbucks around here . . . not like on Robson Street. Guess there are no beautiful people at AA.

There is always a group, though. At least a dozen every time. The grey, metal folding chairs are always arranged in a circle. A circle is for sharing, they say; no hierarchy in a circle.

There is always talking. Lots of talking. It's damn hard to listen to all that talking, but I'm determined. Even so, I sit near the exit, perched on the edge of my chair, ready to take off if the need arises. Sometimes I rock back and forth, just a little. Sometimes I bounce a foot, or wear a path on my jeans by rubbing my hands up and down my thighs. Always I swallow repeatedly. Yep. I force myself to sit, to listen . . . because it helps, knowing I'm not the only one.

The first time I try to speak my mouth dries up. "My name's Justin and I'm an alcoholic," I squeak out.

"Hello, Justin." The group responds like well-trained kids in a kindergarten class.

I peer over the heads opposite me and focus on the wall, on a nondescript stain on the wall. I keep talking. "I lost my home when the market crashed."

A collective moan meets my ears. I glance at the group, forcing myself to look at faces. Some sad. Some tired. All attentive, eyes wide. No judgment. My body feels light, relaxed. It's okay to talk. I check for Steve and see him out of the corner of my eye. He's smiling, nodding.

I like the fact that Steve comes along. I guess visitors are allowed; either that or he's made arrangements so he can help me out until I get a sponsor. I still have time before I have to choose a sponsor. I'm in no hurry. Comfortable with Steve.

I turn toward him, keeping my eyes on him as I talk about Sarah and Bobby and the big house. He listens like it's all new information. Funny thing, that. I thought I had already told him this stuff, but I guess I hadn't. Dreams, maybe. Thoughts. Whatever. The main thing is that he's helping me. I must admit, I like the guy. I always thought we could be friends in another life. Beginning to think we're friends now.

"When I realized that we were on the verge of losing our home, I went to see the loan officer at the bank." Huh. That was easy enough to say. But the next part? I cross my arms, uncross them, and cross them again. I suck in a breath and blurt out the words. "I was drunk when I did that." My eyes shift from one person to another. Their faces haven't changed, not one iota. I let out a sigh. Yep, it's really okay to talk. I return my gaze to the blotch on the wall and just keep talking.

39

REALITY CHECK

June, 2009

A man's home is his castle," I say to the loan officer.

"But you must pay for your castle, sir." He flashes a cold smile.

I cringe. My hand curls into a tight fist and my nails dig into my palm. I force my body to sit still. "If y-y-y-ou . . . " I stop, take a deep breath. *Once more, without the stuttering, Wentworth.* "If you knew we couldn't afford it, why did you lend us the money?" That's better. My voice is controlled, monotone.

"Your choices are not our responsibility, sir. Maybe you should see a credit counselor. We can't help you here."

My face burns as blood rushes to it. *Damn you, asshole.* Credit counselor! Already know about the freaking credit counselor. I have an appointment there in a half hour. I wipe my mouth on my sleeve.

"Did you hear me, sir? We can't help you. I wish you luck." He jumps to his feet, marches to the door, and whips it open. He leans into it, waiting.

I stumble from my chair, through the door, to the front exit. When I get to my car, I grab the parking ticket from the windshield, scrunch it, and toss it. I pull my car keys from my pocket.

Beep! Beep! A push of a button unlocks the door. Yanking it open, I climb aboard, and zone in on the glove box. From there I pull my 7 Up bottle. My vodka stash. Twist. Slurp. A deep breath. I re-cap the bottle and return it to its hideout.

Twenty minutes later, I pull up in front of another parking meter. I grab a piece of paper and a pen from my briefcase. "Meter broken," I scribble and fold the paper. After another "7 Up swig," I pop a mint into my mouth. I'm ready.

Briefcase in hand, I emerge from my Lexus, stick the folded note into a coin slot in the meter, and check the street numbers. I turn right.

My suit itches. Too hot a day for it. Cheap suit, too. Not Armani. No longer Armani. Sold the Armanis on eBay. All five of them.

I stand on a street corner, eyeing the people around me while I wait for the walk sign. I'm jumpy, like a fearful animal. Don't know why. Nobody knows I'm drowning.

The light changes and I cross the street. Ahead is a shiny building, its mirrored exterior glistening in the June sun. My destination. I stride to the door, pull it open and march in. A lobby. A desk. And, damn it all, a security guard. Damn. Damn. Damn. I don't want to ask him where the credit counselor's office is. I need to be anonymous here. Maybe I should leave. I put down my briefcase and bend to tie an already-tied shoe. I take a deep breath. When I straighten, the guard is directly in front of me.

"Anything I can help you with, sir?" The guard folds his arms and stares down at me, his eyes firing question marks.

Jesus. I'm nearly six feet tall and he's looking down? Maybe I'm shrinking.

I adjust my tie and clear my throat. "Er, no thanks." I point to the directory beside the elevator. "Everything I need is right there."

The guard hesitates, then steps aside. "Okay, sir," he says. "But if you change your mind, I'll be over there." He tilts his head in the direction of his desk. He doesn't add, "I'll be watching you," but I hear it anyway.

At the directory, I scan frantically. I have to find my floor and get on that elevator before the eyes of the guard burrow a hole in my neck. There it is—sixteen. Thank God. I push the button and shift from one foot to the other while I wait. An eternity.

Ping! The elevator arrives. I scurry on, turn and catch a glimpse of the guard. Hmmm, he's not watching me at all. I push the button for my floor. As the doors slide together, I see the guard smiling and talking with a few people, clearly business people. Jesus, I'm paranoid. Now I smile . . . maybe they *are* business people or maybe they are pretending, just like me.

The elevator stops at the sixteenth floor. I step off and stand in the hallway. "Room 1605 . . . two doors to the right. Convenient." I walk to the door marked REALITY CREDIT COUNSELORS. Once again, I smile. *Reality* Credit Counselors. Time to leave fantasy behind. I open the door and step inside.

The receptionist's counter is four feet ahead. I approach. A red-haired, twenty-something girl talks into her phone and then, with a well-practiced smile, looks up to greet me.

"How may I help you, sir?"

"My name is Wentworth. I have an appointment with . . ." I search my brain but the name doesn't come. I can't seem to remember things lately. My brain is Teflon. Nothing sticks. Stress, maybe. Or booze. Or both.

"Ah, yes, here it is. You'll be talking to George this morning. He'll be ready in ten minutes or so. Please take a seat."

"Certainly. Thanks." I sit in the closest armchair. Then I count the armchairs in the rectangular waiting area. Ten of them. All brown, all faux leather. Two on the back wall. Four on each of the side walls. An assortment of magazines fans the center coffee table. I push aside *Time, O, Sports Illustrated*. The next one is *Fortune*. A guttural laugh escapes me. I look up and notice that the receptionist is staring. I shrug and check the next magazine. *Money*. I flip through a few pages and settle on an article about credit counselors. Huh. Appropriate.

"Mr. Wentworth?"

My head darts up, my eyes widen, and I drop the magazine.

A young man, clad in jeans and a blue shirt, adjusts his glasses and extends his hand. "I'm George. I believe you wish to see me this morning."

I can't move. *Damn, he's just a kid.*

"Mr. Wentworth?" George raises his eyebrows.

I jerk forward and shake his hand. "Yes."

"We'll go to my office. This way, please."

I pick up my briefcase, and follow the casual young man called George.

Once inside the office, I sit where instructed and place the briefcase on the floor beside me. George adjusts the Venetian blinds behind his desk. "The sun will be barreling in soon," he explains. "It will be fine for me, but the glare will hit your eyes. Now," he continues as he plops into his swivel chair, "how can I help you?"

I peer into the face of this young man who can't possibly know what trouble is. How can he help me? How can he help me when he's barely old enough to shave?

The smooth-faced counselor named George leans forward in his chair. "I know you think I don't understand, Mr. Wentworth, but I do. I see many people every day. I'm here to help, not judge. You tell me what's going on, and I'll do my best for you." He leans back. He pivots in his chair—to one side, to the other side, and back again. He folds his arms. He waits. "You just take your time," he says.

"I-I-I don't know where to begin."

George seems to know. "Do you have a family, Mr. Wentworth?" he asks.

"Yes, yes, I sure do. My wife's name is Sarah and my son is Bobby . . . he's eight." My heart drops. "Bobby," I say again. I look straight into George's eyes. "I'm here because I have to be . . . I'm drowning in debt, George." *There, I've said it.* "I'm drowning. It's so bad that I am afraid I am going to lose everything."

George brings his chair to a halt and leans toward me. He sighs. "I'm sorry to hear that, Mr. Wentworth. Sorry, but not surprised. If you weren't in debt, you wouldn't be here." George pauses. "I hope I can help, Mr. Wentworth."

I shake my head and put out one hand, palm facing him. "Don't call me Mr. Wentworth. Doesn't seem . . . " I sigh and drop my hand. *Why bother to explain?* "The name's Justin." I point at my briefcase. "I brought as much information as I could. There's a lot missing. I lost it or hid it or burned it, I'm sure. What do you need to know?"

George is in motion again, swiveling around, opening a filing cabinet, retrieving a stack of paper which he drops onto his desk. "I will need you to fill these out for me, Justin. But first, I am going to ask you a few questions to help get the ball rolling. You answer me as best you can, okay?"

I nod.

"Do you own a house?"

"Mortgaged."

"Do you have any equity in the house?"

"No. Had a little last year but borrowed against it." I tug at my shirt collar.

"So . . . you have two mortgages on the property?"

The questions are accumulating, latching onto me like tiny leeches. Every response sucks blood. "Yes."

"Do you have a job, Justin?"

"I'm in real estate. I work on commission and you know what that means right now."

"Does your wife work?"

"No. Studying for her master's at UBC."

"Do you have any other outstanding debt, other than the mortgages, I mean?"

"Two cars. Both leased. A Lexus and an Accord—no, wait a minute. Repo guy took the Accord last week. I'm driving the Lexus today but . . . " I shake my head. "Then there's the credit cards—all maxed out."

"How many credit cards?"

"Eight, maybe ten. I'm not sure."

"So, you're making minimum payments?"

My eyes follow the trail of vacuum tracks on the carpet.

George sighs. "Justin, in the last few months, did you go to a bank or a credit union to seek a consolidation loan? To pay outstanding bills and improve cash flow?"

I shift in my chair. "Yes. Credit rating sucks. No home equity. And economy's in the toilet, so I'm not selling any property." I shrug.

George stands, walks around his desk, and pulls up an armchair beside me. He leans in. "I'm not going to lie to you. I have to crunch some numbers, but it looks like you're in pretty deep. I want you to fill out some forms. If you don't feel up to coming back here, fine, but fill out the forms anyway, and mail them to me. I'll examine them but"—he takes a deep breath—"you'll most likely have to declare bankruptcy."

My hands are trembling. George is still talking.

"I know it's hard, but bankruptcy will keep the creditors off your back. What you have to do, ASAP, is liquidate your assets. *All* of them. As soon as you declare bankruptcy, you'll have to sell everything anyway. If you sell now, you can use the money to take care of the basic needs of your family: groceries, clothing, shelter. Understand?"

I try to swallow but my mouth is dry. I should say something, but what? No clue, so I just nod my head.

George leans back, plants his hands on the arms of his chair, and pushes himself to a standing position. "Okay, Mr. Wentworth—Justin—that's it for now. Let me just give you the paperwork." He reaches across his desk, picks up the papers he had dropped there earlier, stuffs them into a file folder, and passes the file to me.

I take it. I try to mouth a thank you but still can't find any words so I just take it, all of it . . . the information, the file, and the humiliation. *Click.* Open my briefcase. Stuff the file in. Close the briefcase. *Snap.* Push the locks in place. In slow motion, I stand and make my way to the door.

"I'll accompany you to the elevator and we can talk some more . . . " George is walking beside me, shoulder to shoulder.

I stop, look at him, and shake my head.

"Okay." He takes a respectful step back. "I understand . . . but please try to get those forms back to me as soon as possible."

I fumble my way through the waiting room with the *Fortune* magazine, past the young receptionist with the red hair, through the door with the "REALITY" sign, to the elevator. I push the call button and wait.

My body is empty of anxiety and empty of hope. What had I expected by seeing a credit counselor . . . salvation, maybe? Had I really thought that a credit counselor was going to swoop down like some debt-avenging superhero and take all this away from me? I sniff. Huh. Guess I did, didn't I? "Idiot." I step into the elevator. The doors close. "Absolute idiot."

At the lobby, the doors open and I notice the guard isn't there. Good. I don't want to deal with him. I exit the elevator and veer right. My vision locks on a trash can near the front door. I walk to it, open my brief case and pull out the bankruptcy papers. I *can* make the file disappear into the green plastic trash can, let it rot there with Styrofoam cups and sandwich wrappers. I hesitate, knowing that the problem won't disappear with the papers. Shaking my head, I return the file to the briefcase. Then I remember the 7 Up bottle in the glove compartment of the Lexus. I charge through the front door. I sprint to the car.

40

THE REAL WORLD

February, 2010

Sure are lots of tourists in town." I zip my jacket as Steve and I exit one of many meetings.

"Olympics are almost here, bud."

"Oh, yeah. Opening ceremonies on Valentine's Day, right?"

"Nope. On the twelfth, actually."

We walk in silence for a few minutes. I like that—being able to walk with someone without feeling the need for a steady stream of conversation. It's comfortable. I need that comfort.

Spilling my guts at these meetings is supposed to help, but it feels like a surgeon has pried open my chest with a rib spreader and knifed his way into my heart. No anesthetic. I want to kill the pain. Or at least bury it. That's where alcohol comes in handy. But there is no alcoholic fog for me now. Now I'm living in the real world. One day at a time. No booze. Hurts like hell. Yeah. But I guess it's supposed to. *Hurt to heal* . . . Isn't that what doctors do?

"Wanna go check out the ice rink?" Steve asks.

"Huh? What ice rink?"

"Robson Square. They opened it just for the Olympics."

"Oh. That. Already passed by a few times. I lived on Robson, remember? Literally."

"Yeah, right." Steve laughs. "Well, I haven't been there yet, so what do you say?"

I shrug. "You're the boss."

We stroll along Robson, winding in and out amid hordes of visitors. Smiles everywhere. Cameras everywhere. The sense of optimism is tangible. It transports me, elevates my mood from gloom and doom to hope and joy. Huh. All that from the bubbly spirits of total strangers. A sudden, childlike urge to play passes through me—my feet actually skip, just a step or two. I smile, amused as hell. The Olympics are not even here yet and already Vancouver has become the Magic Kingdom. Maybe I can relax and enjoy some of this.

It is not long before we get to the skating rink. People swarm about, drinking coffee, putting on skates. We sidle up to the rink and lean against the boards to watch the skaters. The cold bites my nose and stings my fingers; the swish of skates scraping ice reminds me of crisp days spent in hockey rinks. I rub my hands together.

"So, was it worth it?" Steve asks.

"What?"

"Was it worth it? All the stuff you and Sarah accumulated? Were you happy?"

There goes the magic.

Damn it all, Steve. I take a deep breath, turn away from the rink, and lean back, elbows on the boards. "So why are you hitting me with this now?"

"No particular reason. Guess this is kind of a family scene." He points to the rink.

I shrug. "Sarah and I loved each other, if that's what you mean. And yeah, we were happy. Had everything. Each other and Bobby and the house and cars and TVs and travel. Everything."

"Must have been tough to give it all up."

No answer for the obvious. I push away from the boards, inhale deeply and exhale in a whoosh. My breath combines with the cold air to form a nebulous cloud of fog; somehow this amuses me so I repeat the procedure.

"Okay, I get it. Of course it was tough. Sorry I asked."

I turn and look at him.

He's shivering. "It's freezing here, bud," he says. "Want a hot chocolate?" His eyes express apology.

I nod, letting him off the hook.

"Be right back." Steve takes off to a nearby vendor.

I turn to face the rink; I fold my arms on top of the boards and lean in. My lips curl into a smile. Amazing. I am in the center of a metropolis and yet, here, amid a gliding sea of smiling, rosy faces and Olympic-red mittens, I am like a kid again, on a frozen pond, in a small town.

"Vancouver is sure going all out for the Olympics," I remark to no one in particular.

"As long as they get the homeless and the riffraff off the streets," responds a man beside me as he opens the gate and takes to the ice.

The words slice like a guillotine. My head drops to my arms and stays there. I'm still in that position when Steve returns.

"Here you go, bud," he says. "Watch out. It's very hot." He nudges me with his elbow. "You okay?"

It's a struggle, but I manage to raise my head. I turn, and reach for one of the two hot chocolates he's carrying. "Yeah, yeah. Let's get going." I walk to the nearest garbage bin and drop the steaming Styrofoam cup into it.

"Hey! What a waste. Why did you say you wanted it if you are not going to drink it?"

"Let's just get the hell out of here, okay?"

"Justin, what the . . . ?"

I brush past him and hurry away. Steve catches up. I notice that he is no longer holding a hot chocolate. Guess he dumped his, too. Whatever. I lurch into high gear. We are back to silence now. Not so comfortable this time, though. I am anxious to get back to the condo. I shift into even higher speed. I'm only aware of footsteps—mine and Steve's, as he falls into rhythm beside me. The crowds thin considerably as we put distance between us and all things Robson Street. The farther away we get, the better I feel.

The wind gusts and I turtle my head into my jacket. I want to stay that way, sheltered from the world. This is my space. Don't anyone dare enter. My eyes are cast low.

"Windy day. Feels like we're in for a storm," a man, some stupid cheerful man, remarks as he passes. I don't look up. I don't see his face. But I *do* see his dog. The bouncing golden retriever at his side. I avert my eyes. Too late. An unwanted memory emerges, punishing me with excruciating chest pain. I reel and stumble. The ground is closing in when Steve catches me. He pulls me upright. I lean on him.

"What the heck, bud? What's wrong? You want me to call an ambulance?"

"No." I shake my head both in response and in an attempt to repress image and agony. I straighten and push away from him. "No. I'm not sick. It's just the dog."

"What dog?" Steve's turns and looks. "Oh . . . you mean the retriever?"

I nod. "Yeah. The retriever." Sweat oozes from every pore of my body.

"Hmm. I'm guessing you got a golden retriever for Bobby . . . right?"

My head snaps up. "I never said anything to you about that. Not a fucking word. How did you know that?"

"No, you never told me. But I'm not an idiot. Just saw the way you reacted, bud."

I sigh. I shrug. "Yeah. For Bobby. Got a dog for Bobby." My body trembles as cold air meets perspiration. "Need to sit down."

"No problem." Steve points to a nearby green and white sign. "Starbucks on every corner around here." Boy Scout Steve takes my arm and guides me in, to a table at the back. He pulls out a chair and parks me in it. "Wait here."

I sit and shiver. My back is to the door. Uncomfortable. Unsafe. I switch to the other side of the table and watch Steve in the line at the counter. Damn. I just know he's going to ask stuff I have no intention of talking about.

Steve places a coffee in front of me. "Here. You darn well better drink this. Not buying you anything else if you throw this out." He pulls out a chair and sits. "What was the dog's name?"

Fuck you, Steve. Lips clamped tight, I clutch my coffee.

"My guess is Dory for a female, Nemo for a male."

"Ha ha!" Laughter erupts, surprising the hell out of me. Can't help it. I'm smiling. I take a deep breath. "Okay. Okay. Puppy was female. At the breeder's, Sarah asked Bobby if he wanted to call her Dory. Should've seen the look on his face. Eyes wide, staring at Sarah like she was some kind of alien. "Dory's a *fish*, Mommy," he said. "A blue *fish*." Then he held up the puppy. "This is a *dog*."

Steve smirks. "So what *did* you call the dog?"

My laughter is gone now. "Lady. We called her Lady." Just like the retriever puppy Sarah cuddled the first time we visited Gastown. So long ago. My heart aches.

"Like *Lady and the Tramp*?"

I probe my brain, trying to remember when I told him about that trip to Gastown. Doesn't seem to matter. "Yeah. Exactly like *Lady and the Tramp*."

"Breeder's, you said. Purebred dogs cost a lot."

"Huh. Thousand bucks just for the dog. Probably another thousand for crate and toys and leash and vet. Big bucks."

"Must've been hard to keep up with everything."

I shrug. "Visa, MasterCard, American Express."

"Did you get the dog the same year you bought the house?"

"Yep." I'm squirming now, like I'm in an interrogation room. The door to the coffee shop is ajar. Part of me slips through.

"Furniture? Cars? All at the same time?"

I rub the back of my neck and gulp back the urge to spit at him.

"I was listening to everything you said at the meeting. All the credit counselor stuff. Can't help but wonder . . . did it ever occur to you to slow down a bit, maybe wait a while before you bought everything you wanted?"

I glare and spit out the first thing that comes to mind. "Does it ever occur to you to slow down?"

"Huh? What the heck are you talking about?"

"The only difference between you and me, *bud*, is tragedy. If your parents died and left you without a bank account, would you change your lifestyle? You *ever* work for anything, *bud*?"

Steve smiles. "*Touché.*" He leans back, sips his coffee, and taps his spoon on the table. "So, what happened to Lady? Does Bobby still have her?"

My rage fizzles, instantly. All sounds morph into white noise. Steve and Starbucks and street—all garbled nonsense. I inhale. Not coffee I smell, but alcohol. My body no longer shivers; it quakes with need and longing and pain. I want a drink. My vision blurs and images whirl in front of me. Spinning and turning. Booze. *Get out of here and get booze.*

"Hey, bud. You still here?" Steve has a firm grip on my arm.

I shake my head and pull back. "Let's go." I spring to my feet and march forward. There is no stumbling for me this time.

"Sorry, bud," Steve says when he catches up. "Guess Lady is off the table for now, huh?"

I keep walking, through the door, to the sidewalk, toward the condo.

Back in the condo, Steve grabs a Diet Coke from the fridge and goes to the den.

I gave him lots of data tonight. Bet he's in a mega rush to enter it into his computer before he forgets any details.

I hang out in my room. Lie there, staring at the ceiling, creating patterns in the stucco. Dog patterns. Small and golden. Big and fluffy. Many dogs. Then only one. Only Lady. A little boy appears beside her, bouncing along a beach, running in and out of the waves. His laughter rings above the surf and detonates Lady's bark. *Woof! Woof!* I close my eyes and smell salt. Gulls shriek overhead. Sarah's hair waves in the wind. I stand nearby, watching my family.

A jogger passes. "Put that dog on a leash, Mister. There are laws, you know."

I swerve toward him. My body jumps. And, suddenly, without warning or intention, I'm sitting bolt upright on the bed in Steve's spare room.

I slowly drop back onto the pillow and squeeze my eyes together, trying to recreate the memory, the feeling—trying to re-create my family. The only thing that comes easily is tears. I grab my pillow and cling to it like a distraught child latching onto a teddy bear. I inhale, seeking familiar smells— Bobby, wet dog, sea salt, Sarah. But they are all gone. I slam the pillow back on the bed, jump up, and march to the door.

In the hallway, I pause. My heart pounds and my head spins. Maybe I should just forget this. I *can* leave. What's stopping me? I can slip right past the door to Steve's den. I can go to the street. I can drink. Forget. Get rid of this pain. My feet choose to move. Step. Step. Step. Past Steve's den, down the hall, to the front door. There I grab my jacket, put it on and shove one hand into the pocket that holds Bobby's castle. I close my eyes and breathe. Not just one breath. Many, long, slow breaths. What's stopping me? I ask myself again. Bobby. Sarah. My family. That's what. I take off my jacket and pad my way toward the den.

Tap, tap, tap. "Steve?"

"Yeah. Come in."

I push the door open.

Steve closes the file he's working on. "What's up, bud?"

"I gave up the dog."

Steve swivels toward me.

"What do you mean? Did you take her back to the breeder?"

I shake my head.

"Find a new home for her?"

My eyes lock on the ficus tree. A single, dried leaf breaks off, falls. I follow it down to the pool of dead leaves on the carpet.

"What, then?"

I move to a chair beside Steve's desk and drop into it. "SPCA."

41

BEAUTIFUL DOG

September, 2009

What am I going to tell him, Sarah? What the hell am I going to tell him?"

Sarah reaches for the radio and turns up the volume.

"Sssh. Not so loud. He'll hear you." She plops into a chair beside me and leans on the kitchen table. "Bobby will be crushed, but we can't keep Lady. We're lucky we found a small apartment. I don't care about that . . . you know that, don't you? I've told you a thousand times I'd live in a garage to be with you and Bobby. But we have to do something about Lady. The apartment building doesn't allow pets. And we have to move . . . soon."

"Jesus, Sarah . . . "

She jumps up. Plants her hands on the table and leans in so that her face is two inches from mine. Spits the words. "Don't 'Jesus, Sarah' me. You have to get your act together. You promised to stop drinking. You *promised*. I can support you through whatever it takes to get you sober, Justin. And I don't give a damn about all the *stuff* we had to sell. We will do just fine without the big TV and fancy furniture." She drops her head, then lifts it again. Tears stream down her face. "Look . . . it kills me to give up Lady." She chokes back a sob. "But we *have* to . . . and we have to do it *right away*. You know damn well the leasing company will repossess the Lexus any day. You need to take care of this while we still have the car. Call the breeder, Justin. Explain things. You have to take Lady *now*. And *you* have to tell Bobby. Man up, Justin."

I let out a moan.

Sarah sighs and sits. She turns down the radio. Takes a deep breath.

"It's Saturday, so I'm taking Bobby out for the day. You take care of Lady. You'll think of something to tell him, Justin." She stands and walks away.

A few minutes later, Bobby barrels into the kitchen.

"Me and Mommy cleaned the aquarium, Daddy. I took out the castle and now I can't find it. Mom says we have to sell the aquarium. But I want to keep the castle. Did you take it?"

I stare at my eight-year-old. *I want to keep the castle, too, son.* I shake my head.

Bobby shrugs. "I'll look for it later. Mom and I are going out . . . shopping for school stuff. We're taking the bus. Isn't that cool?"

I smile.

"Later, Daddy!" He runs out.

I hear both of them at the front door. Chattering, gathering shoes and jackets. Then the door opens and closes.

Lady whines.

"Laaady!"

She hurries to me, tail wagging. Looks up, brown eyes shining, and places a paw on my arm.

I cringe. "Oh, God." I extend my hand to pet her, but instantly recoil. Can't be too nice to her. Not now.

Using the table for support, I push myself up, shuffle toward the kitchen cabinets and pull open drawers, one after another. Empty. Empty. Empty. Damn. Yellow Pages. Where are the freaking Yellow Pages?

I finally spot the book in a drawer, yank it out, and flip to dog breeders. There it is. I reach for the phone and start to punch in the number. I stop. How the hell am I going to explain this? Must be an easier way. I flip the pages of the phone book again until I find the SPCA. No mention of hours. I try to read the phone number but it keeps jumping on the page so I plant one finger under it and lean closer until it becomes legible. I repeat it over and over, like a mantra, until it registers in my brain. I say it again while I am pushing the numbers on the phone. Someone picks up immediately. My heart races. What am I going to say? Wait, it's just a voice message. A sigh of relief gushes from me. I listen to the recording until I hear what I want. "Noon to five on Saturdays." I hang up.

Only 9:30 now. What am I going to do for the next couple of hours? I drop my gaze to Lady who is following my every footstep. She is just standing there, brown eyes shining, waiting for instruction. *What do we do next, Dad?* Her tail sways, stops, sways again. Jesus. I look away. Can't play with her, too painful to play with her, but want to do something nice, maybe something to prove I'm not evil. Huh. She needs a bath. Maybe the SPCA people won't think so badly of me if I see that she is well-groomed before I drop her off.

Maybe that makes no sense, but I have to do something. Prefer to sit and drink, but I promised Sarah. Make a lot of promises these days. Never seem to be able to keep them.

Not about to groom Lady myself—couldn't stand all that one-to-one. Not when I'm about to give her up. I open my wallet and check my cash. Not enough. So I go to Sarah's hiding place, behind the door in the walk-in closet, where she stashed all the money from recent garage sales. She thinks I don't know. Huh. I open a pink shoe box and remove fifty dollars.

Then I leash Lady, take her to the car, and put her into the front seat. This is not the usual arrangement, but Lady seems very pleased. She has always loved to look out the window, and the front seat gives her maximum view. I don't really want her there beside me, so close that I feel her every breath or see every strand of escaped fur float in front of me like dandelions on a breeze. But today, I have no choice. I need the trunk and back seat for her kennel and dog food. So Lady must sit in the front.

When I'm sure I have everything, I get behind the wheel and, without an appointment, drive to the Pet Smart store which is about twenty minutes away. Know for sure that they groom dogs. Not a chance I'm going to a local groomer today—might see, or worse, be seen by, someone I know.

Lucky for me, it's a slow day in the grooming department at this particular Pet Smart. An eager woman smiles as she records my information, takes my money, and reaches for my dog. With ease, I relinquish the leash to her and watch as she escorts Lady to a step-up tub. Lady doesn't look back; she knows this woman will do her no harm. She trusts me. Lady trusts me. An arctic shiver sifts through my body and tears spring to my eyes. I gulp and turn away. My feet stumble as I head toward the exit.

Once outside, I look around. I need a refuge, a waiting place. Nearby, there is a coffee shop. Good. I hurry toward it, push open the door, go to the front counter and place my order.

While the clerk moves to the coffee machine, my eyes travel the room. I spy an empty table in a far corner and, as soon as money and coffee have changed hands, I rush to it . . . have to move quickly before anyone else spots it. Putting the cup onto the table, I sit facing the counter, and shove my hands into my pockets. While my right hand is twisting off the cap of an airplane-sized vodka bottle in my coat pocket, I again look all around. *No one will notice*, I tell myself. The bottle, completely covered by my hand, emerges. With a deft motion, I add vodka to coffee and return the bottle to its hiding place. Smiling, I lift my coffee cup. Steam rises and the aroma of coffee, just coffee, permeates my nostrils. My smile widens. Vodka is deceptive. Secretive. Like me.

No need to guzzle this drink. Just knowing it's there eases my anxiety. I clutch the cup and blow on the coffee to cool it. Little ripples travel across the surface of the liquid. I blow again. And again. And then I gulp. Once, twice, three times. I let out a sigh as my body eases into the effects of the mixed drink. Great combination, caffeine and alcohol. One kicks, the other calms. Yep, great combination. Right now, it's perfect for me.

It's a tough thing that I'm going to do today. Damn tough. *Not fair that I have to be the one to do this, Sarah. Not fair at all. I need a drink, just to take the edge off.* So, for about forty-five minutes, I sit there, taking the edge off. Sipping my way through one mixed drink. Ordering a coffee refill. Adding more vodka. Sipping my way through that. After I have emptied the second cup, I raise it to my nose and sniff. Just to be sure. Can't smell anything. Even if I could, no one would know it was me. Would anyone even care? I doubt it. I take my cup to the disposal area and place it on the tray with the rest of the dirty dishes.

My bladder complains so I head to the washroom and empty it. Then I stand at the sink, staring into the mirror. I snort in contempt at the man who stares back. Pumping the soap container, I turn on the faucet and wash my hands. When I look back at the mirror, the man is still there, the son of a bitch. I wash my hands again, lathering twice. This time I don't look at the mirror; I keep my head low as I go to the paper towel rack, yank off a sheet and rub vigorously. Time to go back to Pet Smart, to Lady.

It's 11:15 when I see Lady. She looks beautiful, so clean and shiny. When she shakes, her long fur floats around her like the hair on a wind-blown runway model. She wags her tail furiously when she sees me. I pay the bill and claim her. Lady jumps up with excitement. I forget, for just a minute. I forget and I drop to my knees so I can hug her and stroke her and whisper sweet things to her. But then I remember and tears cloud my eyes. I blink them back as I stand.

"You have a beautiful dog," says the groomer.

"Yes, yes, I do," I reply.

All the way to the car, I keep my head low. I open the passenger door. "Up, Lady."

Lady jumps in. I close the door behind her, walk around the front of the Lexus, and get behind the wheel.

It's early when we arrive at the SPCA. Not surprising as it's only a fifteen minute drive. I have no intention of waiting around. I park across the street, get out and remove the dog crate from the back. I'm a robot now as I go to the passenger side, pick up Lady's leash, and pull her out. I slam the car door shut with my foot. Lady jumps.

"Sorry, girl."

With the leash in one hand and the crate in the other, I stand beside the car, checking both directions for oncoming traffic. Safe. I glance down at Lady who is sitting by my side, just waiting for my next move. She raises her head and our eyes meet. God, I love her. Goddamn, how I love her. *Maybe I can turn back. Maybe I can find a way out of this. Maybe we can keep her.* A car whizzes by, jolting me back into reality, and I know it's too late for maybes. I lift my head. No more looking at Lady. I check the traffic flow once again and march forward until I am standing near the SPCA entrance. I look all around. I'm getting good at this . . . looking, lurking, skulking. My life is a series of secrets. As soon as I am sure no one is watching, I drop the crate onto the ground, bend, and unlatch the wire door.

"Go to your room, Lady." A harsh command. Damn it all, I have to look at her.

Lady tilts her head. Question marks in her eyes. Her tail droops. Her body trembles.

"Go to your room." My voice is softer this time.

Lady obeys.

I undo her leash and deposit it inside the crate. My fingers fumble to remove her collar with its telltale ID tags. Can't leave the collar so I slip it into my pocket. I snap the wire door closed and slide the lock. There. I've done it.

Imprisoned her. And now for part two: abandoning her. I straighten, spin on my heel, and walk away.

Lady whines.

I stop.

My gut screams at me to run back and get her and take her home and pretend that none of this ever happened. *Maybe I can* . . . No. There are no more maybes. Can't. Can't go back.

My feet pound across the sidewalk to the asphalt and then to the car. Lady's crying crescendos until it roars in my ears.

As I scramble to open the car, I break into tears. I ram the key into the ignition, and rev the engine to cover the howling from Lady. Sobs rip from my gut. I slam the gearshift into drive and speed off.

Blocks away, I remember: the dog food is still in the car. No way I'm going back to the damn shelter. I pull over to the first Dumpster I see, haul the bag from the back, and toss it into the trash.

The dog collar is burning a hole in my pocket, but I can't throw it out. Have to destroy the tags. I root around in the glove box for the emergency kit. Take out the tiny scissors. Sit and sob as I scrape the existence of Lady from our lives. I climb out of the car again and throw away the collar.

Then I roar away.

How the hell am I going to tell Bobby?

42

SLIM HOLD

February, 2010

What did Bobby say?"

I hold up a hand in a feeble attempt to ward off the question. My throat is tight and tears are not far off. I turn and stare at the ficus. Another leaf drops. "Maybe I should get the tree some water." I glance back at Steve.

He rolls his eyes, picks up his Diet Coke, leans over, and holds the can above the planter. "Should I just give it a caffeine jolt?"

My eyes flash. Somewhere deep inside me, frayed nerves dance like downed wires in a thunderstorm. The hair on the back of my neck stands up. "You trying to kill it?" I ask.

Steve shakes his head. "Not a chance." He leans back. "No more than you were trying to hurt Lady. It surprises me that you actually went through with it, though. I would have been willing to bet you couldn't." He stops and the silence hangs like a broken pendulum. He's dying for me to comment, I know, but I have no words now. After a few seconds, he sighs in acceptance and ticks off the next question on his list . . . "So, how did you tell Bobby?"

I turn my gaze to the tree. Some branches are barren now; some are dotted with leaves—curled, shriveled leaves—which are on the verge of renouncing their slim hold on life. One slight tremor; that's all it would take. One miniscule push and they would all rain to the carpet, to the funeral pile on the carpet. How much damage can one tree take? How much damage can one person take? How am I supposed to fix that tree without repotting the whole thing? How am I supposed to fix me? I swallow and look away. It takes a concerted effort to rise from my chair, but I manage it. I head toward the door.

"Where you going, bud?"

One foot moves, then the other. *I'm walking away*, bud. *Just walking away.*

"What about Bobby? What did you tell him?"

I keep going. Pad my way through the hall. To my room. To my bed. I lie down. Stare up. No images on the ceiling this time. A blank slate.

Steve calls. "Justin? Justin? Justin?"

No need to respond; he'll give up. This I know and I am right. Soon, all is silent.

I focus on the ceiling, pretending that everything's fine, pretending that Bobby is down the hall, playing. I listen for the sounds of his laughter. Here it comes . . .

A distant rumble enters my ears. Laughter, but damn, it is not Bobby's. It is low and slow at first. Then a steady crescendo, escalating until the bulk of my body pulsates. Memory flashes and I'm back in the Dumpster. The laughter, the freight train laughter, thunders through my head. I jump up and pace the room, back and forth, back and forth. Still the laughter roars. I clamp my hands over my ears but the noise escalates. My mouth drops open and a throat-burning scream tears its way out. I gasp, break into sobs, and plummet to my knees.

Suddenly, Steve is there. "Justin, are you okay? Justin?" He drops down beside me and puts an arm around my shoulder.

'Leave me alone." I growl as I push him away.

"Easy, Justin. I just want to help . . . "

"Shut up. Just shut the fuck up."

Steve puts his hands out, palms facing me. He stands, backs up, and hovers nearby.

"Get out, asshole. Get the hell out of here." I pound my fists on the floor and let out another primal screech.

Out of the corner of my eye, I can still see Steve's shoes. Son of a bitch is not leaving. Screw him.

I thrust my hand into my pocket. Nothing. Where the hell is it? I try another pocket and another, all the while sobbing. No sign of it. I suck in a deep breath and hold it. Can't let go. Finally, when I find what I'm looking for, the breath rockets from my body. I wrap my fingers around the castle, Bobby's castle, and clench like a vise grip. More deep breaths. Over and over. Inhale. Exhale. Counting . . . one, two, three . . . six, seven, eight . . . fifteen, sixteen . . . twenty-seven, twenty-eight. Slowly, my body calms. It's okay. Everything's okay. Exhaustion takes over. I crawl to the bed, climb in, start to drift off.

Last thing I hear is Steve's footsteps, retreating.

Steve doesn't ask anything about Bobby the next morning. We're sitting at the kitchen table and he looks at me with inquisitive eyes, but he doesn't ask.

I squirm, look away and focus on my coffee. Greasy, black coffee. Drinking lots of it. Caffeine. Need the caffeine. It's *one* addiction I *can* have. Caffeine. Huh. An image pops into my head . . . Steve with the Diet Coke can, threatening to caffeinate the ficus. I smirk and turn toward him.

He raises his eyebrows. "What's that about?"

"You . . . with your Diet Coke can— locked and loaded. Holding a tree hostage." A guttural laugh escapes me.

Steve's face reddens. "Yeah, well sometimes getting words out of you is darn near impossible. I was getting desperate."

I nod. "Couldn't talk about it."

"I know. Sorry. I pushed too hard."

I pause, waiting for him to question me, expecting my resistance to jump to the fore. But he doesn't ask and I feel no need to struggle. "I went to Douglas Park," I volunteer.

"Excuse me?"

"After I dropped off the dog, I went to Douglas Park." My amusement fades and I know I'm slipping down . . . back to the dark side. I squirm in my chair. Damn. Maybe I should have kept my mouth shut. Too late now.

"I see." He pulls his notebook from his pocket. "Where's Douglas Park?"

"A couple of blocks from the house." Damn again. I close my eyes in an effort to block the pain that I know is coming; in a strange way it works. As the memories of the event surface, so do the feelings. Painful, yes, but, on that particular day, the pain was subdued by alcohol and that's the way I remember it now. Not totally unpleasant. I shrug and let the images slide from past to present.

"I parked the car. Pulled a 7 Up bottle from under the driver's seat and opened it. Let the vodka slide down my throat. It warmed me up . . . *and* calmed me down."

"You just sit there and drink?"

"No. I thought I might look suspicious just sitting in my car. Didn't want any neighborhood watch groups to alert the police, so I got out to take a stroll." My eyes open wide and I stare at Steve. "I was just like other local residents, enjoying a day in the park."

43

DOUGLAS PARK

September, 2009

I stop at the southeast corner of the park and sit on a bench. It's a little after twelve and the sun is glaring down. Feels warm. Hot, actually. I loosen my jacket and stare straight ahead at the maple trees that line the perimeter of the park. The leaves are flooded with color—gold, red, brown. Just like the trees at Mount Allison, years ago. That much colder autumn day when I met, and fell for, Sarah.

Three bicycles whiz past on the gravel trail in front of me: a man, a woman, a little boy. A family. A whole family. The key word there is 'whole.' Clear as glass that they're happy. Resentment churns my gut and I scowl. Damn.

My family is not happy. It's like cracked glass, with spider veins extending, threatening ruin. Maybe beyond repair. One more hit could shatter it completely. Huh. One more hit. Telling Bobby. That might do it. I gulp, wipe my lips, and continue to drink.

Don't know how long I sit there. I only know that when the bottle is empty, I rise and stumble back to the car. I drive to the house and park in the street, only because I am too drunk to maneuver the vehicle into the back lane. As I fumble with the front door keys, I hear an engine rev behind me. I turn. A tow truck pulls up and parks directly in front of my car. Two men emerge. One runs to me.

"Justin Wentworth?"

I nod. Know what's coming.

"Repossessing your car, sir." He thrusts a paper at me and hurries away. The two men ignore me as they hook my car to the tow truck.

Jesus. What am I doing, standing here, swaying like I'm on a boat dock? Can't watch this crap. I unlock the front door and stagger into the house. My lips are dry again. There must be more booze around here somewhere. I head through the house and into the garage where I keep all the 7 Up bottles. Kicking aside junk-filled boxes, I drop to the floor and root around on all fours, sniffing and snorting like a pig searching for truffles.

The odor hits first, the unmistakable, heavenly aroma of alcohol. Damn it all. Did I break the bottles? Panic sweeps my brain.

Gotta find it. Gotta find it. I crawl on a blue tarp, swearing and sobbing as shards of broken glass pierce the plastic and work their way into my knees.

Jesus. It's all gone. I broke all the bottles. I extend my arm, grab the corner of the tarp and lift it. I fall over onto my hip so I can pull the tarp completely out of the way. Relief belches from my body.

Thank the Lord. There they are. All my green bottles. Stashed away in a corner. Safe and sound. Not broken after all. Laughter erupts from the pit of my stomach. Of course, they're not broken, idiot. They're *plastic.* I seize one bottle, twist off the cap and sit and drink.

After a while, I peek under the tarp, looking for broken glass. And there it is . . . remnants of an old whiskey bottle. That explains the smell of booze and the shards of glass. I wonder if my knees are bleeding. I don't feel any pain so I don't bother to check. Dropping the tarp, I continue to drink. Just a few more sips. Then I slide into a curled position, comfortable, clinging, like a contented infant, to my bottle.

Next thing I know, Sarah's voice screams in my ear. "Justin! Justin!" She is shaking me. "Justin!"

I moan.

"Damn it all, Justin, I've been looking all over for you. You're drunk! Son of a bitch. You promised. You just get your ass up this instant. Bobby wants to know where Lady is. You are going to get into the shower and then you are going to talk to your son."

Her words are stilettos, piercing my skull. I moan again.

She pulls me into a seated position.

"Sarah, I love you and I love Bobby . . . "

Thwack! My head snaps to the side.

Jesus Christ! She hit me. Sarah, my Sarah, hit me. I fall back to the floor.

"On your feet, Mister." Sarah pulls me up again.

I don't resist. Up to my knees, then to my feet. I lean on Sarah as she drags me into the house and through the house and to the master *en suite*. Sarah opens the shower door, shoves me in and turns on the water. Then she's in there with me, clothes and all.

"Fuck! That's cold!"

She seizes a fistful of my hair, snaps my head back, and thrusts my face under the freezing spray.

Glug. Glug. I cough and sputter.

Sarah reaches for the top button on my shirt. As she undoes it, I plant my hands on her breasts. "Sarah. Sa-rah." I'm singing now.

Sarah's punches me in the gut. I crumble and throw up.

"Disgusting!" Sarah rips open the shower door and jumps out.

Curled up in a ball now, I watch as water, tears, and vomit spin down the drain. I'm staying here. In a holding pattern. Staying here until I die. Right here. Fully clothed. Cowering in my own shower. Lathered in my own vomit. *Die, asshole, die.* Death means freedom. Freedom from facing Bobby, from telling Bobby that I abandoned Lady. Abandoned her, as she cried out for me. A new wave of nausea hits, and I spew my guts again. Jesus. Maybe I can go get Lady. No way they'd give her back. *Die, asshole, die.*

No such luck. Sarah is back. In the shower with me again. Naked this time. Pulling me up and then propping me up as she unhooks the shower hose from the wall and rinses away the vomit. She returns the shower head to the wall and goes back to undressing me. Opening the shower door, she tosses each soggy item of clothing into the sink. Then she massages my scalp and soaps every inch of my body. She suddenly breaks into sobs and clings to me.

"Dear God, Justin. How can you let this happen? I love you. Jesus, I still love you." She slides against me, encourages me, takes my hands in hers and leads them to her breasts.

Instinctively, I recoil. But Sarah, my Sarah, pulls my hands to her again and I moan in gratitude. My body returns to its senses and responds. I slip into her, allow her to do all the work while I lean on the wall. It surprises me that my cock can even hold an erection and yet, here I am, on the receiving end of undeserved release.

Only once do I glance into her eyes. Only once. In there, I witness something cold, something final. I immediately turn away. I can't help but wonder about the tears on her face. Are they hers? Are they mine? Are they droplets from the shower? I don't know. I don't ask.

Sarah keeps whispering. "We have to get back on track, Justin. We can start over, but you have to tell Bobby. It will break his heart, but you have to tell him." We stay there as the water turns warm, hot, warm, and back to cold again. She twists off the faucet, steps out and puts on her robe. I follow, grabbing a towel which I wind around my body. She shoves a thermal mug toward me. Pungent odor. Coffee. My stomach writhes. Holding my hand over my gut, I turn away.

"Damn it all, Justin. Take the fucking coffee."

In that instant, I know that our romantic interlude, or whatever it was that occurred in the shower, is over.

Sarah sighs. "Justin, you need the coffee." She steps closer. "Here." She thrusts the cup under my nose.

I take the coffee, look into her hard, cold eyes, and nod. I'm not going to die, damn it. Not today. No freedom by death for me. No easy out for me. The only way out of this is through it . . . I have to tell Bobby.

In between gulps of coffee, I blow dry my hair and shave.

Sarah brings me clean clothes. She brushes against me as she passes, and I smile at her but she turns and walks away. A chill hits me. A winter chill. Maybe there has been a death after all. The death of a marriage.

I place the coffee mug on the counter and get dressed, slowly, deliberately. Then I sit on the toilet and finish my coffee.

"Time to talk to Bobby, Justin." Sarah stands in the doorway, fully dressed, arms folded. "After you do that, we'll talk about AA." She pulls a tissue from her pocket and dries her eyes. "I really *don't* want to lose you."

"Even after today?"

"You heard what I said. But you have to get professional help."

I gulp and nod. Thank God. No deaths today after all. "Where's Bobby?"

"He's at the neighbor's house. I just called. He'll be here any second."

As if on cue, the front door slams. "Mom! Dad! I'm home!"

Sarah and I head downstairs. I'm in front. Don't like it, but I'm in front. I'm in charge now. *Yeah, right. Who am I trying to kid?*

At the foot of the stairs, Bobby jumps into my arms.

"Dad! Where were you?"

I forget everything for a few seconds as I hold him. The winter chill hits me again. I shiver and struggle to inhale the scent of my son. Somewhere in my soul I know I am creating a memory. The smell of his shampoo infiltrates, lingers. I remember Lady's freshly-shampooed fur. My body stiffens.

Bobby wriggles out of my arms. "What's wrong, Dad?"

I stare at my empty hands as he slides away from me.

"Dad, what's wrong? Are you okay?"

"I'm fine, son, I'm fine."

Bobby smiles, but not for long. He looks around. "Where's Lady?"

"Son, I'm sorry . . . " I extend a hand but he slaps it away.

"Where's Lady?" he demands again. His eyes darken.

I can't look at him. I cast my gaze to Sarah who is standing beside us. She looks away. She, *my* Sarah, looks away. I am alone. It's winter and I am alone. I have to say something.

"Where's Lady?" Bobby is yelling now.

"Son, I'm sorry," I whisper," but we just couldn't keep Lady. We have to leave this house and move into a small apartment where they don't allow dogs."

Bobby screeches as he flies at me, fists flailing. His punches land, pounding me in the ribs, in the stomach.

I grab his arms. "I had to take Lady away," I yell to be heard over Bobby's screams. I continue to yell, saying anything I can think of just so I can get past this moment in time. "I took her to a place where she will have lots of room. To a farm, Bobby, a farm that has lots of other dogs." The lies take the edge off Bobby's outburst, so I add more. "Lady will have many friends; there are at least five other retrievers there, just like her."

"I want my Lady, I want my Lady," Bobby sobs. He's stops flailing now so I let him go. He runs to Sarah and, as her arms envelop him, his body goes limp. She picks him up, glares at me, and carries him toward the stairs.

"He's heavy, Sarah. Let me help." I reach out my arms.

"You stay away from me!" Bobby pops his head up from Sarah's shoulder and he points an accusing finger at me. "You took my Lady. You promised I would always have Lady. You broke your promise."

"Son, I'm sorry . . ."

"You promised." He scrambles to get out of Sarah's arms. She releases him and he runs. Up the steps. Screaming at me. "You promised. Remember? I promised you I wouldn't tell Mommy and you promised I would always have Lady." His feet hammer the upstairs hallway toward his room. The door slams. His cries echo through the house.

44

FINANCIAL MISTAKES

February, 2010

I sit still, elbows on table, head in hands, as Bobby's agonized screams spiral in my brain. I comb my fingers through my hair and clamp my hands over my ears but the torture persists. *Dear God.* I lace my fingers behind my head, locking them tight. Still no reprieve.

"So, what was the promise?" Steve asks. His voice, although loud and demanding, is welcome for it severs the screams, gifting me with inner silence. Gratitude washes over me and I take a deep breath. In measured motion, I remove my hands from my head and pivot toward him, determined to answer him. But the second I open my mouth, Bobby's screams filter in again. I cringe and drop my head. I don't want to talk any more. Not at all. But I have to try, damn it. I have to try. I lift my head, and open my mouth again, and am on the verge of emptying my soul . . .

"Darn!" Steve glances at his watch and throws his hands in the air. "Darn! Darn! Darn! I really want to hear what you have to say, bud, but it will have to wait. I'm so sorry. If I don't leave this instant, I'll be late. I cannot skip this class today." He leans over, puts a hand on my shoulder. His eyes are shining with apology. "We'll get back to this later, okay?"

"Yeah." Relief goes through me like a landslide, but doesn't last long. Anger rumbles in behind it. *You've taken me down this path,* bud, *and now you're leaving me here, memories dangling?* Huh. I am totally pissed at Steve.

"I really am sorry." Closing his notebook, Steve jumps to his feet.

Screw you. You're not getting away with this, bud. "The promise was no big deal, really," I say, loud, clear, determined.

He pauses, looks at me, and rolls his eyes. "Okay, so you're angry. I get it. But . . . *'no big deal'*? Are you kidding me? You drove your family into bankruptcy . . . " He puts his hands out, palms facing me. "Look . . . whatever the promise . . . the point is, *you reneged.* I'm sure it *was* a big deal . . . to Bobby *and* Sarah." He checks his watch again. "Darn. I'm late. I *really am* sorry, but I have no more time for this now." He dashes down the hall and disappears through the door. *Poof!* Fast as Alice's White Rabbit.

I stare after him, mouth gaping. Huh. Guess I'm stuck here, mad as hell, with Bobby's distress and Sarah's rage revving in my brain. What was it Steve said? . . . *it was a big deal?* I shake my head. No way. I didn't get why Sarah was so mad then and I don't get it now. She never erupted before that . . . not over the spending, the drinking, the bankruptcy. So why that day? Just a minor accident, that's all it was, a minor accident. Bobby only had a little bump. *If it was no big deal, Wentworth, then why did you try to hide it from Sarah?* I shrug. Nah, no big deal. I screwed up, that's all. I screwed up.

Compelled to move, I rocket to my feet and look around for something to do, anything to get my mind away from that day. I rummage through cupboards until I spot a plastic jug. Huh. Guess I can water the ficus. I fill the jug and amble to the den.

As I pour the water, as the ficus welcomes it, I extend one hand and touch a leaf. It drops, just like I knew it would. My fingers recoil and I shudder.

Damn it, my eyes are flooding again . . . like dripping faucets. I can't seem to be able to shut off the tears for any length of time, no matter how hard I try. I drag my sleeve across my face, stare at the nearly-naked branches and then drop my gaze to the crisp, departed leaves on the floor. I put down the pitcher, sit on my haunches and gather up the dead leaves, handful after handful. I rub each handful into dust particles and deposit them into a nearby wastebasket. As I brush dust from my hands, it occurs to me that I may not be able to save this tree. This needy tree.

Hmmmph. What about saving myself? Can I do that? What do I need in order to get my life back? Food? *Check.* Got that. Shelter? Another *check.* AA? I guess. I don't know. Anxiety ripples through me, and my whole body squirms. I grab the pitcher and rush it back to its place in the kitchen. I look around. What's next?

My angst revs up, kicks into near-panic mode. I begin pacing, back and forth, back and forth, in a narrow line, like the caged panther I once saw at the zoo. All that power and might and black velvet beauty, confined, permanently broken. No options. Stuck in the moment, just pacing. What are my options? Beyond Steve and AA? What's next? I don't know. *Only know I have to do this one day at a time, like every other person working the steps.* Yeah, yeah, yeah. AA. Could call my sponsor, if I had one. Got to get one soon. I could go to a meeting. Is there a meeting? I check the calendar. Guess not. Not for a few hours anyway.

I can't stand still so I dash to the living room, snatch the remote, and switch on the TV. I scan the guide. Searching. Searching. All the while shifting from one foot to the other. I have to find something, anything to watch. Need something to take me away. Away from all the worrying and wondering. That stuff can kill a guy. Or drive him to drink. I have to stay away from the booze. *Can't get drunk if I don't pick up.* Yep. That's what they say at AA. *Can't get drunk if I don't pick up.* I wrap both hands around the remote.

No luck scanning the guide so I surf the channels. *Flip. Flip. Flip.* One show to another to another. Nothing. I push the guide button and page through the selections again. Tons of selections. Steve has satellite, every channel known on the planet. Still nothing. I stop shifting my feet. I turn toward the door. I stare.

There's my blue jacket, on the chair where I tossed it yesterday. The condo keys beckon from a hook beside the door. My mouth is drying up and my hands are quaking. I gulp. My body is wriggling inside my crisp, Steve-bought clothes. How easy it would be to slink through the door, slither to Davie Street, step inside the liquor store, suck in the pungent odor of the empties that jangle in the bottle depot along the back wall. . . .

I squeeze my eyes shut. *Breathe, just breathe.* When I re-open my eyes, I'm holding the remote straight out, like I'm making an offering to some pagan idol. The PVR button jumps into view. Desperate, I swerve back toward the TV and push the PVR button. Gotta find something to keep me here, anything to keep me away from the jacket and the keys and the door. I scan: a couple of movies, a few CSI episodes, a smattering of sit-coms. The last thing on the list, the only thing that catches my eye, is some program about entitlement. A documentary? I lean in. *Click.* Select. *Click.* Start.

As soon as I realize that the show centers on overspending, I flinch. Who the hell wants to listen to that? Not me. Yet, the compulsion to run seems to have passed, so I plop onto the couch and sit there, disgusted, sneering, as people divulge secrets. Spending, spending, and more spending. *They want this. They deserve that.* No thought to what they can afford. All of them morons, no doubt.

Despite the current of contempt streaming through my veins, I watch the entire show. I jeer at a man who purchased a luxury car he couldn't afford because his economy vehicle couldn't pass muster at work. When another guest flashes his twenty-five hundred dollar watch into the camera, a watch that he purchased to impress clients, I snort. "Huh. Twenty-five hundred dollars. That's all? My Rolex cost more than that. What an absolute idiot!"

My body shoots to a standing position. Jesus H. Christ! I'm the idiot! I was just like the people on the show, *a thief,* buying all kinds of things I knew I couldn't pay for. Things I was sure I *needed* and *deserved.* Things that would impress other people. I never, ever gave any thought to consequence. *This* consequence. It never occurred to me that I could lose everything.

"You drove your family into bankruptcy . . ." Isn't that what Steve said just before he left? Holy shit! *He was right.* He was right.

I raise my hand to throw the remote at the screen. But I stop in midpitch. I tighten my grip, locking my fingers around the remote until they turn white. I move my thumb only to rewind. Then I sit and watch the whole damn thing again.

When it's over, I turn off the TV and relinquish the remote, dropping it onto the coffee table.

Exhausted, I sprawl on the couch. *I'm not the only one. Can't believe that I'm not the only one.* Maybe I can deal with all of this. Maybe it's time to deal with all of this. Am I ready? My heart is racing like an Indy car. My head's reeling like I'm having bed spins. Jesus. How can I be ready? My body's crawling with anxiety; full-blown panic is not far behind. I rocket from the couch and begin pacing. My brow is sluicing sweat but my mouth is dry, rough, like sandpaper. I slide my tongue over my parched lips. My body freezes. Booze. I need booze. Booze is like a mute button—silences everything. I definitely need booze. The liquor store. The solution.

I help myself to the money waving from the fridge magnet and head to the door. I grab my condo keys from their hook. Huh. Dangling from the hook next to mine is the key to Steve's BMW. Why didn't he take his car? *Maybe I should drive.* I seize the key, charge through the door, and pound down the stairs.

At the door to underground parking, I pause. I wipe my mouth with the back of my hand and realize that I'm still holding the money from the fridge. I shove it into my pocket and, as I'm doing that, my fingers graze something buried there. I take a deep breath, reach in a little further and pull out Bobby's castle. I stare at it for a long time, seeing my boy's smile. And hearing a voice, a woman's voice, not Sarah's. No. Not Sarah's. The voice is my mother's.

'S-o-n and s-u-n,' she says. Just a whisper. That's all.

I take a deep breath, do a slow pivot, and climb the stairs. Back to the condo. Back to the couch. I sit. Then, clinging to Bobby's castle, I lie down, determined to unleash every negative feeling. Feelings pass, they tell me . . .

Shame leaps to the foreground, twisting my gut into knots. I recoil, drawing my knees to my chest and hold them there. I offer no resistance to the ticker tape of transgressions that batters my mind: *Choosing the Rolex over my wedding ring. What kind of ass chooses a fucking Rolex over the symbol of his marriage? Abandoning Bobby's dog. No, you gutless asshole, not just Bobby's dog. Not just Sarah's dog. My dog. My Lady. A member of my family. What family, idiot? All gone now. All my fault. Spending. Spending. In over my head. Spending. No thought to consequence. No thought to losing my family. Bankrupt. Penniless. Homeless. Ruined. Destroyed everything. Everything. Everything.*

I lie there for a long time. Or maybe it just seems like a long time. When the pain subsides, I unravel my body, bit by bit. My hands release their grasp on my skull and then push against the cushions to propel my body into a seated position. My feet swing around and drop onto the floor. I lean forward and look around. I am still here. Sweating, but here. Shaking, but here. And . . . damn it all, I'm sober. Stone-cold sober.

I blink repeatedly, then stand and sway until I am sure of my footing. I plod down the hall to the bathroom where I strip and step into the shower. Twisting the tap, I deliberately let the cold water shock my body.

Along with that shock, a new awareness pricks my brain: All the time that I was spending, spending, spending, I *knew* exactly what I was doing. I chose it. I watched it. *I knew.* I knew what was coming. Yet, I kept doing it. Pushing and pushing the envelope. Why the hell did I do that? Why? I shake my head and water flies from my hair. I have no idea why. *Asshole.*

I plant my hands on the walls of the shower and lock myself in that position as the pulsating water changes to lukewarm, then to hot, then to scalding. Punishing heat. Well-earned, punishing heat. Wash away everything.

As the water cools again, my thoughts return to the documentary. I smile as it occurs to me that Steve recorded that show before he met me. Guess the debt angle is all part of his research. What a hell of a find I must have been for him. A hell of a find. And what a lucky bastard I am.

I don't apply soap until the shower's temperature has turned to ice. Lather and scrub. Lather and scrub. Washing the feelings away. Clean. Shiny. New. Until next time.

Until next time. Yes, there will be a next time. I am sure of that. But now, I know that if I stay with the feelings, the pain will subside. It will leave, for a while at least. *Until next time.* I turn off the shower. Step out. Towel off. I need sleep and I don't fight the need. I just go to my room and crawl into bed where it is comfortable and soft. Don't know how long I sleep, but when I wake up, Steve is home. I can hear him singing.

I smile and stretch. I should go and talk to Steve. I would like to thank him for food, shelter, even for recording the TV program. But sleep beckons, dragging me back into comfort and warmth and peace. Tomorrow. I'll thank him tomorrow.

45

STALL TACTIC

O nly a week left before Olympics now," Steve says the next morning as he examines the calendar attached to the fridge. He lingers there, stabbing his finger at the scrawling red letters that read "Opening Ceremony." He looks at me out of the corner of his eye, and then shrugs. Yanking open the fridge door, he pulls out the orange juice. "OJ?" He planks the container on the counter, reaches into the cupboard, and takes out two glasses.

"Nah. Just having coffee this morning." I'm sitting at the table, watching him. Curious. What was that sideways glance about?

"Okay." Steve returns one glass to the cupboard. He opens the juice and pours it, slowly, deliberately. He's considering tactics. I just know it. He's going to delve into conversation any second. He's going to ask me stuff, stuff I don't want to dredge up. Not now. Not while I'm still feeling good from yesterday. What was my plan? Oh, yeah. To thank him. Got to do it now before Steve steers me down another path or before the gratitude sensation evaporates completely. Got to do it now . . .

"Steve, I can't begin to tell you how much I appreciate everything you are doing for me." There. I said it. Never thanked anyone for anything my whole life. Well, I did; even thanked Steve before, but I didn't really mean it. Never, ever meant it . . . until now.

"Huh? Oh, yeah. No big deal, bud." In slow motion, he closes the orange juice carton and returns it to the fridge. He picks up his glass from the counter and stands there, his back to me.

Damn. He's dismissing me. Just like that. But I'm not done yet. I have to make my point. "It's a big deal to me." My voice is loud. Confident. I like that. I keep talking. "You took me off the street. You could have picked anyone for this research, and you took me off the street. I'm grateful, Steve. Beyond grateful."

His shoulders droop. "Yeah, yeah, yeah, I get it," he mutters, "but maybe I didn't want to pick just anyone."

"What do you mean?"

"Well, maybe someone or something led me to you."

"Oh." The born-again bit. "If you're going all Jesus Saves on me, *bud*, you can just drop it. Not interested."

Steve is silent. His back straightens and his shoulders rise and fall—a conciliatory shrug. "Good enough. So . . . you want to tell me about Bobby today, bud? What promise was he talking about?"

I drum my fingers on the table and stare at the greasy swirls in my black coffee. Out of the corner of my eye, I see Steve swing around. Orange juice sloshes from his glass to the floor, splattering his white, very white sports socks.

"Darn it!" Steve drops down and swishes a white, very white, paper towel over the floor until it becomes sodden and carroty. "Did you hear me, bud?"

I keep my eyes on my coffee cup. How does grease get into coffee anyway?

"Hey, bud. You listening? You gonna to tell me about the promise?"

My head snaps up. "I heard you the first time."

"Well?" He opens the cupboard door under the sink and drops the paper towel into the trash.

"Well, what?"

Steve slams the cupboard door and whips around. "You know damn well what!"

My eyes pop wide. "Did you just say 'damn'— an unprompted 'damn'?"

"You don't have a monopoly on swear words, bud."

Huh. Maybe I'm just angry with the way Steve brushed off my thanks. I don't know, but I am deliberately pushing all his buttons. It's working, too. Born-again Steve is pissed.

Steve rockets to the table and grabs my arm. "Listen, bud, we had a deal. I give you shelter. You tell me your story. Remember?"

End of enjoyment. I glare into his eyes and instantly flash on the hospital. The nurse with the angel tattoo and the compassionate eyes. The doctor with the stethoscope and the pitying eyes. And now, here's Steve with the *Jesus Saves* belt buckle and the . . . what?

"So tell me, Steve, after I finish splaying my guts, after you bleed every piece of information from me, then what? Where do I go then?" Huh. I'm stunned by my own question. I thought I was over the fear of getting kicked out. Guess not. I hold my breath.

He releases my arm, stands straight, and sets his jaw tight. "You can stay here, of course," he says, looking down at me. "When you're better, completely better, I'll help you find a place. And a job."

"I see." I stare up and narrow my gaze. I remember Debra now, searching my eyes, looking for a "tell." I could never lie to Debra. To Sarah either. My eyes always betrayed me. Maybe Steve has a "tell." I peer into his eyes. A nanosecond flash. What is that? Guilt? What does he have to be guilty about? I look harder, but whatever was there, is gone.

"I mean it, bud," Steve drawls, emphasizing every syllable. "You can count on me. I will help you."

Steve's saying exactly what I need to hear. But those eyes? Something glitters again. Damn. What the hell is it? I don't have a clue and I can't ask. Question restricted due to fear of consequence: getting kicked to the curb. I'm a guest here, yes, but I'm a prisoner, too, confined like the panther at the zoo.

I press my lips together and nod, slowly.

There's a deep sigh from Steve. He turns and goes to the counter, retrieves his orange juice glass, and refills it. "Okay, then, now that that's settled, tell me about Bobby. What promise was he talking about?" He pads back from the fridge and drops into the chair across from me.

I sip the coffee. Cold. Ice cold. I know I need to talk now. Something's up with Steve. Something . . . but what? If I say nothing . . . then what? Random pictures flicker in my head: a marshmallow jacket, discarded, replaced; a ficus tree, thirsty, dying; two thugs, kicking, pounding. Damn it. That did it. The Dumpster dream has been detonated. My heart hammers and my body trembles.

Did you hire those thugs to pummel me, bud? Was it just a dream? I don't know. He's staring at me, waiting. I need to talk. To stall. To buy time to figure things out. I don't want to finish my story if it means I'll end up in the street; he says he won't do that but can I trust him? I only know I can't go back to the street. Will never see Sarah again. Will never see Bobby.

Just thinking about my wife and son sends knives of pain through me. Jesus. Will I ever get them back? I shudder as I open my mouth. "I promised Bobby . . . " I clamp my lips together and, through gritted teeth, attempt to change course. "Can we talk about something else for a while?"

"Like what?" Steve's brow crinkles into fine lines, crepe paper lines.

Don't know what. Anything. Anything. I recall swatches of conversation in which *I* was the one peppering him with questions: *Where are you from? Why do you give away money? What does your grandfather have to do with it?* I latch on to the last one. "You said something once about promising your grandfather something. What was that about?"

I hold my breath. Have I created a stall tactic? I sure as hell hope so. I need time. God help me, I need more time.

Steve's eyes widen and he lets out a low whistle. "What? My grandfather? Where the heck did that come from?"

My heart pummels my chest as my thoughts tumble into words. "You remember . . . when we were on the bus and you said you promised your grandfather that you would help people who were homeless or down on their luck or whatever. You were about to tell me more when an elderly lady got on the bus and you gave her your seat. Remember?" I lick my lips and try to breathe slowly.

Steve nods. "Oh, yeah, that. I remember. You're right. I did promise my grandfather that I would help people who were down and out."

"Why?" I relax now and continue to sip my icy coffee. I don't dare move to warm it up. Can't break the moment. A story is coming my way. Distraction created. Mission accomplished.

"Just something that concerned him. That's all. The homeless."

"Did he have anything to do with giving you all this?" I spread my arms wide, taking in the breadth of the open-concept condo.

"No." He shakes his head slowly. "He was pretty much broke when he died. Wouldn't take a penny from my parents. Trust fund is from them, remember?"

"Oh, yeah." I pause. Can't let him stop there. I plunge onward. "So how did it come about that you made a promise to him?"

"I spent a lot of time with him during his final days. He had cancer. Died just a couple of years ago."

"Oh." A fleeting veil of grief slides over, through me. "Sorry for your loss, Steve."

He shrugs. "Thanks. I wish I had spent more time with him when I was a kid. As I told you, I'm from Toronto. He lived further east."

"You never saw him when you were younger?"

"Yeah, yeah, I did. He visited us every couple of years. I think I went to *his* house one summer when I was little." Steve snaps his fingers. "Yeah, that's right. A big house with a yellow kitchen. He loved to sit in that kitchen and talk." He rolls his eyes. "Did he ever love to talk. *That* I remember."

"So, when you were a kid, he made you promise . . . ?"

"Uh uh. Not then. Much later. Before he died. And, he didn't *make* me. He asked and I agreed. But, even when I was little, he yammered on and on about money."

"So? What's that got to do with your helping street people?"

Steve's gaze drops to the floor. "Don't know. For some reason, my grandfather was obsessed with the idea." He raises his eyes and scrutinizes my face. "He told me that the important thing is to take care of your own and to try to help others. And that I should be careful with money. 'You never know when you might need it,' he said. How many times did I hear that? From the time I was very little. The same spiel over and over again. Eventually, his words were just etched into my brain."

Discomfort worms its way up my spine. Can't figure why. I pause—a short break—while I'm trying to comprehend.

Steve jumps in, turning the topic back to me. To my life. "Enough about that. Why don't you just try to tell me what happened? Bobby? The promise stuff?"

I shake my head, both in answer to Steve's question and because I'm trying to dislodge residual cobwebs regarding Steve's grandfather. I shift to a different track. "Watched one of your TV recordings yesterday."

He raises his eyebrows.

"The show about overspending."

"Hmmph. That. Well, I recorded it because it's related to my studies. Spending, economy, entitlement stuff. A hot button topic for you, I guess. Must have been a bit hard to take."

I cringe as I recall the gleam of the twenty-five hundred dollar watch. "Yeah. I bought a lot of stuff I couldn't afford in order to impress strangers if that's what you mean." I let out a laugh. "Really pissed me off when I realized that I was one of them—the entitled morons—but I watched the whole thing anyway."

"Did you always just buy what you wanted right away?"

"Pretty entitled yourself, aren't you, Steve?"

Steve roars with laughter. "Yeah, yeah. We've had this conversation. Thing is, though, this is not about me; I don't have to worry about consequence. Lots of money coming my way. But you . . . you didn't have money. So why did you think impressing strangers was so important?"

"Don't know." My body's getting restless. Maybe it would be easier just to give up stalling, to answer his questions about Bobby. "You want the rest of the story or you want to continue with psychoanalysis?"

"Sorry, bud. Go ahead."

I take a deep breath and let the words whoosh out. "I promised Bobby that he would always have Lady as long as he didn't tell Sarah about the accident."

"What accident?"

Damn. This again. I close my eyes and see the steering wheel directly in front of me, the wipers slamming back and forth. Wait a minute. Wasn't it sunny that day? Jesus. Drinking sure has screwed up my memory. I wave my hand in the air. "Nothing major. I mentioned it to you before, remember? My drinking? My judgment? Bobby got hurt? No big deal, really. I hit a few garbage cans, that's all. But Bobby was in the car. He bumped his head. I didn't want Sarah to worry, so I decided not to tell her."

"Drinking and driving? With Bobby in the car?"

"Yeah."

"Sarah must have been pissed."

"No kidding." Once again, I'm back there, watching Sarah, losing Sarah . . .

46

BROKEN

Sarah falters, steps back. Her face is ashen.

Oh, Jesus, I've broken her. Certain she will collapse into a heap, I grab her arm. She stumbles. Then she yanks her arm away and stands rigid, glaring. With a determined shake of her head, she sidesteps me and climbs the stairs. Her feet pound, pound, pound. Then stop. I know she turns because I can feel her eyes drilling into the back of my skull.

"I'm done, Justin," she hisses.

The words are a whip, lashing at me, encircling my body. I struggle to breathe. *Don't say that, Sarah. Don't say that.*

I hear her inhale—deep, long—and I pray that a retraction is coming. She can't be done. She can't be broken. Not my Sarah. Me, yes, but not my Sarah. She's the strong one. We can't both be shattered . . . not now, not at the same time.

"I told you, over and over again, that I would have lived in a garage to be with you, Justin, remember? But now? You put my son in jeopardy. I'm done!"

I cringe, turn, and begin crawling up the stairs. "Noooo . . . Sarah, I'm so sorry, Sarah. It was just a little bump. It won't happen again. I love you and I love Bobby. You have to believe me, Sarah." I extend my hand and clutch her ankle.

She shakes me off and moves backward, climbing, climbing, away from me.

"I don't know where Bobby and I will go," she announces. "But, wherever it is, we are going without you." She spins around. Her footsteps resume. *Pound. Pound. Pound.* Quick. Steady. Decisive . . . and gone.

An acute chill penetrates, infiltrates, permeates my body. I lie, prostrate and powerless, on the stairs, shuddering. Sounds drift to me from the second floor: Bobby screaming and Sarah soothing. She's taking care of him now. She's not coming back.

I slide my hands to the edge of a riser and push until my knees find solidity on a step. I'm on all fours, and I stay there until I get my bearings. Groping for the banister, I latch on and pull like a toddler trying to find his way out of a crib. I linger for a few seconds, longing to run up the stairs, to win my wife and son back.

Do it, asshole. Just do it. Just shoot up those stairs and into Bobby's room and tell them that you love them; tell them you will take care of them. But I remain still. I can't move toward them. Just can't pull the trigger. Can't do that, but I can't stay here either. I have to escape the piercing screams that emanate from Bobby's room. My wife. My son. They are in pain. I caused it. I turn and stumble down the stairs.

I plod my way through the house toward the garage. The kitchen phone rings as I pass. Without checking the call display, I pick up the receiver.

"Hello."

"Mr. Wentworth?"

"Yes."

"Mr. Wentworth, this is the Vancouver SPCA. We have your dog here. Did you drop her off? It seems that way, but we have to check. Maybe she was stolen?"

My body sags into the counter. *How the hell did they know who owned her?*

"Mr. Wentworth? We checked the microchip, and we thought we should call . . . Mr. Wentworth? Are you still there?"

Microchip. Forgot about the fucking microchip. What an idiot. *Stolen.* I latch onto the word. *Gotta get her back. For Bobby. Gotta get her back.*

"Thank God you found her! I'll be there as soon as I can." I slam the phone down. What a mess! How could I even think about abandoning Lady? But I can fix this before my family leaves. No need to let Lady go, not if . . . I glance toward the stairs and, with a sigh, pick up the phone again.

For a minute, I stare at it. Then I scan the directory and push a pre-programmed, rarely-used number: Sarah's mother.

"Marian? This is Justin. Sarah and Bobby need you . . . . they're okay, but they need you. To stay with you. Will you call back right away, after I hang up?"

I wait, biting my lip.

Her response is immediate, unquestioning. "Yes."

"Thanks, Marian." I start to hang up. "Oh . . . one more thing . . . Lady. Can Lady go with them?"

By the time, I get to the garage, the phone is ringing. Once, twice, three times . . . then, nothing. Good. Goes to message after six rings. Sarah must have answered.

I busy myself looking for my car keys. Reality hits. No car. How the hell am I going bring Lady home? *Home.* My body doubles over in pain.

Get it together, Wentworth. Got to get Lady back. I straighten, check my pockets, locate some cash. Not tons, but enough to get a cab. There's bound to be a taxi that will take us. I head through the door to the bus stop. *I'm coming, Lady.*

47

HOPE

February, 2010

Figured as much."

"Huh?"

"Lady. I knew you'd get her back somehow."

Bobby's face flashes in front of me, his eyes dark, tear-filled. I cringe. "Should never have taken her away. *Never.*"

"But you got her back, bud. Bobby must have been thrilled."

"Yeah. Still wouldn't look at me, though."

"He'll forgive you eventually."

I shake my head. "I doubt it."

"Time heals. Don't give up hope."

Hope? Tears flood my eyes and my body slumps into the chair.

Steve pauses. When he speaks again, his voice is low, tinged with concern. "You okay, bud?"

I swallow and drag my sleeve across my eyes. "Yeah, yeah. Keep going."

His sigh is long, rippled. After another brief bout of silence, he continues. "So, Sarah and Bobby went to her mother's? In Ontario?"

"Yeah. Ajax, Ontario."

"Why did *you* call Sarah's mother? Why not let Sarah do it?"

I straighten my back. "Check your notes, Steve. Sarah gave up on her family long ago, when Marian married Thomas Herrington. Sarah contacted them now and then—Christmas and birthdays. But, in all our time together, she never asked them for anything. Not a darn thing."

"You think she would have called them that day . . . I mean, if you hadn't?"

I nod. "Damn straight. Sarah would do anything for Bobby. I made the call because . . . well, it was the least I could do. I knew Sarah would accept their help. She had no other choice. I left her no choice."

"So, before that, you couldn't see that your actions were destroying your family?"

"Drunks don't have clarity, bud. I only knew that everything was chaotic, collapsing. I couldn't stop it. In the end, I just wanted my family to be safe. They're safe with Marian."

Steve reaches out and puts a hand on my arm. "You did a good thing there, Justin."

I pull away. "I screwed up. They suffered enough."

"Yeah." Steve nods. "Guess so. But, the fact that you helped them . . . that counts for something, doesn't it?"

His words catch light inside me. "Maybe. Maybe you're right. I was sure I'd lost them. But now . . . " Optimism leaps, zipping my heart into high gear. " . . . now, thanks to you, maybe there *is* hope. I'm not drinking . . . maybe I can get them back." My eyes latch onto Steve's.

Steve blinks, nods. "Maybe." He takes a sip of orange juice. "In fact, I bet you can. If you want, I'll contact them . . . "

I raise my hands, palms out. "Hell, no! Not yet. More time. I need more time . . . "

"Okay, okay. Don't panic. More time. I get it. But maybe you should give me the number . . . for later?" He slides the notepad and pen toward me.

I eye him suspiciously.

"Don't worry. Won't use the info without your say-so."

I reach for the pen but don't pick it up. "Can't remember it." I shove pen and notebook back to him. "Next question?"

Steve tilts his head. "You can't remember?"

I make a spinning motion with my arm. "We're on a roll here. Let's keep going." I stare at the notepad, heart racing. *Should I trust him, jot down the number?*

"Fine." Steve grabs the pen. "What happened next? Did Sarah and Bobby leave right away?"

My eyes are still locked on his notebook.

"Justin? Did you hear the ques . . . ?"

"Yeah, yeah," I jump in. "I hear you." I blink and lift my head, releasing notebook and pen from both view and thought. "They left a few days later. It's all a blur. Kept myself lubricated most of the time. Do know that Marian couriered airline tickets to Sarah. Paid for Lady, too."

"Were you and Sarah even on speaking terms at that point?"

"Hmmph. Not a chance."

"What do you think she told Bobby?"

"No clue. She wouldn't come near me and wouldn't let me near him. All I know is I woke up one morning and they were gone."

"They just left? No good-byes?"

My eyelids slide shut, my head drops, and the answer sighs its way out. "No. No good-byes."

"That must have gutted you. Look, you don't have to regurgitate that hell . . . "

I wave away his concern. "Already there, bud, already there." I lift my head and open my eyes . . .

48

A CAR DOOR SLAMMING

September, 2009

When I open my eyes, I hear a car door slamming. Or maybe I open my eyes *because* I hear a car door slamming. Whatever. The sound has no meaning. I'm safe inside that blank instant of awakening: no thought, no feeling. My eyes blink . . . once, twice, then a prolonged squint. I rub both eyes, propel myself from the garage floor, and plough my way through the house—mudroom, family room, and kitchen—to the bay window in the living room.

There I crouch low, very low, and peer over the window ledge. Like a spy—secretive and skulking—I watch as my wife, my son, and my dog board a Yellow Cab. The driver holds the door and then slams it. A punctuation mark. The cab roars away.

My heart plunges and my head thuds to the ledge. My body slithers down the wall and crumbles into a heap on the hardwood floor. The shiny, hardwood floor. In the house. My dream house. Huh. The dream house is an empty shell now. No furniture. No footfall. Nothing but an echo chamber for the *tick-tock, tick-tock* of the forgotten pendulum clock that hangs in the foyer. I listen as it marks the seconds.

Soon another sound joins it, a primal wail that rips from my gut and burns through my throat. Gasping for air, I scramble to all fours and struggle to my feet. Wobble, step, wait. When my footing is secure, I wander through the downstairs rooms, stopping in the kitchen when I see the empty dog dish. I stumble over, pick up the bowl, and hug it tight.

Aware of every step, I plod the stairs to my son's former room—or is it my former son's room? Through blurred vision, I see blue fish and clown fish on the wallpaper—Dory and Nemo—dancing and smiling. I run my hand over the wall and remember the high-beam grin on Bobby's face when he first saw this room. A smile tweaks at my lips.

I spot something on the floor in the corner. My smile disappears.

The "something" is the small, plastic castle that recently lay embedded in sand in my son's aquarium, his Dory and Nemo aquarium. I drop to my knees, tuck the dog bowl under my arm, and crawl across the oak floor. Scooping up the castle, I sit, my back against the wall. I stare from the bowl to the castle. No dog. No son. I look at my naked ring finger. No wife. How had this happened?

I hurl the dog dish across the room; it thuds against the wall and lands on an edge, rotates, wobbles, and comes to a standstill. I hoist my other arm to throw the castle, but I can't do it. I squeeze my fingers around it, pull it to my face, and inhale. Hoping for what? I don't know. Perhaps a scent? A memory of Bobby? I jam the castle into my pocket.

Using the wall for balance, I rise, and continue wandering. Downstairs. Through the kitchen. The living room. There is a business card turned upside down on the carpet. I pick it up. Vladimir. I remember him. The real estate agent. The *prince*. Like me. Huh. Right. I glance at my watch. No wedding ring. But still have the damn watch. Yep. I'm a prince, for sure.

I toy with the business card. Stare at the name. Prince Vladimir. Not his fault. The red, FORECLOSURE sign that screams from the front door is not his fault. Vladimir was just doing his job. Not Vladimir's fault. Mine. It was all me. My fault.

Does it matter anymore? It's gone now. All gone.

I trudge past tumbleweeds of dog hair which dot the hallway like a scatter graph. The breeze created by my footsteps sets the fur balls in motion and they roll along behind me, haunting, taunting. I raise my eyes and confront more dots, nail holes in the wall, the barren wall that once displayed family photos.

My body trembles. I inhale. Exhale. Inhale. Exhale. I stand very still and reach out one hand to lean on the wall. Jesus Christ. Can't handle this. Have to get the hell out.

I stumble to the mudroom and retrieve my backpack. Then I forage. I manage to scrounge up a few things— an extra pair of jeans, a toothbrush, an old towel—and stuff them inside the pack. In the kitchen, I locate an apple, some crackers, and two small containers of juice. Bobby's snacks? Guess Sarah forgot them. I pull Bobby's plastic castle from my jeans and shove it into the side pocket of the pack.

Then I rifle through my wallet. I count all my cash—ninety-six dollars. The full extent of my wealth—ninety-six dollars. I roll the money into a tight wad and tuck it into a pocket in my jeans. I hunt through the wallet again, probing every crevice. No more cash. Am about to discard the wallet when I eye my driver's license.

WENTWORTH, JUSTIN MICHAEL. Bold letters. Glaring, bold letters. WENTWORTH, JUSTIN MICHAEL. The name has no meaning. I grab the license from its transparent pocket. Drop the wallet. Attempt to tear the license in two. Impossible task.

Scissors. Where the hell are they? I storm around the kitchen, clawing at cupboards, jerking at drawers, exposing everything. But everything is nothing. All drawers are empty.

Damn it. I slam every door and drawer, one at a time. *Bang. Bang. Bang.* The noise reverberates through the house like gunshots cracking the night.

No scissors. Now, what? I hover, contemplating my next step. The wallet is still there, on the counter. Still fat with cards—membership cards and rewards cards and medical cards—all useless. All belonging to WENTWORTH, JUSTIN MICHAEL. Bold letters. Glaring, bold letters.

Destroy the damn cards! The impulse is irrefutable. I yank all cards from the wallet and toss them on the counter. What next?

My eyes dart around until they fall on the fireplace in the adjoining family room. A wood-burning fireplace. I nod.

Matches? Where are the matches? They are where they are supposed to be, on the mantle, high up, away from a little boy's reach. I am not a little boy; I am a man. I laugh at my own arrogance.

Scooping up the cards, I march to the fireplace and drop all pieces of identification on the floor. Grabbing the matches, I plop to the hearth, open the flue, and systematically light and burn all evidence of the existence of WENTWORTH, JUSTIN MICHAEL. When I have gone through everything from the wallet, I scour the house, searching for any piece of paper containing that name. Just like *The Terminator*. Seek. Find. Destroy. Unaware of anything but the mission.

Eventually, with evidence located, cremated, I sit by the fireplace and stare at a heap of black ash and molten plastic. A funeral.

Dark. Empty. Final.

There's nothing else for me here. I stand, go to the kitchen, get my backpack and head toward the front door. I place my hand on the doorknob. I twist it and pull the door open. The FORECLOSURE sign jumps at me. I avert my eyes, step out and close the door. Keep my head down. Stare at the front walk. Down the steps. One foot. The other foot.

At the end of the walkway, I turn right. Keep going. One foot. The other foot. At the end of the street, I turn left. Keep going. I just keep going.

49

WANDERED LIKE MOSES

February, 2010

You didn't look back at all?"

"Why would I? Nothing there anymore."

"What happened to the house? You even lock it?"

I shake my head. "Not mine. Didn't care."

Steve jots down the last comment and looks at me. "So, when exactly was that?"

"September. Last year."

Steve nods. "So, you were on the street for what? About half a year when I found you?"

"Yeah. Guess so. Maybe four, five, six months. Why?"

"Just trying to get the dates down, bud."

I narrow my eyes. *Should I ask?* "Why me?" The question pops out.

"What do you mean?"

Jesus H. Christ! What the hell am I doing, asking him that? Don't know, but the question is out there. Sequence locked in. Irreversible. I lick my lips. "I mean, why me? Lots of homeless people to choose from. Why pick me?"

He folds his arms, leans back. His eyes spark with . . . what? Indecision? Not sure. "Good question." He nods.

Stalling, bud? I scrutinize his face.

"Guess I was looking for a 'type,' " he begins, as he sits up straight.

Damn. He's revving up for a speech. Arms will be raised in *maestro mode* any second.

Sure enough, Steve's lifts his arms and begins waving them in the air. "Some people are permanently homeless—they live on the edge of society due to addiction or neurosis. Some are periodically homeless—they end up in shelters and soup kitchens repeatedly, perhaps due to family violence. And, for some, it's short-lived—they are displaced, or misplaced for weeks or months. A one-time thing. Maybe due to bankruptcy or divorce or disaster, like an earthquake *or* like the housing market crash."

He stops. A breather. I leap in. "And me?" *Damned if I'm buying this academic crap*, bud, *but I'll play.* "I take it I'm the last type?"

"I think so."

"Not the addict type?"

"Maybe, but I'm guessing you're redeemable."

"Why?"

Steve shrugs. "At first, it was just a hunch. Thought you looked pretty together for a guy living in the streets. Figured you couldn't have been there that long."

"Huh! A few months, fifty years. All the same to me. A fucking lifetime."

"I get that. Anyway, now I figure I'm right. You're redeemable. You want help because you want Sarah and Bobby back. Right?"

There's that lump in my throat again. I swallow, blink, nod.

"You *need* help. I *can* help. Simple as that. Satisfied?"

NO! I want to shout . . . *NO!* But I can't say it. *Not yet.*

"Satisfied?" Steve presses, raising his eyebrows.

"Guess so." The words just skate over my tongue. Easy. *Damn, I'm an expert at the lying thing.* Guilty about it in the past, grateful for it now. Next step, another practiced skill: change the subject. "What do you plan to do with all this research?"

"I'm writing a thesis, bud, remember?" He checks his watch and closes his notebook. "Speaking of which, I gotta get moving."

"What's the rush?" Damn. A second ago, I pushed him away. Now I'm clinging like a leech. *What the hell . . . ?*

"Have an appointment with my thesis advisor at UBC. Thesis outline due Friday." He looks at the calendar and then back at me. "Five days from now."

"Why the appointment?"

"I want to discuss the fine points, make sure I'm doing it right, get it in on time."

"What difference does it make? They give extensions, don't they?"

"I don't want an extension. Like I told you, my parents handle everything. Pay for everything. Least I can do is be responsible."

I look around. "Yeah. Guess you're pretty lucky."

Steve taps his fingers on the table. "Guess so."

I shake my head. "Tough life, dude."

Steve shrugs. "No, it's a blessed life. I appreciate my parents. They want me to learn the value of hard work. They keep saying "There but for the grace of God . . . yada, yada, yada."

I tilt my head. "So you're doing all this—studying and research—to please your parents?"

Another shrug from Steve. "That's part of it."

"Oh." I drop my gaze to the table. *How the hell do I fit into all this?* I'm desperate to know, afraid to ask. *Am I just a research subject?* A chill snakes through me. A winter chill. Just like the one I felt the last time I attempted to hug Bobby and he wriggled out of my arms, leaving me staring at my empty hands.

Steve leans across the table and whispers, "Justin."

I don't respond.

His hand grasps my arm. "Justin, look at me."

I gulp. I look up.

"You don't have to worry, Justin. I'm not going to dump you." He sighs, pulls away from me, and runs his hand through his hair. "Can't blame you if you don't believe me, not after everything you've . . . " He leaps to his feet and paces the floor. "Look, Justin, the thing is . . . you're not just primary research; that's not why I chose you. It's about . . . ." He stops and looks at me. "Remember my telling you about my grandfather?"

I nod. *Now we're getting somewhere.* "Yeah . . . he wanted you to help the homeless."

"Well, there's a lot more to it than that." He pauses, scratches his head.

I wait.

"My money comes from my parents. My *nouveau-riche* parents. My grandfather wouldn't take a cent from them, not a cent, even though he was living in poverty. "Steve shakes his head. "I never understood that . . . at least, not until just before he died." He is silent now, contemplating.

"And?" I prompt, leaning forward, hungry-like.

He returns to his chair, plops down, settles in. Just as his mouth opens, his cell phone rings.

Damn! My fingers grip the edge of the table. *Don't answer . . . don't answer.*

He yanks the phone from his belt. "Darn! Gotta take this. It's my thesis advisor. Be right back." He jumps up and heads toward his room. "Dr. Jenkins. What's up?"

His door clicks shut. I hear the intermittent murmur of his voice. No discernible words.

Left to dangle, I just sit. Five minutes. I go to the sink, pour my coffee down the drain, refill my cup, and return to my seat. Ten minutes. I pick up the newspaper from the table and thumb through it. Fifteen minutes. His door creaks open. Footsteps pad the hallway.

He reappears, notebook in hand, sits, and drums his fingers on the table. "Prof had to cancel our appointment so we just ironed out details over the phone. I still want to get to campus, but do have time for a few more questions . . . "

I sniff. "Uh uh. What about *your* story? Your grandfather?"

He waves a hand in dismissal "Lots of time for that. Got to finish the research first." He thumbs through his notebook. "Oh, yeah . . . how did you adjust to living in the street? I mean, after you walked away from your house, where the heck did you go?"

I frown. Minutes ago, he was about to tell all. Now . . . complete shutdown. What's that about?

"Where did you go?" he repeats.

I blink in disbelief and open my mouth to protest, but the determination in his eyes stops me dead. My confidence implodes. Can't push it. Whatever his game is, I gotta keep playing. No choice. "Nowhere in particular," I say, responding to his question. *Where did you want to go,* bud? *What the hell did you want to say?*

"Yeah, but you ended up someplace. Can't tell me you just wandered for days, like Moses in the desert."

"Days? No. Well, maybe a couple of days. No awareness of time, of sound—nothing, until I came to the pedestrian tunnel at the south end of the Granville Bridge. I paused there for a bit and then just kept going."

"Going where?"

Damn. *What about you*, bud? *Where were you going?* Damn. Damn. Damn. I let out a long sigh. Guess he'll tell me when he's ready. Fact is, I believe him when he says he's won't dump me. A good guy, Steve Jameson. Pretty sure of that at this moment . . . maybe.

"Where did you go when you reached the tunnel?"

50

DUMPSTER DIVING

September, 2009

I pause at the tunnel because it creeps me out. Strange that I have lived here for years and didn't even know the pedestrian tunnel existed. I drove over the Granville Bridge countless times. Never walked it.

Many people hustle past me, into the dark, no hesitation. I follow them, my eyes shifting side-to-side, suspicious of everything. Luminous spray paint designs—gang tags—jump from the walls. Paper, cigarette butts, and used condoms litter the ground. I shudder and pick up my pace.

Relief slides through me at the first hint of light from the other side. I'm moving so fast now that I almost crash into a stationary shopping cart. An overloaded shopping cart. Guess someone abandoned it. Or just parked it. Whatever. *Homeless riffraff and their shopping carts.* I angle away from it and keep going.

I walk and I walk, *en route* to nowhere. I run across many street people. Where do they spend the night? What do they do for booze? My need for that would come soon. Huh. Interesting. No thoughts about food. Only booze. Maybe I *am* an alcoholic.

I pat my pocket, checking for my roll of bills, and wander on. In front of a liquor store, I stop, look around. I'm in the West End. On Davie Street. How the hell did I get here? Damn, my feet hurt. Shifting from one foot to the other, I stare at the liquor store. My lips are dry. I wipe them and go inside.

On automatic pilot, I aim for the vodka. Once there, I check the price tag. That much? I move to the wine aisle, grab a cheap bottle, and head to the checkout.

"Would you like a bag for that, Mister?" the cashier beams at me. She's young, this checkout girl. Somebody's daughter. Too young to be selling booze.

"No, I'll just put it into my backpack, thanks," I reply, twitching, anxious to get out.

I exit and head toward the open beach. Too many people. I opt for the seawall, walking, walking, eventually hobbling, until I arrive at Lumberman's Arch. There I skulk around, like a burglar casing a building until I spot a grove of cedar trees. I saunter into its center and drop onto the cool grass.

My brain churns at breakneck speed, spitting static images, unwanted images of loss: Mom, Dad, Sarah, Bobby, home . . . *Gotta make it stop.* I'm whimpering as my fingers struggle to unscrew the damn wine bottle. When the familiar alcoholic haze finally comes, my brain slows, the pictures fade. I lie on the grass, stare through the treetops, and watch the clouds meander. Somewhere in the back of my mind, I wonder where I will sleep.

Not an issue. Next thing I know, morning light awakens me. Gotta take a leak. What do people do about that? Where do they go? Public washrooms? I passed one on my way here, didn't I? I stumble to my feet. My clothes are saturated with dew and my body's shivering. I pull my coat around my torso. September? Huh. More like January. Damn near freezing.

I find the washroom, rush in, and relieve myself. I avoid the mirror as I soap up and wash my hands, furiously wash them. More soap. Then I scrub my face. It feels so good, I do it again. *Lather. Rinse. Repeat.* What was that commercial, anyway? Can't remember. What I'd give for a heated shower, but it's not an option. Or is it?

I could couch surf, I guess. There are friends, acquaintances . . . but no. Damned if I want them to see me, not like this. I doubt I'd be welcome, anyway. Lots of them are living on the precipice of a financial abyss, just like I was. None of them would want to look at me. Too close to home. I sniff. "Home." *Good one, Wentworth.*

I vacate the washroom and head to the beach. This is it now, I figure, gazing at the ocean. I'm here, alone. For how long? How will I spend my time? I fumble in my pocket and extract money. Still have some wine. Maybe I should buy some food. I remember the snacks, Bobby's forgotten snacks, in my backpack. I pull out the apple and nibble as I turn to examine the city skyline.

What next? Guess I'll roam, see where it takes me. I fling my apple core to the sand, where it is instantly scooped up by a screaming gull. Huh. Wonder how many screaming opportunists prowl the streets of Vancouver? I shudder, tighten the straps on my backpack, and launch onto Beach Avenue, up Nicola, toward Davie Street.

I pass lots of people, busy people, people with jobs and responsibilities and appointments and families. Concerns that I no longer have. No sense of relief, though. In fact, no feelings at all. Numb.

All day long I wander, stopping intermittently to have a drink. When the bottle is empty, I buy another. When I tire, I park on a bus bench, but when the buses halt and expectantly wait for me to climb aboard, I make a mental note: no loitering at bus stops.

At dusk, I am somewhere between Granville and Broadway. Downtown. Vancouver. With the indigents. And with darkness approaching. I pass an alley and see a Dumpster. I am so tired that I am tempted to hide behind it to rest for just a little while. But I can't bring myself to do it. I don't belong with these indigents, I tell myself. I am better than that . . . and too terrified to approach the Dumpster.

I keep going until I am back in the park at Lumberman's Arch. I slept there last night. Can do it again tonight. As I near the ocean, I feel the cold wind blowing from it and wish that I had thought to stuff a blanket into my backpack. But I do have a towel. I use that to stave off the cold as I settle into the cedar grove.

It is a couple of weeks before I start Dumpster diving, looking for food or the dregs of wine bottles. I have no money left now. My filthy jeans are sagging, and it's obvious that I am losing weight already. I don't care about that; don't care about anything except where my next drink is coming from. I figure I can live like this indefinitely.

51

CATCH-22

February, 2010

So, did you beg for money?"

"Yeah."

"Did you drink the whole time?"

"Pretty much. Boring as hell in the street. Gotta do something in order to pass the time."

"Why no drugs?"

I shrug. "No reason. Probably would have done drugs after a while. Like I said, boring as hell."

"Try to get a job or anything?"

"Ha! You kidding me?"

"No, I'm not."

"*Catch-22*, bud. You can't get a job without an address and you can't get a place to live without a job."

"Oh, yeah, that makes sense." Steve sighs. "So that's it, then? To this point, I mean. Nothing else to tell me?"

I throw my hands up. "That's it."

"Hmmm."

"Hmmm . . . what?"

"Well, I guess we're done then." Steve jumps to his feet. "I'm heading for campus . . . soon as I grab my laptop. Later, bud." He charges from the kitchen to the den, from the den to the door. A jangle of keys, a click of the deadbolt, a slam of the door: gone.

"Hmmph! Yeah, later," I reply to no one. "Later." I look around. Now what? He'll be gone for a while. I could go . . . where? Nowhere to go. Guess I'll make myself useful: do some cleaning, head to the den, water the ficus. Huh. Wonder if the tree is root bound. I could check. Sarah taught me how to fix that. Yeah, I can handle that. But first? Coffee. That's what I need. Coffee. Then I can confront the ficus.

As I wait for the coffee to perk, I wonder what info Steve was about to drop, why he aborted the effort. Huh. Not a clue. Eventually, he'll tell, I guess. I can wait it out. Got no choice, really. I'm going to stay here as long as it takes. For Sarah and Bobby. I nod. *Yes.* Going to get Sarah and Bobby back. Definitely. Not right now, but it will happen.

Abruptly, the condo door whips open. I jump and swerve. "Jesus, Steve! You scared the hell out of me. What are you doing back?"

Steve remains near the door, shuffling his feet. "Don't know, really. I guess I was afraid you'd take it upon yourself to leave, or something. You don't have to go just because the research is done. You're welcome to stay here, bud. I need you to be sure of that."

"Okay," I manage slowly, nerves taut as the skin of a drum, "I hear you, but . . . whatever you need to tell me . . . can you tell me when you get back?" Both my heart and my speech speed up. "I mean . . . I'm on track now. I want to stay on track. I want to stay here."

"Good." He gulps, opens his mouth, gulps again. "We'll talk later." He nods like a bobble head. "Yeah. Later. Guess I'll be on my way." He slips through the door and pulls it shut.

A wave of relief hits me, almost knocking me over. I grasp the counter and lower myself to the floor. It's safe on the floor: can't fall off the damn floor. *"We'll talk later,"* he said. Okay, then. At least, he's agreed to talk. I can live with that. I take a few deep breaths and sit there for a while. Then I scramble to my feet and look around.

Now, where was I?

Picking up my coffee, I stroll to the den and stare at the ficus. Yep. Maybe I can save this tree after all. Hmmm. Let's see. Got to get garbage bags and newspapers, spread them out, lift the plant out of its container, and loosen those roots. That will help. I can get a bigger pot later.

I gather discarded newspapers and plastic bags and spend about an hour fumbling, cutting and tearing so that I can create a protective covering for the carpet. Once the carpet is shrouded, I collect my tools: a mismatched butter knife, a castrated dinner fork (missing two center tines), and a pair of rubber gloves, brand new, still in the package.

I drop to my haunches and hesitate: the cutlery is dispensable, yes, but what about those rubber gloves? I glance at my nails, my chipped and gnawed nails. My shoulders jog with laughter. How long has it been since my days of manicures? I grab the gloves, return them to their snug little shelf under the kitchen sink, and roll up my sleeves. Wait a minute. No need to get the good clothes dirty. I run to my room, squirm into my street clothes, and rush back to the den.

The plant weighs a ton. I wriggle it onto the newspaper and use the butter knife to loosen the dirt from the sides of the pot. Putting down the knife, I grasp the main branch and lift. The whole thing comes up, plant, pot, and drainage tray. Damn.

I drop the stubborn monster onto the floor and try again. Nothing. The plant doesn't budge from the pot. Back to the butter knife. I plunge it deeper this time. Then I grasp the trunk and lift a third time. My fingers slip . . . the whole thing hits the floor, scattering leaves and dirt. The side of the drainage tray splits, releasing the tray from the pot. More dirt. Damn again. It's going to take forever to clean up this mess. As I reach for the dislodged tray, something glistens up at me.

"What the hell . . . " In slow motion, I pick up a dirt-covered, Ziploc snack bag, and give it a shake. Caked, dried earth disintegrates into powder and feathers to the floor. My eyes glaze, vacuous, uncomprehending, as I stare on the shiny object shielded within the plastic. Letters are visible. I blink, once, twice, and the letters slide together forming words. An engraving—*From Pauper to Prince* . . .

52

UNDERSTANDING

U nderstanding creeps like a sloth from my brain down through torso and limbs. When full awareness comes, my knees buckle and I drop like a stone. *This can't be. Steve wouldn't do this. We had a deal, a bargain, he was helping me and I was helping him.*

I stay there, on the floor, locked in position like a discarded mannequin, staring at the Rolex. No awareness of time. I just stay there—a few seconds or a few minutes. Don't know.

Eventually, I remove my watch from the Ziploc, slide it onto my wrist, and crawl to the front door. There, I stand, get my jacket and keys and charge out. Realizing that I need money, I go back, head to the kitchen, and remove the two twenties that my benefactor habitually leaves beneath a magnet on the fridge. I'm going to Davie Street. I have a purchase to make. And then, I'm coming back because I want to see Steve—Born-again Steve, Marshmallow Man Steve, Good-Samaritan Steve—one last time.

The walk there is easy. As is the purchase. Not cheap wine today. Not vodka. Whiskey. I'm getting decent whiskey. Not for immediate consumption, though. Oh, no. I tuck the brown bag under my arm and hold it close. On the way back to the condo, I let my brain churn, allowing the anger to set in.

By the time I unlock the condo door, hurt and rage are tunneling into a tornado inside my body. Building and building. I continue to nurture it: it has to peak at the exact second that the bastard gets back. *Yep. Gonna have one fucking F-5 storm waiting for you*, bud.

I hole up in my room, unscrew the bottle, and revel in the aroma that sails up my nose. I pause. *Can't get drunk if you don't pick up.* Fuck that. I ram the bottle into my mouth and tip it back. Once. Twice. But wait . . . I have to slow down. A little at a time. I have to control this. I'm on a mission. It's important to drink just enough. I don't want to drown the anger, don't want to mess up my coordination. Can't meet the task at hand if I'm too drunk. I put the cap back on the bottle, and wait a few minutes before opening it again.

I'm so intent on the bottle, on my focus, that the next thing I hear is Steve's voice, yelling at me. "Oh, God! Justin! Are you here? Justin!"

I rocket to my feet and the bottle plunges to the floor. Valuable golden liquid splashing, splattering. Fuck it! The goddam son of a bitch is back. I bolt through the bedroom door like a racehorse through a starting gate.

I see him, my benefactor, sagging against the doorway to the den, gawking at dirt and limbs and leaves and litter. I stop dead. Got to get my bearings, prepare my attack.

Steve's head jerks toward me. He thrusts his arms out, palms facing me. "Justin. I'm so sorry. I tried to tell you. God in heaven, I tried. I'm so sorry. Really. I never meant for them to hurt you. I was waiting for the right time to give the watch back. I was afraid you'd leave if you found out. Justin, I really do want you to stay. Say something, will you?"

Not a chance. *No more words for you*, bud. All I see in front of me is a target, an outlet for billowing rage. I don't give a damn about his pleading. I zone in.

Steve backs up, pivots his head to see where he's going, and, in the process, drops his arms.

Thanks, bud. I pull my fist back and drive it forward, nailing the right side of his face.

He teeters and then drops to his knees, cradling his head in his hands.

"Get up, asshole," I taunt, but he doesn't oblige.

"For God's sake, Justin!" He's crawling away from me now. "My grandfather took money from your parents . . . "

His words have no meaning. I grab his shirt, drag him to his feet, and prop him against the wall.

All the while, the son of a bitch rambles on. "Grandfather took money. Your parents were not broke, Justin. Mr. Cormier . . . "

Like always, he's still talking. His words have no significance whatsoever. *Shut up!* I unleash a flurry of fists onto his torso, pummeling him until he slides down the wall into a shapeless heap on the floor.

He gasps, moans, and curls into a fetal position.

I retreat. I wait, fists still raised. I'm bouncing side-to-side like I'm fucking Mohammed Ali. "Come on, just get up, *bud*. Just get your ass up."

He groans and looks up, eyes glazed. "Grandfather took money. Justin! Listen to me! My grandfather took money from . . ."

"Shut the fuck up!" His words mean nothing. Not a damn thing. I step back, pull my fists in front of my face, preparing to jab. The sight of my bloody hands and ballooning knuckles makes my gut lurch and my body freeze.

I can't bring myself to look at Steve, my savior Steve, lying there, in a ball. Just can't look. I *can* hear him though, damn it, whining and whimpering. Why is there no satisfaction in the sound of his pain? And what the hell is he saying? I don't know. I don't know. All I know is that I have to get the hell away.

I stumble from my paralytic state and, using the wall as support, stagger past Steve. Once I'm sure I can walk solo, I thrust myself down the hall, jerk open the condo door, and barrel toward the stairs. Down, down, down. To the first floor. The lobby door. My attempt to glom onto the door handle fails. Damn. I look at my hand. Huh. No wonder. My bloody fingers are curled into a fist. I unlock my fingers and a jingling object tumbles, clinking onto the concrete floor. My eyes follow it. Steve's key ring. Steve's keys. Don't remember grabbing them. Huh. I sniff. Guess I'm taking a ride.

I retrieve the keys, veer away from the lobby door, and continue down the stairs to the parking garage. Once inside, I pause. Strange terrain, this. I've taken lots of buses since I've been here and I've walked a freaking marathon, but I've never ridden in Steve's car. I narrow my eyes and look all around. Where the hell is his car anyway? I grin. Easy find. I raise the key ring, push a button and the car responds. *Beep! Beep!* There it is. All silver and shiny.

In seconds, I'm in the driver's seat, jamming the key into the ignition. The engine roars and the noise reverberates, ricocheting off concrete walls and pillars. From the dash comes a steady pinging sound, warning me to buckle my seat belt. "Buckle up," I used to say to Bobby, just like my parents said to me. Huh. Screw the seat belt. I ram the car into reverse and squeal to the garage entrance. There, I stop and push the button to open the wrought iron gate.

Directly across the alley, looming like a fortress, is the green Dumpster, the one that I can see from the bedroom window in Steve's condo, the one that taunts me daily. A green Dumpster. Just like the one that the son of a bitch Steve had me tossed into. As soon as the gate is open, I pull across the alley and squeak past the monster, close enough that the corner of it makes contact with the fender of Steve's car. I laugh in response to the gratifying screech of metal on metal. Feels so good I have to fight the temptation to sideswipe a parked vehicle as I veer right onto Nicola. Forget that. Could attract attention. I'm going downhill, to the beach.

At Beach Avenue, I pause and stare at the waters of English Bay. Grey day. Granite ocean. Far off, a wave is forming, building, sucking in every droplet of water within reach. Fingers of foam claw at the shore, reluctant to be pulled into the rolling giant. At its peak, the wave looks hunched, like it's poised for attack. It lingers, then pounces, heaving its guts to the shore. My body shudders. I shake my head. Not going to the beach.

I turn right, onto Beach Avenue, and keep a watchful eye on the ocean. *Think it's gonna attack you, Wentworth? Idiot.* But I keep it in my sites and plant both hands on the steering wheel: ten and two for safety. A scornful laugh escapes me. *Safety, my ass.* I've been drinking for Christ's sake. Don't give a damn. Where am I going anyway? Beach Avenue morphs into Stanley Park Drive and the question is answered. Stanley Park. I'm heading into the core of Stanley Park. I zoom past Denman and follow Stanley Park Drive until the car is flanked by towering walls of cedar. Green, green, everywhere.

Bobby is on my mind now: he loved it here. He and I drove this exact route to find the Hollow Tree. "His castle," he called it. Maybe I'll go see that castle. Is it still there? I frown, remembering the wind storm a few years ago, the one that wreaked havoc on the four-hundred-hectare park. Almost destroyed the Hollow Tree. But didn't they repair it? I think so. I'm going to check it out. Yep, that's what I'm doing.

The sky, gun metal grey, is spitting rain in pearl-sized droplets. *Dot, dot, dot, dot, dot . . .* they splatter the windshield, increasing in size and speed, forming into rivulets, obscuring my already shaky vision. My heart hammers and my hand trembles as I activate the wipers. The blades leap into action. Back and forth, back and forth. A metronome. My eyes chase them. Back and forth. Water beads. Wipers sweep. Back and forth. Back and forth. And suddenly I am lost . . . no idea of place or time.

Bewildered, I glance at the passenger seat and realize that someone is sitting there. Is it Bobby? Panic rises, sending bile into my throat. *Oh, God. Sarah will kill me. I've been drinking. Can't have Bobby in the car.* I catch my breath. Wait a minute. Steve's car. Not mine. My son is not here. My son is gone from my life. No one else here. *Calm down, Wentworth.*

I take a few deep breaths and glance to my right again. Damn. I *do* see a face. *Dear Jesus, don't let it be Bobby.* I widen my eyes and I pivot my head. No. Definitely not Bobby. On the heels of gushing relief hangs the obvious . . . Who? Who the hell is it? A woman. It's a woman. Wearing a three-quarter, beige trench coat over black slacks. She leans forward and deposits a brown paper bag on the floor. It rests against her shoes—small, patent leather pumps. I drag in a breath and the odor of Chinese food assaults my nose. I cough it out. Jesus. My eyes fly back to the black pumps. I can't stop staring at those black pumps.

A horn sounds, the highest point of its Doppler effect telling me it's too damn close, and I swerve to avoid an impact. Bullets of rain bombard the windshield, and I accelerate the wipers until the suicidal raindrops are whipped away the instant they make contact. I inhale, exhale, and again turn to the passenger seat, dread billowing inside me. I choke back a sob. I know that face. Damn it all. I know that face. *Mom?* I glance into the rearview mirror; my father is there, hands gripping the back of the seat, eyes glazed with terror, jaw flapping like a marionette. I shake my head, but the horror movie plays out. Over and over, my father's stiletto shrieks lacerate my eardrums. My name, he's screaming my name. I blink, unable to do anything but watch as the scene plays and replays. All in slow motion. Then, without warning, all is dark.

The wipers swish, the rain pounds, but the engine is silent. Did I stop the car? Steve's car? I guess not, but the air bag is inflated. Something stopped the car, but not me. I hear groaning, like the twisting of a wooden beam on a doomed ship. I open my eyes. The windshield is cracked, veined like a web, and the window beside me is gone. I am still breathing, though, still breathing, inhaling the scent of a cedar branch that is slap, slap, slapping my face. Where the hell am I? In Stanley Park. Yeah. That's right. Stanley Park. Crashed into a cedar tree. Yeah. A cedar tree. But I'm seeing another tree. Another time. Another place. I'm remembering my father coming out of the Chinese restaurant. His arm around my mother. His car keys in his hand. The keys flying through the air, the key ring with the Maple Leafs symbol flashing. *"Here, son,"* he says. *"You drive. Only had one drink, but one is too many. No drinking and driving in this family.*" The memory is strong, it is real, and it fills the void. For twenty years, I did not know. Now I do. My father, Jason Wentworth, was not at the wheel the night he and my mother died.

Shock and disbelief trigger a further deluge of memories: crushed, twisted metal and flashing police cars and countless questioning faces. The police must have known. If so, then how did I not? Did my mind obliterate more than just the accident?

My torment ruptures into a throat-searing scream which serves to jettison the flashback flood. The hows and the whys don't matter. A single piece of information floats to the surface and remains. My truth.

I was driving that night. I killed my parents.

Sirens wail in Stanley Park, and I, thankfully, fade to blackness.

53

SON AND SUN

My eyes snap open and I don't know where I am. At first. Myriad sounds creep in: murmur of voices, rattle of a smoker's cough, clatter of trays. Out of the corner of my eye, I see an angel, not a real one, but a tattoo. And I know I'm back in the hospital, back with the nurse with the angel tattoo. Relief slips in. Closing my eyes, I inhale, long and slow. I'm on the cusp of exhalation when memory pierces. My body gasps and goes into defense mode: craving alcohol. I sniff. *No.* No more. Time to deal. I lie still, inhale again, and let the memory run . . .

"Buckle up, s-o-n and s-u-n," said my mother, as she slumped into her seat, leaned against the car door, and closed her eyes.

My father and I laughed . . . we knew she was going to drift into sleep any second. "A single glass of wine and she's off with the angels," Dad said.

I wrinkled my brow. Strange choice of words. I shrugged it off.

I started up the engine and glanced into the rearview mirror. Dad's eyes glinted with humor as they stared into mine. We talked about A Fish Called Wanda *and the* Toronto Maple Leafs *and the broken cap on the newel post in the front hull . . . he would repair it tomorrow. Then the conversation switched to my leaving for university and a curtain fell between us. We both let out long sighs. He leaned back. I leaned into the wheel.*

Rain had been spitting until now. Without any rumble or warning, the heavens unleashed a deluge. I flipped a switch and the wipers launched into overdrive. The road meandered, snakelike. I maneuvered a curve and the glare of high beams blinded me, just for a second. I swerved. Dad screamed my name.

I jump, sobbing, shaking, clinging to the rail of the hospital bed like a drowning man to driftwood.

A slight pressure, gentle fingertips on my shoulder, stills my body. A soothing voice filters into my ear. "It's okay. You're safe here, remember?"

I look up, into the face of the nurse with the angel tattoo. Compassion there, same as before, compassion that splinters my pain. I'm here. In the hospital. Safe. The memory of the accident slides into its place, into the past, where it belongs. I've denied it long enough. Knowing is better. I inhale and exhale easily now. I'm free, a man who has been released from a twenty-year prison.

"Great to see you again, Vladimir . . . or should I say Justin?"

I open my mouth to speak but the words don't come. I clear my throat, hawking up a disgusting globule of mucus which I barely manage to keep in my mouth.

The angel smiles as she places a stainless steel, kidney-shaped tray in front of my face. I obligingly spit into it and she, without leaving my bedside, whisks it from view. An angel and a magician. Huh. I clear my throat again, this time without the unpleasant side effect.

"How did you know my name?" I croak out.

She shrugs and steps aside. Suddenly, in her place, is Marshmallow Man. Battered.

"Damn, dude. You look worse than Stallone at the end of *Rocky*. What the hell happened to you?" But before the words are out, the answer hits. I cringe. "Jesus. I did that?"

He waves a hand in dismissal. "Doesn't matter. I'm just glad you're okay, bud." He pauses.

I start to respond, but he stops for only half a beat. I miss my opportunity and, like always, he yammers on. "When you walk out on a guy, you sure do it with a bang. Not hard to find you, though."

For once, I'm glad he's still talking. He can't be hurt too bad if he's still talking. I don't want to deal with him now, though. Enough to deal with. I need time. Time alone. Time to think. "What are you doing here?" Inside, I'm searching, searching, trying to locate the rage that made me pound him in the first place. It's gone. Interesting.

Steve slowly shakes his head. "I had to see you. I promised my grandfather . . . "

I sigh. "What the hell does your grandfather have to do with any of this?"

Steve points to a chair in the corner. "Mind if I sit?"

I say nothing. I look away.

He grabs the chair and plops it down beside me. "My grandfather," he says, "and your Mr. Cormier were one and the same person."

My head swerves toward him. "What?"

He nods. "I tried to tell you, but I left it too late. Should have told you long ago, but . . . " He shrugs. "You trusted him. And I was loyal to him. He cheated you, Justin; he didn't mean to. He was desperate, that's all."

Snatches of conversation are coming back to me. Maybe he did tell me this . . . while I was pounding him. Can't remember for sure. "I still don't know what the hell you're talking about."

"Okay, okay. I get that." He puts both hands out, palms facing me. "I can explain. If you don't think you're ready for all this yet, I'll wait until you're better. You beat yourself up in that accident. You're not going anywhere for a while. Lots of time to tell you this. Your call . . . now or later?" He sits back and folds his arms.

"Later, my ass." My life has been a freaking puzzle for too long. I want all the pieces in place. I fumble for the remote that controls the hospital bed. Can't find it. "Raise the head of this damn bed, will you? And then, start talking."

Steve hurries to oblige. He even fluffs my pillow. Gets up close and personal, so close my nose cringes at the acrid smell of his aftershave. So close I can count the stitches under his eye . . . five of them; both eyes are the color of eggplant. Remorse starts in my chest and hemorrhages outward.

"I'm sorry, Steve. Shouldn't have beat you up."

He sniffs. "Oh, I think I gave you plenty of reason. Don't worry about it. I'm fine. Bruises will fade."

"Huh. You really do go in for the 'turn the other cheek' stuff, don't you?"

He smiles and points to his face. "Maybe this is my karma. I deserved it after what I did . . . Look, I'm the one who should be apologizing to you. I'm sorry about the Dumpster and the thugs. Never meant for them to hurt you."

"Why didn't you just tell me what you wanted that day you woke me up on Robson Street? Why go to such trouble?"

He tilts his head. "Would you have walked up to someone in your position and said 'here . . . my grandfather owes you this' and given him a hundred and fifty thousand dollars?"

Thunderstruck, I stare, blinking repeatedly. "How much?"

"You heard me. Plus interest."

"A hundred and fifty thousand . . . " My voice trails off. We're both silent for a while, staring at each other.

He steps back, reclaims his seat. "Ready for the rest of *my* story, now?"

"Damn straight."

"Okay then. My grandmother was dying and my grandfather was in denial. He was willing to do anything . . . wanted to try treatment someplace in Mexico, but couldn't afford it. Your father financed it. My grandfather intended to pay him back, but couldn't. He lost everything and wound up in a dingy apartment. He didn't want my parents' help, the stubborn old coot. Didn't want to take money from anyone, ever again. Not even his daughter. Mom and Dad tried to convince him to move to Ontario. Not a chance. He had to be near my grandmother's grave. Instead, he agreed to reside in an assisted living facility in Moncton. I went there every summer and stayed nearby. Spent hours talking. When he died, I made the arrangements."

"What year did he die?"

"Think I mentioned it before. A couple of years ago . . . July, 2008."

"And he talked about me?"

"Yeah. He told me everything. Repeatedly. Started a few months before he died and then recited the same story over and over. I promised him I'd find you. Had no idea how to do that, but you know what they say . . . the good Lord works in mysterious ways." Steve stands, goes to the foot of the bed, stares at me, and waits.

"Okay, I'll bite. What was the miracle?"

"Not *what. Who.* Debra. Remember her?"

My brow knits together. "Debra? My Debra from Moncton? Haven't seen her in two decades. You know Debra?"

"Not really. I met her, though. She read the funeral announcement in the *Moncton Times,* came to the funeral home, and marched right up to me. Told me about you, your parents, and your relationship with my grandfather." He tilts

his head. "She kept track of you through friends who attended Mount Allison."
He hesitates, and then adds, "If I were the gambling type, I'd bet that she
showed up at the funeral looking for you."

I shake my head and let out a sigh. "That was all a long time ago, bud. Debra
was a great girl. She just wasn't . . . "

"Just wasn't . . . Sarah?"

I shrug. "Yeah. Pretty much."

He nods, moves on. "Anyway, my grandfather took, not *took, borrowed*
money from your father. A gentleman's agreement, apparently. No paperwork.
Medical expenses mounted, his ability to repay dwindled. So he convinced
himself that you were young and you could handle it. You got debt. He got
guilt."

Huh. I say nothing, just lie still, expecting Steve's declaration to detonate
gut-churning rage. Nothing comes.

Steve waits, eyes wide, lips pressed together.

I'm waiting, too. Where's my anger? No anger, no resentment . . . nothing.
Why is all of this information like an afterthought?

Steve breaks the silence. "Are you listening to me, bud? Did you hear what I
said? My grandfather cheated you."

I shake my head slowly.

"Do you want me to repeat all of that?"

"No. No need. I got it. Every word. What strikes me is that it doesn't seem to
matter. Mr. Cormier would have paid me back if he could. He was a good man,
Mr. Cormier. My father always told me so. My problems were my fault, not
his."

"How do you figure that?"

"If my parents hadn't died, they would have found a way to sort out the
money. It's all my fault."

"Not making sense here, bud . . . "

I jerk my body up and lean on one elbow. "I'm the screw up here. Not your
grandfather. Me, just me!" My body is shaking again. I fall back onto my pillow.

Steve puts one hand on my arm. "Bud, Justin, want me to get the nurse
back? What the heck is wrong with you?"

"I was driving."

"Oh, that." He waves a hand through the air. "Don't worry about my car, bud. I don't care. No big deal, anyway. I'm certainly not pressing charges. I can repair it."

"No. No! No! Not your car, damn it. My parents' car. The accident. I was driving that night. I killed them." I cover my face with my hands. Confession filters through. "I killed my parents and buried that memory for twenty years. And Bobby? I almost killed my own son. I thought it was no big deal, drinking and driving, my son in the car. Sarah was right to leave. Damn it all, she was right to take Bobby and leave me. How can I expect her to forgive me?"

With that, the rage I was seeking earlier, detonates. It explodes in my gut, spewing jagged bits of shrapnel that pierce my every pore. I recoil, curl into a ball, wrap my arms around my torso as excruciating, hard-earned pain wracks my body. I suck in a deep breath and emit a guttural scream. Another breath. Another scream, this time in the form of hate-filled words. The target is self, but my eyes are wide now and locked on Steve. "Get out," I shriek. "Just get the fuck out of my life!"

Voices surround me. Steve. The angel nurse. Some doctor, maybe. I feel the blankets rustle, a quick prickling sensation in my hip, and then . . . nothing.

The next morning, when I wake up, the nurse is there, hovering. No sign of Steve. Hmmph. I can't blame him for that. Collateral damage. Sorry, Steve.

I struggle to slough off blankets. "What day is it?"

"Hello there. Good to see you."

"What day is it?" I rub my eyes.

"Sunday. The twelfth. Opening ceremonies for the Olympics today."

"Oh. I see." Bet that's where Steve is. I guess I won't be seeing him for a while, if at all. My fault. Told him to get the hell out, didn't I?

The nurse checks my blood pressure.

I look up at her. "Still no track marks." I smile and check her nametag. "Jennifer." Just like my mother. Why hadn't I noticed that before? A fleeting pain pierces my chest.

"Yes, that's my name."

"Thanks for helping me." I almost say her name again, but decide to avoid the sting.

"And helping's my job." She pats my arm.

I'm remembering something about her now, about the concern in her eyes the first time I was here. "More than just your job. I remind you of someone, don't I?"

"Aren't you the curious one?"

"Maybe. Am I right?"

Jennifer drops her head and lets out a sigh. "Yes, you're right. My son. You remind me of my son. He was the light of my life but . . . Died on the street. Drugs. Did everything I could but it wasn't enough."

I nod. "Sorry for your loss." I want to tell her that I lost my son, too. Want to say that it was all my fault. I spiraled into debt. Drank. Drove drunk. But I could have changed things, couldn't I? I was stupid. For some reason, I don't want the angel to judge me, so I keep my mouth shut.

She looks at me, puzzlement in her eyes. "What makes people do it? I don't understand. How can someone just ignore his family . . . " She turns her head. "I'm sorry," she says. "Not your responsibility. Not your place to explain."

"I'm not in much of a state to explain anything. Don't even think I could. I screwed up my life big time. Don't think my family will ever forgive me."

"You'd be surprised what people can forgive, Justin. I'd have done anything for my son if only he were willing to do the work that would heal him. Anything."

"Had my chance. Blew that, too."

"What about your friend, Steve?"

I look around. "That was the chance I blew. Don't see him here, do you?"

"Oh." She nods. "Gone for good, you think?"

"Wouldn't be surprised."

She pats my shoulder again and then goes about her business, checking my temperature, writing numbers on a chart. She turns on the TV and I spend the day watching Olympians, people whose whole lives are dedicated to greatness. Nothing to do for the next few days, but lie there and watch. Be in the moment. No future to think about, not yet. Got to deal with the truth of my parents' death. Then, maybe, I can find a way out of the hell I have lived in for twenty years. On my own now. Pretty much. No Steve anywhere. I catch myself glancing toward the door. Oh well. Maybe if I scan the crowds on TV, I'll find him. Maybe he'll turn up and give me my money. Doubt that.

Don't know exactly when, must be a few days into the Olympics, Steve actually does come back. I'm mobile now. It feels good to be able to go to the bathroom on my own. I'm walking out of the can, and there he is, parked beside my bed. Shocked, I halt. "Damn it all. Didn't think I'd ever see you again." My innards are dancing.

"You're the one who told me to . . . " He pauses and makes quotation marks in the air. " . . . get the eff out."

"Touché." I walk over and plank my butt on the bed. "So," I grin, "enjoying all the Olympic venues?"

"Haven't been there yet."

Huh. Puzzling. "I figured that's where you were hanging out."

"No. I went to see my parents."

"They come for the Olympics?"

"Uh uh. They didn't want to deal with the crowds so they opted for TV."

"So you were in Ontario?"

He nods.

"Why did you come back?"

"Unfinished business."

I grin. "Ready to give me my hundred fifty grand, and take off, are you?"

He shakes his head. "Not a chance."

"Why not? My money, isn't it? Isn't that why you looked me up in the first place?"

"Ha! Got me there." He smiles. "After my grandfather's funeral, my plan was to find you, give you money, and split. I entered the grad program at UBC and spent all my spare time here looking for you. By the time I found you, you were on the street." Steve stands, serious now. He moves in close, and puts a hand on my shoulder. "I wasn't kidding when we first met, when I said I wanted to help you. A place to live, a companion for AA. . . whatever you want, whatever you need, you've got." He removes his hand and folds his arms. "But I'll be damned . . . yes I said damned, if I'm just going to hand you money and walk away. I'll walk . . . eventually. Guess I'd do it now, if you could convince me you're ready to do all of this on your own."

My gaze hits the floor. "I want to get back on track, Steve. I screwed up big time. All I really ever wanted was family. I thought I would always have Sarah and Bobby, but she will never forgive me for putting Bobby's life in danger." I shake my head. "No, she'll never forgive me. Never. And I don't blame her."

"You'd be surprised what people will forgive, bud. I'd be willing to bet that things are going to work out."

Huh. Someone else said that to me recently. Oh, yes. The nurse with the angel tattoo. The nurse with my mother's name. I look directly at Steve. "I still don't get why you would go to so much trouble for a complete stranger."

"Told you already. I loved my grandfather. And, unlike you, I believe in the hereafter. I want him to have some kind of peace. Do you get that?"

Do I? A picture of my parents flashes. Hereafter? I don't know about a hereafter, but I know I want my parents to be at peace. I nod, slowly. "Yeah, I guess I do."

"I didn't go to Ontario just to visit my parents, Justin."

I stare at him blankly.

"I went because . . . " His cell phone rings, he pulls it from his pocket and glances at the screen. "I have to take this. Be right back." He slips into the hall and I am left staring at the door.

What did he mean? Why did he go to Ontario? What did I tell him about Ontario? Did I tell him Sarah and Bobby and Lady were in Ontario? Does it matter? Sarah will never let me near her, never let me near my son. Why is my heart pounding? Get the hell back in here, Steve, and tell me why you were in Ontario.

Steve returns, holding his phone to his chest. "I found her, Justin. I went to Ontario and I found her. I told her everything. You would be surprised what people are prepared to forgive."

I stare from him to the phone which he is now extending to me.

"Someone wants to talk to you, bud," he's saying.

I try to lift my arm but it doesn't cooperate.

Steve moves closer and puts the phone to my ear.

Unable to utter a sound, I blink and wait. The silence extends until my muscles are so taut I think they will burst. Finally, I hear one word, one pivotal, hope-filled word . . .

"Daddy?"

04/06

Painful morning following too
much activity Friday. Standing & sitting
is still o.k. Need to see Boyd on
17th. That's 3 mo. During past 5-6 days
there have been times that showed
improvement. I guess it really is
good & bad times for about 6 months.
HOPE, HOPE

04/07 Sitting @ Mindy's - pains up ↗
Most of the pain is pushing foot forward
Keep doing stretches. Watched FAME & got
nostalgic about old life/friends - USA.
Certainly much stronger about being
with myself. It's funny my own company
sets a high standard for being with others.
Perhaps being an only child plays a
role here. Also guitar/singing continues
to save me - ALWAYS. There's a lot more talent
there than I ever knew. It's good training
for living at the last residence & being O.K.

+ Seeing Boyd on 17th will be a turning
point. Can't deny that @ time there is
segments of progress - so what is the question
Remember - time is needed to see where
it will go. Medicine for the blues:
• It is what you have / can do that counts.
• All is indeterminant.
• Keep working on - love myself & hate
• Leg pain is defining me now - hate to be
   a victim. Stronger drugs maybe -
to kill Lyrica @ 150/day possibly

4/12 Fri - feeling down. Tired of leg issue.
   Claim: Hard to believe that more time makes better.
√ All literature tells me 6 mo. is earliest wait time. FACT
√ It is better now than 6 weeks ago - FACT
√ WCS: Wait for January 2014. FACT

ABOUT THE AUTHOR

Annie Daylon was born and raised in Newfoundland, Canada. She studied music at New Brunswick's Mount Allison University and education at both the University of Manitoba and the University of British Columbia (M.Ed.). After thirty years of teaching, she decided to pursue her passion for writing.

Annie's work has appeared in Alberta's *FreeFall* literary magazine, Ontario's *Wynterblue* anthologies, Newfoundland's *Downhome* magazine and in Maine's *Writers Weekly*. Annie's has published another novel, *Maggie of the Marshes*, and a collection of short stories, *Passages*.

Annie lives in British Columbia, with her husband, David, and their dog, CoCo. You can find out more about Annie at www.anniedaylon.com.

17928927R00150

Made in the USA
Charleston, SC
07 March 2013